Austin's thu ❦ **P9-DLZ-235** e
of Willa's chin, tilting her face gently up
to bring her gaze to his.

"Are you all right?"

She stared into his blue eyes. They were kind and filled only
with concern.

Her hand seemed to lift of its own accord and land on the
center of his chest. Not to push him away or to act as a
barrier between them, but simply to touch him.

"I'd like to stay."

"You sure?"

She nodded. It was hard not to be tempted by the kindness
on his face and in his voice—tempted to believe in fairy
tales. If she were a different woman, she might think she
was starting to fall in love.

Willa kept her hand on his chest. His heart thudded reliably.
It was an intimate thing, to feel it beat, that made the
moment between them real and changing. Austin was no
longer a stranger, but a man she wanted to know.

* * *

Montana Bride
Harlequin® Historical #1099—August 2012

Author Note

Writing stories set in Montana Territory is one of my favorite things. It's fun to put aside my daily troubles—the laundry needing to be done, the checkbook I keep meaning to balance, the errands I've been putting off—and sit down with my laptop. I sink into a different time and place where life is slower paced, where there is no traffic noise—just the tweet of birds and the wind whispering through an old-growth forest—and where the things that really matter in life are the same. Love and belonging, duty and family. These are the themes I found myself exploring when I wrote the first few sentences of *Montana Bride*.

I was touched by Willa's tragedy—both her abusive marriage and being a pregnant and penniless widow—and by her strength to face marriage to a stranger again, knowing what kind of man she could end up with. A young woman who has never known love, she worries what kind of mother she'll make, but she clearly wants to do her best.

Austin Dermot is a character from my earlier Moose, Montana Territory, stories who was passed over every time a new lady came to town. I started wondering about him and felt sorry for the poor man—surely a nice guy like that deserves to catch a nice woman of his own. He is a man who wants to love and be loved—but unfortunately for him he has chosen a mail-order bride who doesn't believe her scarred heart can ever love.

I hope you enjoy this story about Willa finding her heart and discovering the wonder and renewal that love can be.

Thank you so much for choosing Willa and Austin's story.

JILLIAN HART

MONTANA BRIDE

HARLEQUIN®

entertain, enrich, inspire™

Recycling programs for this product may not exist in your area.

ISBN-13: 978-0-373-29699-6

MONTANA BRIDE

www.Harlequin.com

Printed in U.S.A.

**Did you know that these novels are also
available as ebooks? Visit www.Harlequin.com.**

Chapter One

Montana Territory, April 1884

"The town of Moose, next stop!" The blue-uniformed train conductor strolled through the rocking passenger car with the ease of a man used to riding the rails. Sparse gray hair poked from beneath his cap as he grabbed the bar overhead, stopped in the aisle near her seat and offered her a fatherly smile. "Would you like help with your satchel, miss?"

Willa Conner straightened her spine, clasped her hands together in her lap and shook her head slightly. As nice as it sounded to have the kindly man's help, she was used to doing things on her own, especially since her husband's sudden death. If marriage had taught her anything, it was to never rely on someone else.

"Thank you, but no." She offered what she hoped passed for a polite smile, but the edges of her mouth felt tense and stiff. The train was already slowing, and the great shadowy expanses of forested foothills and mountainsides whipping by the window were not flashing by quite as fast. Moose, Montana Territory. She was almost there. Terror beat in her chest with bone-rattling force, but she set her chin and hoped her fear did not show. "I can manage."

"All righty then." He tipped his cap to her and moved on, offering help to the pair of older ladies toward the back of the car.

The whistle blew a long blast, nearly drowning out the ear-splitting squeal of the brakes. Willa perched on her seat, looking beyond the haze twilight made on the window glass to the break in the trees. She caught glimpses of a tiny log shanty, a sod stable and split-rail fencing before the trees closed back in—her first peek at the outskirts of the town she would be calling home.

Maybe I have made a mistake. She laid her hand on her reticule, thinking of the letter within. A written proposal from a stranger, from a man she had found through a newspaper advertisement. He'd sent her a train ticket and so she'd come to marry a man she'd never met. As her ma used to say, beggars can't be choosers, and her heart skipped a beat as if threatening to fail. She was a widow with no family and nowhere else to go. She had no more choices. Penniless and alone, she only had this door open to her, the only path in a cold and lonely world.

What would he be like? She grabbed the seat-back in front of her as the train jerked to a slow, screeching stop. As she'd wondered and fretted all the way from

South Dakota, she tried to imagine what kind of man would propose to a woman sight unseen? A desperate one, that's what. One who could not convince any woman able to set eyes on him to be his bride.

Fear gripped her as she hauled herself to her feet with what strength of will she had left. Would he be cruel? A drunk? Did he work hard, or was he a lazeabout? Terrible visions flew into her head as she hauled her satchel from the overhead rack by one strap, pulled on her wool coat and followed the fresh sweep of chilly air to the open doorway.

"You take care, miss." The conductor seized her firmly by the elbow. Her shoe hit the step and then she next made contact with the icy boards of the platform. He released her before she could thank him, turning to aid someone else off the train.

A tiny snowflake brushed her cheek, icy against her skin. She shivered against the wintry world where strangers hurried by to greet one another warmly, where families were reunited gratefully or hugged desperately, about to be torn apart.

"Excuse me." A man bumped her shoulder on his way to board the train, marching past her as if she were nothing more than a bench at the edge of the platform.

Feeling out of her element, she stumbled farther into the shadows, clutching her satchel's grip in both hands. Which man was Austin Dermot? She searched the faces of every male on the platform. Several were in the company of wives and family, so she didn't wonder about those. Mr. Dermot was a bachelor. When a shadowed figure paced in her direction, her pulse stalled. Was that man her betrothed?

He was short of stature and the bald skin of his head reflected the light from the train's windows. His eyes, the color of coal, reflected no kindness. His rough hands curled naturally as if used to being balled into fists.

She shivered, fear clawing around her insides like talons. *Please, not that man. Please don't let it be him.* Air caught in her lungs, making it impossible to breathe as he stalked nearer to her. To her relief, he marched past her, casting a sneer in her direction.

"Willa?" A baritone voice rumbled behind her, low and deep and as richly warm as buttered rum. The only soul who would know her name in this unfamiliar place had to be him. It had to be her husband-to-be.

She pivoted on her heels, unable to stop the hope taking root in her heart. A man with a voice like that might not be unkind. Another snowflake struck her cheek as she faced him. He was cloaked in shadows, a tall man with brawny shoulders. Her entire being jittered with a rapid-fire tremble. Her throat went dry. "Mr. Dermot?"

"Call me Austin."

She still couldn't see him. He stood between the bars of light from the train windows, lost in the twilight. She caught the impression of a burly man, which made sense since he owned a livery stable and did heavy work. This was the moment of truth. If she wanted to change her mind, it would have to be now.

"Let me take that for you." Was it her imagination, or were notes of kindness layered in his voice?

She hoped so. Before she could collect her breath, he lumbered out of the shadows and into the wash of light. Golden lamplight bronzed him, illuminating the thick brown fall of his hair, bluebonnet-blue eyes, high cheekbones and chiseled rugged face.

He was handsome. That completely surprised her and her mind shut down. She had been prepared for anything—unfortunately none of it good. She had learned to expect the worst, which had generally been the way most things in her life had worked out. So, what was wrong with this handsome man that he had to settle for a mail-order bride?

His hand clasped around the grip, taking the satchel from her. He smelled pleasantly—of hay and wintry wind, soap and man—and his irises had light blue sparkles in them that lit when he looked at her. "The train doesn't stay here for long. We had best make sure we get your trunks from the baggage car."

"I don't have any trunks." She swallowed, wondering for the first time what he might see when he looked at her. She smoothed a patch in her wool overcoat. "Everything I own is in the satchel."

"Is that right?" Realization etched compassion into the hard planes of his face. Maybe he felt sorry for her poverty, or maybe he was attempting to hide disappointment.

You are no prize, Willa. The words swirled up from the past. She shut out her late husband's voice, but she could not deny the truth of his words. She might not be a prize but neither was she a disgrace. She lifted her chin and gathered her dignity. "I did not exaggerate. In my letter I said I had nothing to bring to the marriage."

"You are enough."

His kindness was unexpected. Her throat burned, and she looked away. The earlier hustle and bustle on the platform had died out, families reunited with loved ones had gone on their way and only one couple bid a tearful goodbye as the conductor tossed a trunk into the baggage car. An icy wind drove snow before it in falling waves.

"Looks like there's a storm on the way, which means we had better head for the church." He held out his other hand—it was big and well-shaped with long blunt fingers and a wide-callused palm.

If she took his hand, their deal would be set. There would be no turning back. She pressed her hand to her still flat stomach, torn. Her every instinct screamed at her to run. She had made this mistake before in marrying Jed. But if she did not marry Austin, where would she go? Who would hire a pregnant woman, and alone how would she provide for the baby once it was born?

Willa swallowed hard, knowing she had no real choice. She laid her hand in his, realizing he was much larger than she'd first thought. His fingers engulfed her hand as they closed around her, but it was gentleness she felt as he led her along the platform.

"Is the reverend waiting?" Cold panic slid through her veins.

"He is. I didn't tell him your story." He paused at the steps leading down to the street. A faint haze of lamplight drew him in silhouette. He towered above her, making her feel small and protected from the drive of the wind. He kept a good hold on her—in case she slipped on the ice—and continued speaking. "It wasn't my place to say anything, although I think Reverend Lane has his suspicions. He's agreed to marry us, unless you've taken one look at me and changed your mind."

"Me? No." She couldn't afford to do that. Austin Dermot may be a complete stranger, but he was her salvation and much more than she expected, perhaps much more than she deserved. She'd never had anyone escort her down a set of steps before or protect her from a driving arctic wind. "Have you?"

"Changed my mind? Not a chance." A smile shone in his voice as the darkness swallowed him. He was a faint impression in a background of snow and night as he helped her into a covered buggy. A horse blew out his breath, as if impatient standing in the cold.

"There now, we're almost on our way," Austin rumbled low to the horse as he untied him from the hitching post. "No need to get huffy."

The horse snorted, and Austin's roll of brief laughter was the warmest sound she'd ever heard. A man who laughed was not what she had prepared for.

"That's Calvin. He's never been one to withhold his opinion." The buggy swayed slightly as the large man settled onto the cushioned seat beside her. Not a crudely made cart behind an ox, as she was used to. Not even a more serviceable wagon, but a fine buggy.

Oh, he is definitely going to be disappointed in me. In the light of the church, when he would be able to get a good look, he would change his mind then. As the buggy rolled smoothly to a start, she knew the tables had turned. She'd spent a good deal of her journey worrying about the man. Now she was the one in question.

"We're a small town but a friendly one." He held the reins lightly, talking with ease as if he picked up strange women at the depot and drove them to church all the time. "Let me correct that. We're a *very* small town. Five whole blocks, as you can see."

"Oh, my." Five blocks? She couldn't see much in the evening storm, only the hint of a roofline and a glimpse of a second-story lamp-lit window that blinked out of sight as they rolled on.

"You're disappointed." His voice knelled with understanding, as if he were not surprised.

"Not at all." He truly didn't understand, did he? She swiped snow from her eyelashes with cold fingertips. "I'm used to small towns. I like them. I'm only afraid this is a great deal more than I am used to."

"More?" They drove out of the reach of the town's main street, where tall trees threw them in deep shadow.

"The nearest town to my husband's South Dakota farm was just a mercantile, a tavern and a stage stop." She felt the wave of unhappiness begin to crest and she banished all memories from her mind. Jed had been a man with great faults. She had been young and naive, marrying at sixteen and expecting a fairy tale. Reality had driven that notion from her mind, and the blame had been hers alone. Marriage was hard work, it was often a disappointment and took patience to bear.

She blew out a small breath, determined to find the inner strength to endure marriage again. To do that, she would think of the positive. She would have a roof over her head, a home to keep and after the thaw she would plant a garden where flowers bloomed. "Is your house far from town?"

"On the outskirts. I have one hundred acres. Never wanted to be a rancher, but I like the solitude. I built the cabin myself."

"Wonderful." She had spotted many such dwellings in her life in South Dakota and on her journey here. Small, often crudely made but snug against the elements. It sounded like heaven to a woman who had spent more than a few nights homeless. "The views must be lovely. I have never seen such beautiful country. I sat transfixed at the window most of the train ride."

"It is rather pretty." He reined the horse to a stop. "We're here."

The hint of a steeple rose up against the faint illumination of the veiled sky. Light burst into existence as a door flung open wide and a man in a dark coat and white collar gestured with one hand.

"Hurry up out of the storm, Dermot!" the reverend called out.

"Got to blanket my horse first. Can't have him standing for long in these winds." Austin hopped to the ground, his friendly voice rumbling as he exchanged a few words with the minister.

Nerves fluttered inside her. At least she hoped it was anxiety and not the nausea that plagued her each morning and lasted throughout much of the day. She took small breaths, wishing she had something to nibble on, something to put into her stomach. She swept snow off the seat beside her and swung her feet around.

"What do you think you are doing?" Harsh words admonished her. Austin broke out of the shadow beside her, but his rugged face wasn't pursed with harsh displeasure. A merry light twinkled in his eyes. "You wait for me to help you down. If you are to be my wife, you will have to let me be courteous to you."

"Oh, I—" She fell silent, her tongue refusing to work, her mind going blank. The back of her eyes burned as she placed her hand on his palm. Her knees shook as she hopped onto the running board and landed on the ground with a jolt.

He towered over her, brawny and substantial and powerful enough to break the bones in her hand if he squeezed, but it was only his gentleness she saw. Her throat closed up entirely and she could not thank him. She could not speak as he offered her his arm.

"It's slick, so be careful." He shortened his long-legged stride to accommodate her as he led her down a snow-covered path and into the shelter of the church's tiny vestibule. There was no darkness to hide in and no falling snow to veil him. In the fall of the bright lamplight, he was even more handsome. The pleasant lines of his face, the wide intelligent eyes and the hint of a smile upturning his mouth, naturally took her breath away.

Why would Austin need to write away for a wife? The question ate at her again, undermining her confidence and feeding her fears. And worse, he could see her clearly. Was he regretting his decision? Was he trying to hide his disappointment as he led her into the sanctuary?

"I'll be right back," he promised, the low, resonate tone full of an emotion she could not name. "I need to tend to the horse."

"Yes." She watched him go, then wrapped her arms around her middle, feeling intensely alone as the door swung shut behind him. His opportunity to escape, she thought, shaking her head. Snow tumbled from her plain dark hair as she stared at the closed door.

"Austin tells me you're a widow." The reverend's sympathy appeared genuine. "But you aren't wearing black. Your mourning period must be over?"

"My husband died six weeks ago." She flushed and stared hard at the plank floor, where a dust of snow lingered, the building too cold for it to melt. She could feel the stranger's scrutiny. How did she admit she did not own a black dress and she couldn't begin to afford the fabric to sew one? She was sad Jed's life had ended but she did not miss him. She wished she did. "Brain fever took him."

"I'm sorry to hear that." Compassion, where others might judge. The minister's gaze lingered at her waist, wondering.

She tightened her arms around her middle, unable to speak of something so private to a man she did not know. Ridiculous because she could not hide her condition forever. The door swung open, icy wind swirled past her and Austin returned. The snow on his shoulders accentuated his physical power, his breadth and height and strength, but it was the kind gleam of concern in his blue eyes as he focused on her that affected her.

"You must be cold clean through." He pulled off his gloves. "I should have noticed earlier you didn't have any mittens."

They had worn out beyond repair, but she didn't tell him that. In the bright light he must be able to see the patches on her clothes and shoes. He must be able to see what she was, and still the kindness in his gaze remained.

His boots knelled on the planks as he paced closer. She shivered when he drew near. The tiny hairs on her arms and the back of her neck stood straight up and tingled. Air caught in her chest as he gently slid his gloves on her hands. Way too large, they dwarfed her, but the sheepskin lining was toasty warm from his heat.

"Are you ready to get married?" he asked.

Too choked up to answer, she managed a single nod. On jelly knees and shaking like a leaf, she followed the minister to the front of the church with Austin at her side.

Chapter Two

"In sickness and health until death do you part?" Reverend Lane paused, allowing silence to fall in the small church. The gust of wind outside battered the eaves, sending a chilling breeze through the already unheated building.

This wasn't the way Austin had envisioned the ceremony, but the train had been late and he was a man of his word. He had promised Willa he would marry her the moment she stepped foot off the train, to provide for her and her unborn child and to keep her safe from harm of any kind. He wanted to show her the man he was. He unclamped his teeth, afraid they would chatter, but managed to speak in a strong clear voice that carried the power of his conviction. "I do."

Her hand, so small within his much larger one, trembled even harder. The poor woman, hardly more than a girl, with her blue doe eyes and soft-faced vulnerability.

Several rich molasses locks had escaped her chignon to curl around her cheeks and chin. Her high cheekbones, small sloping nose and dainty chin must have been carved by angels they were so flawless.

It was her unassuming beauty and soulful eyes he liked the most, but he had not expected a woman so comely or, he hated to admit, one so young. He was in his late twenties and she could not be eighteen. Age was not something he had asked about in their brief correspondence.

"I pronounce you man and wife." The reverend said the words with a hint of gravity and sympathy that rang like a bell tolling in the quiet sanctuary. "You may kiss the bride."

Tension shot through the small hand resting in his. He felt the cool wedding band on her finger when she jerked away. She gazed up at him, vulnerable and so small, half his size. Such a petite slip of a girl, and he must seem like a giant to her. He felt like one as he leaned in, feeling the air snap with tension. Uncertainty passed across her face. He recognized the plea in her big beautiful eyes, the look he'd come to know so well as a blacksmith. He worked with horses all day long, animals subject to a man's whims of temper and thoughtlessness.

A thousand vows rose into his heart, ones he could not find the words to say. He hoped he had the chance to show her every one so she would no longer be afraid. So in time she could see some promises were made to be kept. Some anxiety slipped from her face as she watched him tilt to the side, away from her rosebud lips that were so tempting. But there would be time later for that.

Her silk tendrils brushed his forehead as he dropped a kiss against her satin cheek. Unprepared for the tenderness that swept through him, he jerkily straightened and settled his hand protectively against her shoulder blade.

"We should get home where it's warm. You too, Bill." He could feel Willa trembling through her worn, wool coat. "Thanks for staying late for us."

"Drive safely," the reverend called out, his words echoing in the high ceiling as Austin opened the door and Willa disappeared ahead of him into the blinding night.

Was it disappointment that dug into him as she forged ahead without him? He rubbed at the painful spot on his chest and followed her tracks through the deepening snow. He caught up to her at the buggy and seized her forearm.

"Thought you could get away from me, did you?" He helped her onto the seat, making sure there was no hint of his disappointment in his words, just the warmth he wanted her to believe in. "The drive home isn't far. Are you warm enough? I can give you my coat."

"Oh, no." She wrapped her arms around her middle. "Thank you, but I'm used to the cold."

"Fine." He patted her arm once before stepping away to remove the horse's blanket. The wind disbursed the warm impression he left, and she felt alone. She was not used to sitting in a buggy while a man worked.

No, not just any man, she thought. Her husband. She

gulped, drawing in air to stay the kick of panic in her chest. She had given him back his gloves in the middle of the ceremony, when he had produced a smooth gold band for her to wear. The ring felt foreign on her finger and cold against her skin. Jed had not been able to afford a wedding ring, although he had been able to find the money to buy bottles of whiskey.

She had married Jed straight off the stagecoach. He had met her at the stop, treated her to a fine lunch at the small town's only hotel. He had been on his best behavior then, too, behavior that had covered his true self like a fine, fancy veneer. She'd learned the hard way men showed you what they wanted you to see. She huddled into herself as the spikes of cold on the wind became bitter.

Austin's low baritone mumbled, his words indistinguishable as he uncovered the horse. He was nothing more than an impression in the dark. She caught a glimpse of the crown of his hat, the solid line of his shoulder and the blur of movement as he folded the blanket. This inclement night was vastly different from the hot summer day Jed had tossed her trunk into his battered wagon and driven her across the vast, lonely Dakota prairie, yet she recalled it vividly. The following two years had gone by slowly and unhappily. She lifted her chin, determined to handle this marriage differently. At least she knew the truth. She would be realistic. She no longer believed in a man's good side or in the fiction of romantic love.

"Calvin is none too happy with me." With the hint

of a wry grin, Austin climbed up and settled onto the cushioned seat beside her. "I've spoiled him."

"Have you?" She wished she could be the girl she once was, one who could look at a man hoping to see the good. She could tell Austin wanted her to see he took fine care of his horse, but the way he sat so straight, shoulders back, reminded her of Jed's self-pride that had known no bounds. Her insides clenched tight. *Please, let him not be like that.* Austin seemed kindly and pleasant, but how deep did those qualities go?

Her heart stammered as if she were standing on the crumbling edge of a very high cliff with no way to save herself from falling. She was about to find out. She was about to discover exactly how her life would go. As the horse pulled them down the snowy lane, she fought the urge to leap out and stop the future from happening.

But it was too late. She was bound to this man for as long as they both drew breath. She had to be prepared for silent evenings made longer with a man's displeasure at her and for long days of physical work.

Night had fallen, making the trees towering on either side of the road look like frightening creatures of the night. A wolf's howl called eerily through the forest, reminding her they were in wild, high mountain country. Every passing mile reminded her how much her life had changed only to stay the same. She was still a wife, she still carried a child she might not be able to love and she was still convenient to a man who had chosen a mail-order bride because he could find no other.

"Calvin isn't used to standing in the cold," Austin

explained. "He's never been up this late before. He's old and set in his ways."

She heard the note of humor in his voice but did not smile. She curled her hands into fists. "Have you had him for a long time?"

"Since the day he was born. He's like a brother to me."

"A brother?"

"A horse brother, then." Austin's chuckle rumbled deep, a sound that tried to reach out to touch her heart.

She inched back on the seat, needing distance. Shyness washed over her. She felt small, and he was so big. The dark night world surrounding her echoed with a vastness she could not see or measure. She did not like being vulnerable. *How much farther to the cabin?*

"Sometimes you meet someone and you just know." Austin's conversational tone held a note of strain. Perhaps he was nervous, too. "That's the way it was for Calvin and me. Has that ever happened to you?"

"No." The word sounded abrupt, and she winced. She was stressed, that was all, and she hated that it showed. "I was close to my mother and grandmother."

"Was?" His deep voice gentled, asking for more information. He turned toward her with a hint of concern in his posture as he loomed on the seat next to her.

"Scarlet fever." She swallowed hard, holding back the memories of being fifteen and their sole caretaker. "We all fell ill, but my case was light compared to theirs. My mother went first. It was—" Words failed her. She didn't know how to begin the story about her mother.

"I lost my ma, too." He swallowed hard and although the night hid him fully from her sight, she could feel the essence of him and the strength of his heart. "It was like the sun going out. Like morning without a dawn to light it."

"Yes." Her jaw dropped, surprised this giant of a man understood. Not that she dared believe him too much. "Gran never recovered. She said she'd lost everything."

"Everything? What about you? She still had her granddaughter."

"Two days later, she was gone, too." How did she explain? The circumstances of her birth and her existence were a shame to her grandmother and a tragedy for her mother. She laid her hand on her stomach, thinking of the babe within. Life was complicated and love was a myth.

"We're here." Austin's announcement broke through her thoughts, scattering them on the wind like snowflakes. "This is home."

"Home." Relief ebbed into her. She saw nothing but a slope of a roofline against the iridescent black sky. A good strong roof, by her guess, one that would keep out the wet and the cold. Sturdy walls that would provide the shelter her baby would need.

"You wait for me to help you." He sounded stern, but the harsh notes did not ring true. He hopped to the ground, hurrying around the buggy to offer her his hand. Such a strong hand. He'd swooped her off the seat and onto her feet before she could blink.

"It's not much," he said, grabbing her satchel. "I've

already spoken to Mrs. Pole over at the mercantile to add your name to my account. You can buy all the frills and fabric you want to make curtains and such. I remember how my ma was, and my sisters are always stitching something pretty for their homes."

"You have sisters?"

"It's slick here." His boots thudded on wood steps. "I'll have to get this shoveled off. Yep, I have one sister and two sisters-in-law, which means I have two brothers as well."

"And they live in the area?" Her soft alto was calm and carefully controlled, but he heard the curiosity.

"Hard to believe, isn't it?" He kicked the snow from his boots against the siding and opened the door. The scent of freshly cut wood met him. "You would have thought having so many ladies around me would have civilized me better."

"Is your sister older?"

"Younger." He winced, wondering what she saw when she looked at him. A man older than she'd expected, no doubt, and that pained him. He'd known it was unrealistic but when he'd met her at the train he'd hoped she would instantly like him. That there would be a spark, some recognition between them that would tell him he'd made the right decision. It had been an impulsive decision to offer her marriage, one he wanted neither of them to regret.

He struck a match and lit the wall sconce. The wick leapt to life and the flame chased away the darkness to reveal the sitting room, full of windows with old sheets for curtains. His sister was always offering to sew for him, but he didn't need frills. Now, as he studied the sparse room, he fought off a sense of shame. He wished he had been able to build a bigger home for Willa.

"I'm afraid there's a lot of gussying up for you to do." He covered his feelings with a grin. "My sister offered to sew and fancy up the place, but in the end I thought you might want to do things your way. Make this good and truly your home, too."

"I see." Her eyes widened like a deer facing a hungry hunter. She said nothing more, gazing at the sofa he'd ordered from Chicago so his wife would have a comfortable place to sit with her sewing, and at the furniture he and his pa had made long ago before Ma's passing. End tables, a rocking chair, two deep wooden chairs and a window seat.

"This isn't the only room." She gestured toward the closed doors along the end of the room.

"No." He lit a table lamp. "There's a kitchen and two bedrooms. We can add on as more children come."

She blushed, dipped her chin and focused on working the buttons on the tattered coat she wore. His wedding ring glinted on her slender hand, moving a little because it was a bit too big. He'd had to guess at the size. In the end, his sister and sisters-in-law had helped him and he'd simply gone with their advice. They had offered their advice on more than the ring, and those words drove him now.

"Come, sit and warm up." He rose and held out his hand, waiting for her to come to him. "You have had a hard journey and you need to rest."

"Rest? There's supper to make. Is the kitchen through

one of those doors?" She gestured toward the wall where three doors led to the different rooms of the house. The last button released and she shrugged out of her coat.

"First things first. You need to warm up." He lifted the worn garment from her slim shoulders, breathing in the scent of roses and sweet, warm woman. Tenderness welled up with a strength he hadn't predicted and shone through like a light in the dark.

The coat she'd worn had hidden so much, he realized as he folded it over his arm and helped her settle on the sofa. She was smaller than the bulk of the garment had suggested, a wee wisp who looked overworked and underfed. He noticed the patches on her dress were carefully sewn but there were many. He hung up her coat, frowning. Her advertisement had said she was in great need of a husband and a home. She had not exaggerated.

"I want to tell you right off. I am not the best cook." She gazed up at him apologetically. "Although, in truth, I am not the worst."

"I'm not picky. I will be grateful not to eat my own cooking for a change." He knelt at the hearth to stir the embers. "You don't have to worry about it tonight. My sister brought over a meal to warm up. She wanted to make things easier for you."

Disbelief pinched adorable wrinkles around the rosebud mouth he'd been trying not to look at. Because when he did, he had to wonder what it would be like to kiss those petal-soft lips. The thought made blood roar through his veins. He was thankful the embers caught to the wood he added, so he could retreat to the relative safety of the kitchen before his thoughts got ahead of him. He shoved to his feet.

"You wait here." He tossed her what he hoped was a smile. "Get comfortable."

"You have a nice home, Austin." She watched him cross the room, unable to look away.

"It's yours, too. You may as well start planning how you are going to change it." A dimple flirted with one corner of his mouth before he disappeared through one of the doors.

She caught a glimpse of counters and the edge of an oak table. An entire room for the kitchen. She had never lived in such a grand house, a real house and not a shanty, with more than one room. She had never sat on a couch before. Wooden furniture, yes. Homemade furniture, of course. But a real boughten couch. She ran her fingertips across the fine upholstery, a lovely navy blue color that she would have no trouble finding shades to match. She could make curtains and cushions and pillows. Austin said he had added her name to his account. A charge account. How about that? She'd never had such a thing before.

Any moment she would wake up to find this was all too good to be true. The train's jarring would shake her awake and she would blink her eyes, straighten on the narrow seat and smile at the pleasant dream she'd had, a dream that could not possibly be real.

Heat radiated from the growing fire. The cheerful crackle and pop of the wood was a comforting sound. She tilted her head to hear the pad of Austin's boots in the next room, a reminder that this was real and no dream. She wrapped her arms around herself, wondering what was to come. How long would Austin's kind manner continue? What would happen after the supper dishes were done and the fires banked? She tasted fear on her tongue and shut out that one terrified thought of being trapped beneath a man on a mattress.

Her mouth went dry. The wedding night was still to come. Panic fluttered like a trapped bird beneath her rib cage. Austin was a man, and a man had needs. She braced herself for what was inevitable and tried to focus on the positive. Maybe tomorrow she could select fabric for curtains at the mercantile. She would choose something cheerful and sunny, something that would give her hope.

Chapter Three

Evelyn's fried chicken was as tasty as always but he couldn't properly enjoy the good food his sister had prepared. The mashed potatoes sat like a lump in his gut and he'd dropped the chicken leg he'd been gnawing on twice. Across the small round table parked in the center of the kitchen, his wife looked as if she were having a case of nerves, too. All the color had drained from her face and a green bean tumbled off her fork and into her lap.

"Oops." Covertly, she tucked it on the rim of her plate.

"I do that all the time." He wanted to make her at ease. He wished he knew how to make the worry lines disappear, but they remained, etched deeply into her sweet face.

"I thought of this moment so many times on the train ride." She stuck the tines of her steel fork into the mound of potatoes. "What it would be like here."

"I reckon it's mighty hard to wait and wonder, not knowing what you might walk into." He knew that feeling. "Truth is, I've been so preoccupied with meeting you, for the last week I found myself walking into walls. Going into a room and forgetting what I meant to fetch. Even Calvin had a few choice neighs for me."

"You were nervous?" She looked up at him, meeting his gaze squarely for the first time. Shy, she dipped her head again, breaking the contact, but that brief emotional touch was like a sign.

He squared his shoulders, seeing a way to lessen the uneasiness of two strangers sharing a meal. "I can't tell you how much. I had no idea what to expect. I imagine it was the same for you."

"Yes." Relief telegraphed across her pretty face, framed by soft dark bangs. "Why did you choose to find a wife in an advertisement?"

"Didn't have much of a choice, really." He took a bite of chicken and chewed. Did he tell her his woe when it came to women? "There aren't a lot of marriageable females in this part of the territory. It's rugged and remote, and the railroad coming through hasn't changed that. Every woman I knew up and married someone else."

"Why?" Her blue eyes were like a whirlpool pulling him in.

"I was not enough for them, I guess. In case you haven't noticed, I'm not the dashing type." He shrugged, pushing away that old pain. "I own the livery in town. I run a business. I am no slouch when it comes to being able to provide for a wife."

"Of course not." Her eyes gentled, a hint of the woman within. "How could that not be enough?"

"I am average, I guess." It was tough being an average man. He did fine in school, but not stellar. He had passable enough looks, but no woman had ever thought him handsome. "The few marriageable women who have come this way have tended to look right past me, so I thought, why not bring out my own pretty girl, and here you are."

"You are a charmer. I'll have to keep my eye on you." But she blushed rosily, and it was good to see a glimpse of color in her cheeks and the promise of her smile.

Enough about him and his troubles. He didn't have to feel looked over anymore. His days of being a lonely bachelor were gone. He had a beautiful wife to call his own. She grew more comely every time he gazed upon her. He couldn't believe his luck. He set the gnawed chicken leg on his plate. "Why did you choose my letter?"

"You were the only man who wrote me."

"What?" That surprised him. He wiped his fingers on the cloth napkin, stumped. "The only one?"

"Yes." She set down her fork with a muted clink against the ironware plate. "I suppose admitting I was a pregnant woman looking for marriage wasn't the most popular thing to say in my advertisement, but I had to be honest."

Her words penetrated his stunned brain. He tried not to feel let down, that there had not been, as he'd hoped, a spark of something special in her when she'd read his words. She was truly here because of necessity only. He blew out a breath, holding back his emotions, and focused on her. "You must have been disappointed when you heard only from me."

"I was grateful." Across the width of the small table, she straightened her spine, sitting prim and firm, her chin up. "Very grateful. I had no place to live. The bank took the farm after Jed's death."

"And you had no relatives. No place to go." Concern choked him. He popped up from the table, feeling mighty with his rage. It wasn't right that she'd had no one to care and no one to protect her from the harsh aspects of life. His boots pounded on the puncheon floor and he filled the washbasin with hot water from the stove's reservoir. "How did you get by?"

"The bank had locked up the house but not the barn, so I slept there for a spell." She hung her head, heat staining her face. Her chair scraped against the floor as she stood rapidly. "You can see why I am so grateful to you."

He wasn't hoping for gratitude in a wife. He didn't know how to tell her that. He eased the heavy basin onto the work counter in front of a pitch-black window and frowned at his reflection in the glass. His worry that she was disappointed in him returned. He was certainly disenchanted with the situation and concerned on her behalf. It was April, no doubt nights were chilly in South Dakota, too, and she was pregnant. His hands bunched into fists, and he was unable to know exactly why he was so angry.

The action made Willa shrink against the counter. Alarmed, she stared up at him with an unspoken fear in her eyes and her dainty chin set with strength. Confirming everything he'd suspected about this Jed she'd been married to. He felt sick as he grabbed the bar of soap and a knife and began to pare off shaves of soap into the steaming water.

"I should be doing that." She might be afraid of what he could do with his anger, but she was no willing flower. She reached for the soap, her slender fingers closing over his.

A jolt of physical awareness shot through him, hot and life-changing. She gazed up at him, clear-eyed and unaffected, concerned only with the fact he was doing her housework and not trembling from the shock of touching him.

He swallowed hard, gathering his composure. "I will take care of the dishes. You must be exhausted."

"I am fine. I *have* to do the kitchen work, Austin. I want you to see I'm not a lazy wife." Gentle, her show of strength, but she braced her patched shoes on the floor as if ready for an argument.

"Your being lazy never crossed my mind." He swallowed, confused by the tangle of softer emotions sitting dead center in his chest. "I am more concerned about your condition."

"Oh, the baby." It was almost as if she'd forgotten the babe's existence. A quick pinch of dismay down turned her Cupid's-bow mouth. In a blink, it was gone and she drew herself up, as if searching for fortitude. "I'm fine. I'm a good worker, Austin. Just like I said in my letter."

He could see that attribute was important to her, so he nodded and let her take the dishcloth from his hand.

At the whisper of her fingertips against the base of his thumb, another electric shock telegraphed through him with enough force to weaken his knees. "For the record, I'm a good worker, too."

"I see." Her tense shoulders relaxed another fraction and what almost passed for a smile tugged at the corners of her mouth. In the lamplight, with tendrils of dark curls framing her face, she looked like some magical creature out of a fairy tale, too beautiful and sweet to be real.

His throat closed and he was at a loss for words. He felt disarmed, as if every defense he'd ever had was shattered by her touch. He felt too big, too rough, too average to be married to a woman like her. He still couldn't believe it was his ring shining on her finger. His bride. The last ten years of loneliness felt worth it because they would come to an end tonight.

"I'll go see to the fire." He blushed—he couldn't help it—as he eased through the kitchen door.

"All right." She nodded timidly, a vision in patched and faded calico. She plunged her slender hands into the soapy water, intent on her work. There was nothing else to do but to put one foot in front of the other and set about bringing in enough wood for the morning's needs.

He hesitated at the door, casting one last look at her. The little splashing sounds, the clink of flatware landing in the bottom of the rinse basin, the swish of her skirts and the gentleness of her presence made the tangled knot of feelings within him swell.

Tonight. Tonight he would not sleep alone. She would lie beside him in his bed, his bride to have and to hold.

This was his chance to truly belong and matter to a woman. His turn to find the meaningful, enduring love he'd watched his parents share.

Happiness lit him up like a slow and steady light that would not be put out. He turned on his heels and paced through the house, hardly noticing the bite of bitter cold when he stepped out to fill the wood box.

"How are the dishes coming?" The door opened to the pace of his steps returning to the kitchen.

"I'm done." Willa wiped the last plate dry and set it on the stack in the cupboard. "It took hardly any time at all. I need to thank your sister for the meal."

"No need to, as I've already done it." He sidled up to her, bringing with him the scent of wood smoke on his clothes. His big hands hefted the washbasin off the counter. "You look pale as a sheet. Are you all right?"

"It's been a long few days." She hung the dish towel up to dry, avoiding his gaze. Why was he being so courteous? He walked away with the basin without explanation and opened the back door. He disappeared in the swirl of snow that blew in and returned dusted with white. "I think I made a bigger mess than I meant to."

She shrugged and spotted a broom leaning against a nearby wall. A few swipes took care of the stray snow, but he was still covered with it. The need to brush off the ice from his face surprised her. She stepped back to let him do that for himself. She'd learned her lessons well in her first marriage. Men had a way of punishing you for trying to care about them. At least this time she understood that. At least this first wedding night would not be spent like the last one…full of misery, disillusion and silent tears.

"It is nine o'clock, if you can believe that. The day flew by." He shrugged out of his coat and hung it by the door. "I spent all day getting ready for you. Hard to believe, I know, but I'd left a lot to do until the last minute. Like getting new plates. I didn't want you to show up and have to eat off the chipped ones I was getting by with."

He had an amicable way about him. She had to take care not to fall victim to it. She rescued the basin he'd emptied and set it on the counter to air dry. The kitchen was toasty warm from the stove, warm enough to have chased away the cold from her bones but not the trepidation. If not for the new life she carried, she would never have remarried. She never wanted to be pushed and pulled by a man's manipulations again, but the ring on her finger was a reminder she had made a commitment to Austin until death parted them. She would make the best of it.

"Could you show me to my room?" She held her breath, fearing what was to follow.

"You mean, our room." He watched her intently without a hint as to what he might be thinking. "It's the first door to your left. Come, I'll show you."

"Thank you." She felt self-conscious, and every step she took through the door he held for her felt like the toll of an executioner's bell. The front room's crackling fire and pleasant furnishings were no comfort as she approached the wall of doors.

"I thought this smaller one would make a good room

for the baby." Austin opened the one farthest away, stepping aside for her to inspect the space. "Evelyn brought over a crib as a welcome gift. She is thoughtful that way."

A crib. Her throat closed at the shadowed sight of carved rails and polished oak. Her head swam and Austin's words sounded far away.

"It is the one Ma used for us. Pa made it for her when they were expecting me. You will like my father. I took over the livery from him when he retired." His footsteps echoed against the bare floor and walls, seeming to grow in the shadows. "He's looking forward to meeting you."

"Of course your entire family knows about the baby." She hadn't even considered his family. She hadn't thought further ahead than meeting Austin Dermot. She was still taking one moment at a time. The next moment loomed ahead of her like a ghost in the dark, the moment when Austin would lead her from this room and into the one they would share for the night.

Together.

She swallowed, not sure if she felt strong enough to face that. Worry had worn away at her like water on rock and she felt frail. Maybe it was from seeing the crib with its sweetly carved spools. She tried to imagine the time it had taken to make and could not imagine a man sitting patiently for the hours upon hours it would take to whittle, sand and stain each piece of wood.

"No, only my sister, who has sworn to keep your secret until you are ready to tell it." He shrugged. "I did not tell them. Evelyn showed up with this yesterday.

I suspect when she was cleaning for your arrival, she found the newspaper with the advertisement I'd circled. My sister is nosy."

His grin was infectious and she found the corners of her mouth turning upward. "The crib was a thoughtful gift."

"She cares about you already." He chuckled. "I hope that doesn't turn out to be overwhelming for you, since you're not used to so much family."

"No, I'm sure I will like her." She blushed, awkward with the intensely private subject of her pregnancy. "I suppose we will have to break the news, but I don't want to tarnish your reputation. I know how small towns can be. People can leap to conclusions and think the worst things."

"There's no shame in your situation. It must take a lot of courage to marry a man you've never met for the sake of your child." The shadows hid him, but not his essence. That shone as solid and unmistakable as the lamplight tumbling through the threshold from the other room. "I meant what I said in my letter. I will treat the baby as my own. Your child is our child now, just like the others that will follow."

"The others." That wasn't something he'd written about in his letters. She gulped, feeling dizzy. The future wasn't something she looked at. It was something best left unexamined. Of course there would be more children. He was a man. He would expect certain affections from his wife.

"Maybe I'm getting the cart in front of the horse." He chuckled and his big hand closed around her forearm as if he knew how weakly her knees knocked. "We will focus on getting this baby into the world safely. One thing at a time. How's that?"

She nodded, overcome, shocked by the possessive heat of his hand banding her like a manacle she did not know how to break. She let him lead her from the room. Her head swam, her heart thrashed against her sternum wildly as she stumbled toward her destiny, toward her fate as this man's wife.

One of two bedside lamps was lit, tossing a sepia glow over its bedside table and onto the wide four-poster bed. A patchwork quilt in the colors of spring draped the feather tick, and snowy white pillow slips covered plump pillows. She'd never dreamed of such a room, with a window seat and a bureau to match the carved bed's foot and headboards. A looking glass reflected back at her and she ran her fingertips across the polished wood frame. A real mirror.

"Of course, you will want to change all this. My sister said the curtains are a shame. But my mother made the quilt. You might want to replace it, that's fine by me, but I thought it was pretty. Better than the wool blanket I had there before." Bashfulness had him dipping his head as he backed from the room. "Your satchel is on the window seat. I'll leave you to get ready for bed."

She waited until the door closed before she released her breath. She sank onto the chest footing the bed, shaking so hard she felt sick. In the other room she could hear the fall of the bolt in the door and Austin's boots crossing the room. The sharp sound of the fireplace utensils told her he was busy banking the fires for the night. She would not have much time before he came back through the bedroom door and she had no intention of being caught undressed.

She changed in a hurry into her nightgown. With fumbling fingers, she washed at the basin stand, cleaned her teeth and brushed out her long dark hair in front of the looking glass. The face reflected back at her was ashen, thin and afraid. By the time a quick rap sounded on the door, she was steps away from the bed.

"Come in," she called, pleased at his politeness, and pulled the covers over her. The bed was the most comfortable thing she'd ever felt, both soft and firm at the same time, with flannel sheets. The door whispered open and Austin stalked in, perhaps shy also because he did not look at her as she rearranged her pillow.

He was a more decent man than she'd dared to hope, than she could even now believe. He turned his back to her to pour fresh water into the washbasin. "You're comfortable?"

"Oh, yes." She rolled on her side, facing away from him. The splash of water, the rustle of clothing, the pad of stocking feet on the floor marked the minutes ticking away until his side of the bed dipped beneath his weight. She closed her eyes, cold with fear over what was to come.

Chapter Four

The bed ropes creaked beneath his weight. She felt the mattress dip. Fear skittered through her and she held her breath. She tried to close out the memories of the nights when Jed had roughly pulled her into his arms. She drew in a shaky breath listening to the sheets rustle and feeling the mattress shift as Austin stretched out on the bed beside her.

Just don't forget to breathe, she told herself. *Relax, it hurts less that way.* This was the price to pay for being a man's wife. She thought of the cold nights huddled in the barn so hungry she could not sleep. She thought of the babe growing within her. *You can do this,* she thought. *It will be over before you know it.*

"I've got an early morning." His buttery baritone rang softly as the bed ropes squeaked again. The lamp went out and darkness descended. "The livery opens at six."

"I'll be sure and have breakfast ready for you." Yes, concentrate on what needed to be done tomorrow. That would give her mind something to focus on. Preparing breakfast, taking stock of the pantry and planning her meals for the day. Don't notice he's moving closer.

"How has your morning sickness been?" His big hand lightened on her shoulder and she jumped.

"F-fine." Think about the curtains. With pretty little ruffles around the edge. She braced her body, every muscle drawing tight. Yes, those curtains would look so nice in the front room. Cheerful.

"Willa?" His voice rumbled through her thoughts, like a lasso drawing her back. His iron-strong form lay a few inches from hers, so close she could feel his body heat on hers. Terror struck, making it hard to breathe.

She blotted out what she knew was to come. The roughness, the pain, the humiliation, his weight holding her down until he collapsed on top of her. Her first wedding night rolled back to her like a nightmare. The innocent girl expecting love and romance died that night, too wounded to even cry out. At least this time she knew what was coming. She knew what marriage was about.

"Willa?" His voice gentled. "Darlin', you're shaking the entire bed."

She was? "I'm s-sorry."

"I don't think it's good for you or the baby to be this upset." His hand left her shoulder to brush a strand of hair out of her face. A tone she'd never heard before rang low in his words. It was soft and warm and it made her turn to face him. "I take it your first husband wasn't a gentle man?"

"No. Jed drank far too much for gentleness." She laid her ear on the pillow, making out Austin's face in the darkness—the tumble of his hair, the line of his jaw and the curve of his chiseled mouth. His eyes were black pools with depths she could not read.

"What was your first day married to him like?"

"He was a stranger, too." The words rushed off her tongue, impossible to stop. Maybe it was easier to talk in the night, where she felt hidden. "I answered his advertisement in the territorial newspaper."

"This isn't your first time as a mail-order bride."

"No." She swallowed hard, thinking of the girl who'd kept staring at her left hand, a new bride wishing for a wedding ring. Maybe one day, that girl had thought hopefully, still seeing only blue skies ahead. "I had such dreams of a happily-ever-after. Jed had written a charming letter and I was immediately smitten. He seemed so funny and confident, he made me laugh and I thought, what a nice way to go through life alongside a man with a good sense of humor. But his humor lasted as long as it took to reach his farm."

"What happened then?"

"He ordered me down from the wagon, gave me the reins, told me to put up the horses and fix him supper." She could still remember standing in shock in the scrubby grass by the leaning ten-by-ten shanty, with the reins dangling in her hands. "He took a bottle of whiskey from the wagon bed and shut himself in the shanty. He drank his way to the bottom of the bottle by the time I had supper on the table."

"I see." He reached out again to touch her cheek and rub away the remains of her single tear. "He was a drunk."

"He was a mean drunk." She remembered setting down fried salt pork and potatoes on the rickety table in the light of a single battered lantern. It was dark, the ride from the stage stop where the church was had taken much of the day and she'd been still desperately clinging to her illusions.

Maybe he doesn't drink like this very often, she'd thought, filling two tin cups with water. Maybe once he slept off the whiskey he would be back to his charming self.

I don't want no water, woman. He'd knocked the cup away from his plate and stood up to slap her cheek. Hard. *Get yer lazy ass out the door and fetch me another bottle or I'll teach ya who's boss.*

"He was abusive to you." Austin's voice cut into her thoughts, leading her out of the past and the remembered sting against her face.

"After a while I became numb to it." Her throat knotted up, refusing to feel all that it had cost her to learn to cope with Jed's cruelty. "I learned to be grateful for the good days when he was more himself."

"I see." The darkness polished him like sculpted stone, accentuating his handsome looks in a powerful and masculine way. Silence settled between them and he loomed beside her, big and strong. He was brawnier and larger than Jed had been; there was no way she could stand up against Austin's physical strength. She'd also learned the hard way fighting only made the inevitable worse.

Why hadn't he moved toward her? Fear and dread knotted together in her chest, making her shiver harder. The bed ropes creaked with tiny squeaks in rhythm to her quakes. She could not stop them. She gritted her teeth, willed her muscles to relax while nausea swam in her stomach. The waiting was killing her.

"Do you know how long I've been reading women's advertisements for husbands?" Instead of grabbing for her, his mellow baritone broke the stillness. Instead of wrenching up her nightgown, he levered himself up on one elbow. "A year and a half. I started regularly perusing them, wondering about the ladies who were looking for marriage. Several caught my eye, but I never acted on any of them. Not a one."

She wanted to ask why but the words wouldn't come. Cold beads of sweat broke out on her forehead and rolled down her face. She needed all her strength to stay in that bed with him and not bolt to her feet and start running. Memories pulled her backward into the past, where she'd been a naive bride turning on her side to go to sleep. No one had told her what a husband would demand in the dark of night so she'd been unprepared when Jed had risen over her in bed and grabbed her roughly by the shoulder, reeking of whiskey and anger.

Don't you dare close yer eyes on me, woman. Yer my property now. He knocked her onto her back and ripped her knees apart. *You'll do as I say.*

"Why did you write to me?" She shook away the

past and focused on the question, hating how small her voice sounded in the night, how lost in the dark. She felt small next to him. He seemed to shrink the walls of the room and take up every available inch on the bed. The memories of Jed haunted her as she watched Austin's face move in the darkness. He furrowed his brow, and the corners of his mouth went down.

"There was just something about your written words that caught me." Honesty rang in his voice. "Something about you stuck with me long after I'd put the newspaper down."

"I seemed desperate." No, there was no doubt about it. "I *was* desperate."

"No, that's not what stayed with me." Low and soothing, that baritone, mesmerizing enough to ease some of her fear away.

Did she dare hope that when he reached out for her and pressed her to the mattress with his body weight, that he wouldn't be as rough as Jed had been? She blocked out that ghostly memory haunting her, of that old terror and helpless and tearing pain that left her sobbing. She died that night and every night he'd forced himself on her. A wife's duty, she knew, but she dared to hope now that maybe Austin wouldn't hurt her as much.

"I'd be cleaning stalls at the livery or pounding a horse shoe at my forge and I'd think about you, alone and pregnant." His confession came closer as he eased a few inches nearer. "You didn't go on like a lot of women about your virtues or your beauty. You didn't make promises. You didn't try to seem too good to be true. Your honesty touched me."

"It did?" That seemed an odd reason to her. "You could have had a more beautiful wife."

"Beauty is in the eye of the beholder. You are plenty beautiful enough for me. If I'd known you were homeless and living out of a barn, I'd have answered faster."

"I'm grateful for what you've done for me and the—" She hesitated, her burdens weighing heavily on her. "And the baby."

The baby. What kind of mother would she make with her heart gone and worn away? "What if you hadn't chosen my advertisement? I don't know what would have become of me."

"That's over now. This is your home now." He leaned in, the bed sheets rustling, the mattress dipping, the bed ropes groaning with his movements. Her pulse slammed to a stop.

This is it, she thought. Austin might be kind for a man, but he was still a man, with a man's appetites and strength. The act of marriage was terrible for a woman and she screwed her eyes shut. It would be best if she didn't have to look at him. If she could think hard on shopping for fabric for the curtains. There might be plenty of choices in material in a town like this. The mercantile looked like a big store and she might be able to find a pretty calico or maybe something with daisies on it....

"Good night, Willa." His kiss brushed her forehead as soft as a whisper. That was all, just one kiss and he moved away. The sheets rustled and the bed dipped as he settled onto his pillow to sleep.

She opened her eyes, staring unblinkingly into the

darkness, waiting. Waiting for what, she did not know. For him to launch at her, to manhandle her into submission, to force himself on her until she sobbed with humiliation and pain? That the moment she relaxed, then he would surprise her cruelly the way Jed might do.

But minutes passed by, measured in the faint muted ticks of the clock in the front room. Austin's breathing slowed into the rhythm of sleep and she dared to watch him. Dark hair tousled over his forehead, he expelled air in quiet huffs. Austin was so big he took up more than half the bed, but he hadn't hurt her.

He hadn't done it.

Tears burned behind her eyes with the memories of a long string of nights of misery and pain. The hopelessness as Jed's wife had wrapped her in a thick cocoon on that first wedding night, when she'd been too wounded and shamed that not a single tear would come. She'd lain awake half the night, too hurt to move and felt the girl she'd been wither away and all her hopes for happiness with them.

Love did not exist. It was a falsehood, a story told to girls so they would want to get married in the first place. A lie to trick them into a life of servitude and bleak survival, trying to make the best out of a bad situation.

But at least she knew her married life here would not be as hard as it had before. Tears filled her eyes, ran down her cheeks and tapped onto the pillowcase, tears of relief and gratitude she could not stop.

The poor gal sounded real sick this morning. Austin shrugged out of his coat, scattering snowflakes to the wood floor. The fires crackled in the cookstove and hearth as he hung up the coat, wincing in sympathy as he heard Willa retch once more behind the closed bedroom door. Following his sister's advice, yesterday he'd left a clean chamber pot in easy reach of her side of the bed. Hating that she was ill enough to use it now, he stepped into the kitchen to fix his breakfast. Let her go back to bed, he thought, and rest up after that.

He put coffee on to boil and filled the teakettle. The scrape of a door opening surprised him. Willa stood in the threshold, white-faced and shaky, in a faded and patched blue dress that was so old it was hard to see printed flowers on the calico.

"Good morning." He set the kettle on the stove. "You don't look as if you ought to be up."

"I'm fine." A dark lock of hair escaped her neatly plaited braid and swept across her forehead. She looked too beautiful for that poor sad dress and too young to be a wife twice over. Not a lick of color could be found in her ashen face. Halfway to the kitchen she stopped, placed a hand on her stomach and swallowed hard, perhaps debating a dash back to the chamber pot.

"You don't look fine, darlin'." His bride. His chest swelled up at that thought. He crossed over to pull a chair out at the table.

"I just need to get a little tea." Big blue eyes avoided his, but she hesitated at the chair he'd drawn out for her. She studied it for a moment, as if considering it, before slipping onto the cushion.

"My sister gave me an earful about expecting women." He resisted the urge to tuck that stray lock of hair behind her ear or to give her shoulder a squeeze of encouragement. "That's why I've already got the kettle on."

"That's good of you, Austin." She tipped her head back to look up at him. The sorrow in her eyes got to him. No woman, especially one so young, should have eyes like that. As if she'd known a world of sadness. In the full light of morning, he could see her clearly, more than he'd been able to in the lamplight last night.

She was hardly more than a girl, a young woman who ought to be sewing on her hope chest and giggling with friends her own age about fashion and parties and attending her final semester at the schoolhouse. Tenderness wrapped around him, making her sorrow his.

"If I don't treat you right, my sister will have my hide." He chose humor and put distance between them, when he wanted to move closer, and lifted a fry pan from a bottom shelf. "Evelyn may be smaller than me, but she can enlist the help of my brothers' wives and as a combined force, they outnumber me."

A hint of a smile curved the corners of her mouth. Sagged in the chair, she was wrung out and weak. He set the pan on the stove and cracked an egg on its rim, thinking of Evelyn standing in this very kitchen giving him the what-for on pregnancy.

"A man just can't understand," Evelyn had said, one hand on the small bowl of her stomach barely visible beneath her skirts. "The babe wears on you. The sickness takes you over and drains everything from you those first few months. You make sure to let her rest when she needs it and fix on doing for the both of you.

At least until she's back to her strength in around her fourth month."

"I'll do my best," he'd promised.

"Even then, you help out with the housework." Evelyn gave him a piercing look. "You don't want her to regret marrying you. You're lucky she's settled for the likes of you."

Remembering her laughter, he shook his head, cracked a final egg and gave the mixture a stir. Scrambled eggs and toast might be nice to go along with Willa's tea. The kettle whistled, he whisked it off the stove and poured steaming water into Ma's old teapot.

"I can take over now." Willa stood at his elbow and took charge of the spatula he'd abandoned in order to pour her tea. She stood so close he could see the soft porcelain texture of her skin, the luxurious curve of her lashes and the contour of her Cupid's-bow mouth.

A mouth made for kissing.

A bashful rush of desire ebbed into his veins as he watched her, heart pumping. He drank in every movement she made stirring the eggs—the sweep of her arm, the turn of her wrist, the placement of her slender fingers on the wooden handle—and was amazed by the sight of her in the soft gray morning light. Lamplight found her, drawing gleaming ebony highlights in her dark hair and kissing her face with a golden glow.

His bride. He still couldn't believe it. He hadn't quite known what to expect when he'd written his proposal to her and enclosed a train ticket in the envelope. All he'd known at the time was a deep abiding commitment to her he couldn't explain and the soul-deep hope that because she needed him so much, she might love him more than all the rest—the way he wanted to love her.

He swallowed hard, set the kettle on a trivet and debated trying to talk Willa out of possession of that spatula. For a wee bit of a thing, she looked determined to hold her ground and he remembered her words last night, how doing the dishes had been important to her to prove her worth to him.

Darlin', you don't need to prove a thing, he thought, a ribbon of tenderness wrapping around his heart. Just being here was enough. He left her at the stove to unwrap the loaf of bread Evelyn had baked for them. As he sliced, bread knife in hand, he had to admit it was fine sharing the morning with Willa. Her presence changed everything. There would be no more empty mornings spent alone in his cabin. When he came home from work tonight, she would be here to greet him. His long span of lonesomeness had come to an end.

"Evelyn said to make sure you had toast in the morning." He moved to her side to open the oven door. He liked the sound of her petticoats swishing as he knelt to place the slices of bread on the rack. "She also brought ginger tea to help settle your stomach."

"That was mighty thoughtful of her." When Willa spoke, her dulcet alto held him like no other voice ever had. "And thoughtful of you. I can smell it steeping."

"Here, let me hold the plates for you." He closed the door and stood, intending to whisk around her but something stopped him. The sight of the ridge of bones along her back. Through the thin cotton of her dress he could count her vertebrae, the poke of her shoulder blades and the faint hint of her ribs.

She wasn't merely too thin, as he'd thought when he'd gotten a good look at her in the church. She hadn't been only homeless living out of a barn, but she'd been hungry, too. Very hungry. His hands fumbled with the plates, nearly dropping one. He swallowed hard, hating the circumstances Willa had endured.

But no longer, he vowed, as he watched her load one plate with the bulk of the fluffy scrambled eggs. He would move mountains to provide for her. No wonder her big blue eyes shone somberly. Everything he learned about her broke his heart.

"Is that enough for you?" Her gaze found his, and the look on her face asked a deeper question, one he understood somehow without words.

"Just fine," he said. "Fact is, I hate eating my own cooking. You could be the worst cook in all the world and I would still be grateful for you in my kitchen."

"If I'd known that, I wouldn't have taken such care *not* to burn the eggs." A hint of humor played along the edges of her lush mouth, just a hint, before a flush of embarrassment crept across her cheeks.

"I highly appreciate that you didn't." He winked at her, hoping to make her bashful, hesitant smile bloom into something more.

She lowered her eyes, as if self-conscious, and concentrated overly hard on adding the small remaining portion of eggs onto the second plate. The promise of her smile faded and she seemed to retreat into herself. He tried not to be disappointed. He remembered how hard she shook last night, fearing his touch. The last thing he wanted was to think about what had been done to her by another man, one who'd married her and failed to cherish her.

"Oh. No." She set the spatula down in the pan with a thunk, covered her mouth with both hands and her eyes widened. She looked a little green around the edges as she spun, racing toward the bedroom. Her skirts swished, her patched shoes beat against the floorboards and the door slammed shut behind her.

He was alone again.

Chapter Five

The house echoed around her as she dragged herself through the kitchen. The tea—lukewarm by the time she'd been able to take a first sip—had calmed her stomach enough for her to finish drying and putting away the breakfast dishes. New ironware dishes and she took the time to appreciate them, running her fingertips around the dark blue rim. She took extra care wiping the counters and the table. There was so little she could do to repay Austin's kindness. Regardless of how weak she felt, she wanted to be a good wife.

A knock rapped on the front door, a cheery *rat-rat-rat* that echoed through the silence. Willa turned, the soapy dishcloth fisted in one hand, and spotted a woman waving through the small window next to the door. Her red hair tumbled in ringlet curls from a bright blue wool hood and her button face was round and merry. When she smiled, it was Austin's smile. Austin's sister had come to pay a call.

Midmorning. Willa wilted, realizing the house wasn't swept nor had she washed away the dried smudges on the floor from last night's falling snow. What a poor impression she would make, but there was nothing to do but to open the door.

"Willa." Evelyn burst in, hands out to grip Willa's in a firm welcoming squeeze. The fullness of her skirts tried to hide the small round bump of a growing babe. "Let me look at you. Not at all what I expected. Heavens, you are just breathtaking, but how old are you, dear?"

"I turned eighteen in January." She watched as the bubbly woman looked her up and down, perhaps taking in the patched shoes and the faded, wash-worn fabric of her calico dress.

"More than a few years separate us, so you must think of me as your older sister. Just think. We're going through our pregnancies together. I suppose Austin told you I snooped and discovered that information all by myself?" Evelyn closed the door, shrugged out of her coat and hood and gave her red ringlets a toss. She didn't pause for an answer as she draped her wraps and her reticule on the nearest peg, quite at home. "I know the hour is early, but you're here all alone, you don't know a soul and there's so much to be done setting up your home. Are you queasy, dear? You look a little pale."

Overwhelmed might be a word. But she'd never had a sister before and nobody could seem friendlier or easier to like. "I'm okay. Let me pour you some tea."

"No, no, don't fuss over me." Merrily, Evelyn tapped

into the front room and didn't seem to notice the unswept floor. "Do you feel up to a trip to town?"

"I was planning on cleaning the house." She wanted to make everything shiny and nice for Austin when he came home.

"That can wait. My dear brother asked me to take you to the mercantile. We might be a small town, but we have a fine selection of fabric."

The curtains. Brightness filtered through her as she thought of the charge account Austin had set up for her. "You're taking me shopping?"

"What are sisters for?" Evelyn's laughter was contagious and confident. She looked as if she didn't expect to take no for an answer.

"But what would Austin say?"

"He stopped by on his way to town this morning and asked me to look after you. He's concerned because you were so sick."

"It's passing now. It always begins to fade by midmorning and it's hardly much through the rest of the day."

"My morning sickness plagued me constantly. It troubles me some in the evenings still." A soft glow flushed Evelyn's oval face as she brushed a gentle hand across the bowl of her stomach. "Other than that, the fourth month has been wonderful. I'm feeling like myself again. Soon, that will be true for you."

"I hope so." Encouraged, she managed to push aside her shyness. "I haven't had anyone to talk with about this."

"You have us now. Delia and Berry are busy with

their little ones this morning. Berry's youngest has a fever and Delia's babe is teething, so we thought it best not to expose you to that circus, at least not on your first day." Evelyn's cheer filled the room as she made herself at home in the kitchen. The oven door opened. "Go on, pull on your wraps and we'll get going. It's a cold one out there. Here we thought spring had come, but no. We had to have one more snowstorm."

"You shouldn't go to the trouble of banking the fire." Willa gripped the fireplace shovel and knelt before the hearth, refusing to let her sister-in-law do all the work. "It's my job, Evelyn."

"One thing you've got to learn about me right off, Willa, is I'm pushy." Clatters rang from the kitchen. "Always have been, always will be. You'll get used to it. Everyone else has."

"Even your husband?" She couldn't quite imagine that as she shoveled gray ashes from the fringes of the hearth onto the red-hot coals. Flames sizzled and smoked, the burning wood crumbled and she kept shoveling, wondering what Evelyn might say to that.

"Charlie, most of all. That man knew what he was getting into before he married me, so I don't feel sorry for him in the least. Not one bit. He has no one to blame but himself for proposing to me." After one final clank, Evelyn strolled into sight. Something deeper shone in her blue eyes, a light of happiness and caring that was something Willa had never known.

"Charlie was sweet on me since we were young." Evelyn marched ahead to unhook Willa's coat from the wall peg by the door and held it out for her. "He and I walked to and from school together every day from the time we were six until we were eighteen."

"You must know him so well." Willa thought of all the children she'd watched when she'd been able to attend school, how they laughed and played together, how they developed bonds of friendship and sometimes, more. "I can picture it. How you walked together side by side, talking the whole time."

"Our siblings were there too, but we were largely able to ignore them. For whenever Charlie spoke, I had to listen. It was an unstoppable force in me. I always had been taken with him." She handed over the garment and reached for her own much finer, beautifully made coat. "That force turned out to be love and so I married him."

"A love match?" She didn't believe it. She'd read of them as a girl, building the idea up like a fairy tale. The lonely child she'd been had ached for such a match, with the hopes that perhaps someday in the future she would be finally loved and have a family of her own, a husband who cherished her.

Evelyn seemed so happy. How could she actually like being married? Willa slipped her arms into her coat. Maybe Evelyn was just a very optimistic sort, making the best out of a difficult situation.

I've done the same, too. Willa finished her last button and pulled up her hood. She watched as Evelyn looked her up and down again, sympathy on her face.

"I'm glad Austin found you, Willa, dear." Evelyn held out her gloved hand. "I have a hunch that no one could deserve him more."

"He's been very kind to me." She laid her hand in Evelyn's and no longer felt alone. When her baby came, it would have cousins to play with. Friends. A normal childhood because it would not be born out of wedlock. Her baby would have the kind of life she never knew.

Oh, how she owed Austin for that. With a smile, she let her sister-in-law pull her out the door and into the lightly falling snow.

"How's it feel to be a married man?" Wallace Pole asked as he gave his big Clydesdale a pat, framed by the open double doors of the livery barn. Behind him, snow drifted down like pieces of heaven onto the frosty street. The mercantile owner tugged out his pocket watch to check the hour. Probably worried about getting his deliveries out on time.

No problem there. Austin buckled the last harness. The horses were ready to go. "Not much different," he admitted. "It hasn't been twenty-four hours yet. Ask me after I get home for supper. That will be a nice change."

"There's nothing like a woman's cookin' after you've been making do for yourself. And as for the other kind of comforts a wife can give a man." Wallace winked. "No need to say more, my boy. I'm not so old I can't remember what it was like to be a newlywed."

Heat inched across Austin's face as he handed over the reins. He thought of Willa and how charming she'd looked in the morning's light. The memory of her lush, rosebud lips sent shivers of heat into his blood. He desired her, no doubt about that, but he couldn't forget how hard she'd trembled last night in their bed, afraid in the one place she should always be safe.

"There she is." Wallace took the reins, nodding over his shoulder in the direction of the store across the street. For an instant in the gleam of the wide front windows he caught sight of Willa's dark hair in the lamplight, shimmering like ebony silk.

The warmth in his blood spread from simply watching her. Slim and willowy in her faded dress. Her hair swept across her back as she shook her head, no. His sister marched into view, displeasure twisting her mouth into a frown. Evelyn's eagle eyes caught sight of him across the street; she stalked toward the window and crooked her finger in an unmistakable "come here" gesture.

"Uh-oh." Wallace climbed up into his sled and plopped onto his cushioned seat. "That sister of yours don't look happy."

"No, and I'm afraid she's about to take it out on me." He grabbed his hat from the peg by the door and waited until Mr. Pole's delivery sled lumbered out of the straw and into the snow.

What on earth could be wrong? Austin glanced over his shoulder, checking to make sure all the stall gates were secure before he crossed the street. Not many were out in this weather, where the wind blew like the arctic north through the trees and barreled straight down Main with a mean howl. If Willa hadn't been in such need, he wouldn't have wanted her out in this, either.

Willa. He caught sight of her through the glass in the door. With her head bent to study the bolts of fabric in a display, she didn't see him coming. Her profile might be the prettiest he'd ever seen, a finely sculpted work of art with a sloping dainty nose, those soft lips and a dear little chin.

His very own wife. Tenderness took over as he made his way into the store. He hardly noticed the ring of the bell overhead or Mrs. Pole's cheerful greeting. All he saw was Willa. He could barely breathe drinking her in. How he'd gotten so lucky, he didn't know.

"Your bride is not cooperating." A sharp hammer-strike of a heel sounded near his elbow. Evelyn paraded into his view, her hands on her hips. "I don't know what to do with her. She's stubborn."

"Is that so?" Amusement tripped through him as he watched Willa lift her gaze, turning her attention to him. Once she spotted him, tension crept in. A line of worry furrowed across her porcelain forehead and quirked the corners of her kissable mouth.

How he wanted to kiss that mouth. "What exactly isn't Willa doing?"

"She's not picking out a single dress or a scrap of fabric to make one. For that matter, not even yarn for a pair of gloves." Evelyn looked perplexed. "She doesn't want to spend your money."

"I see the problem. A frugal wife. It's a travesty, all right." He understood Evelyn's upset. Anyone taking a good look at Willa would see she needed new clothes two years ago, something her first husband had failed to provide for her.

But not this one. His boots rang hollowly on the wood floor as he circled around the pickle barrel and toward his bride. Anxiety carved lines into her face and she bit her bottom lip, her teeth white against the pink. A question resonated in her expressive eyes. *Are you upset with me?* she asked without a word.

He shook his head. No. If nothing, her reluctance to charge anything she wanted made him like her more.

"That's pretty." He nodded toward the butter-yellow fabric she'd been fingering when he'd walked into the store. It was dotted with brighter yellow flowers and blue blossoms. "It would make something nice for you."

"It's for the curtains."

"Nice. It's just what the house needs. I hope you get plenty of material so you can make them up real nice, the way you want. I'd like that. Do you know what else I'd like?"

"No. Is there something you need?"

"Yes. I need you to come here." He laid a hand on her shoulder, ignoring the hard ridge of bone beneath his palm. "These ready-made dresses are nice and I want you to choose three."

"Three?" She could not be hearing him correctly. She looked into his eyes, somber and kind, and saw he meant what he said. Three new dresses. She couldn't believe it. "I don't need anything."

"A coat, too. Mrs. Polc, get her the warmest gloves you have in this store. And the fabric she wants for the curtains."

"Will do," the shopkeeper's wife promised, bustling around the counter to fetch and measure the material. "You might want to get your bride new shoes. Honestly, Austin, you're a businessman in this town. What will folks think?"

"New shoes it is." Austin's hand remained on her shoulder, a reassuring pressure that seared through fabric and skin to the bone beneath.

Was he embarrassed by her? She bit her bottom lip, gazing down at her dress. The patches were neat. The dress had been a hand-me-down her mother had found for her years ago, and though worn, it was serviceable. But he didn't seem to think so. This was another sign that Austin may have hoped for more in his mail-order bride. A businessman like him might have wished for someone fancier and not so plain.

"I want you to have what you need, Willa."

I'm not in need, she wanted to argue but Austin's hand skimmed down her arm, leaving a warm trail on flesh and bone. She shivered, not at all sure why his touch affected her like this, as if fire burned on her skin. That fire scattered her thoughts, making it impossible to think. She stared down at the toes of her patched shoes, remembering the day her mother had brought them home.

"They were left behind at the hotel." Ma had slapped the pair of shoes down with the look of disdain she always had for her daughter. "They ain't much, but they're about your size. Not that you deserve 'em. Patch the hole in the toe and wear 'em, girl, cuz that's all you'll be gettin' from me."

The vestiges of the past whirled around her, threatening to drain the light from the cheerful store. Willa blinked, bringing the present back into focus and fighting down the memories and the shame that still clung to her, the shame of being the ruination of her mother's life. She did not want Austin to be ashamed of her, too. His fingers curved around hers to lift her hand, and he drew the pad of his thumb across the golden sheen of her wedding band.

"I ask this for me." His sculpted face turned thoughtful before he fixed his gaze on hers. "I want this for you. No more patches, Willa. I think you deserve more."

He really was a nice man. He surprised her with his gentle blue eyes and dimpled smile, with the friendly squeeze of his strong fingers around her hand as if to say things really were all right.

"It's still too expensive," she leaned in to tell him, aware of Mrs. Pole and Evelyn nearby. "A good wife doesn't spend all her husband's money on the first day of their marriage."

"I've waited a long time to find a bride." Something glimmered deep and private in his words, something that reflected in his eyes and whispered in his voice. "For better of worse, you are it. Three dresses, do you hear me? This one is pretty. It matches your eyes."

She couldn't look at the garment he'd taken from the shelf, caught up by the man. She'd been too afraid of being a bride again to truly consider what he'd been telling her. But standing in the cheerful store, with Evelyn's and Mrs. Pole's merry conversation in the background and with handsome Austin towering beside her, holding the nicest dress she'd ever seen, she understood the look in his eyes. She heard the silent question he asked.

She knew what loneliness was. She'd grown up in a

home where she had to blend in to the background because the sight of her upset her mother. She'd married a man whose best friend was a whiskey bottle. She'd been lonesome as a daughter and as a wife, and she knew how loneliness could eat at you, leaving you longing for a place to really belong, where your heart could be safe.

She couldn't see how that place existed, but she could read the hope for it in Austin's eyes as he held the dress up to her, a dress far too fine for her. She did not want to be an embarrassment to him. Clearly his sister did not have a single patch on her dress, so Willa found herself nodding. The garment would be fine.

"And it's the right size for her." Evelyn bustled over, eager to help now that the problem had been solved. Now that the man had put down his foot—kindly, but it had been done all the same. "You're right, Austin, look what it does to her eyes. I can take over now. Stop staring at her like you'll never see her again. You'll get her back when I'm done with her."

"You make sure to take care of her." He handed the dress to Mrs. Pole, who had rushed over to make the sale, but he didn't move away. "You brought so little with you, Willa. You need to buy here what you left behind. Knitting needles, an embroidery hoop. Whatever makes you happy."

"I'm overwhelmed, Austin. Thank you." She thought of her days as Jed's wife, blinking back misery and ignoring the latest pain from his most recent beating. She'd scrubbed his clothes on the washboard, head down, while he supervised, determined to watch her every move and make sure it met with his approval.

Marriage was a prison, but this was better than most. She caught Austin's hand before he moved away, such a big, strong hand. The calluses rough on his palm proved he was a hard worker. The light blue sparkles in his eyes gleamed gently when he gazed down at her. A question arched his eyebrows, and that emotion flickered into his eyes again, a vulnerable wish her heart could not answer.

Perhaps he did not yet know there was nothing lonelier than marriage.

"Promise me that you'll have fun." He reached out to brush a stray lock of hair out of her eyes. His touch blazed across her forehead like a comet through the sky, lighting up the darkness, but only for a moment.

"I promise." Because it would make him happy. He towered tall and manly over her, so near she could smell the hay clinging to his shirt and the warm clean scent of him, somehow comforting. A comfort she couldn't let herself believe in.

Her duty was to be a good wife to him. That's what she owed him. Her hand crept to her still flat stomach and thought of the babe within. With a final encouraging smile, Austin turned and ambled away, wide shoulders braced, outlined by the windows, looking like a dream she'd made up.

A dream she might wake up from any moment. This isn't reality, she told herself, as Evelyn chose another dress from the shelf.

Chapter Six

Austin had taken a lot of teasing all through the afternoon from his customers, Reverend Lane, who dropped by to ask how he was faring, and even Mrs. Pole. The merchant's wife had crossed the street a few minutes before closing with a big bundle of purchases for him to cart home for Willa.

Good thing he'd asked Evelyn to help her out, or he suspected his bride may not have bought more than the few things he'd ordered her to. After he'd returned to the livery from the mercantile, he'd watched for glimpses of Willa through the store window. Images of her and Evelyn talking, images of his bride choosing between one pair of gloves and another and the flash of her sparkling smile—the first he'd seen of it—when she'd tried on a new pair of shoes, those pictures accompanied him out of the livery and into the cold evening air.

Calvin blew out a huff of disapproval and stomped

his front hoof. Snow covered him and he tossed the white stuff off his ear with a flick.

"I know, it's coming down pretty hard. I'm hurrying, buddy." He gripped the little mare's reins, led her out of the barn and closed the back door. Knowing the livery was snug and safe for the night, he tromped through the deep snow. Spring felt far away, as if it would never return. He shivered as he tied the mare to the back of the wagon box, swiped the snow out of his eyes, walked to the front of the wagon and patted Calvin's nose. "Just think. Tonight when I step in through the front door, Willa will be there."

The gelding tilted his head, listening intently the way only a good friend could.

"No more empty house, no more lonely nights." He dropped onto the seat and gave the reins a tug, but Calvin was already moving, eager to get home to his warm stall.

The town's main street swished by in a swirl of white and dark shadows as the storm blew itself into a temper. Mean winds tried to hold them back, blowing hard enough to slice through every layer of clothing until even his bone marrow felt numb.

No matter. This was April. Winter couldn't last forever. He clenched his teeth to keep them from chattering and bowed his head into the storm. Snow battered him like wind-driven nails, but its misery faded when he thought of his bride. How lovely she'd looked today in the store's lamplight with her teeth dug into her lush bottom lip, worrying about the expense of a new dress.

He'd been right in choosing her. There was something extraordinary about her. His heart skipped five beats remembering her reaction when he'd held the blue dress up to her. Her physical good looks had captured him at first, but she possessed an indefinable quality, a strength down deep that held her up. That beautiful strength he appreciated the most.

Miles passed in an instant while he thought of her, while he imagined her standing in the doorway welcoming him home. He couldn't wait to listen to the fire crackling in the hearth and watch lamplight flicker over her. For the first night since he'd been on his own, he had someone to welcome him home. He could picture it. His very own bride in a pretty dress. The scents of supper cooking would fill the air as he stepped into that warm house made into a home because she was there. His Willa.

Calvin's abrupt turn off the main road startled him. Then he recognized the twin firs marking the entrance to his driveway and the quiet drifts of snow sheltered by the forest on either side. Anticipation thumped in his chest like a trapped bird. He couldn't wait to see her.

His chest ached with longing. He wanted to make her smile like she had today in the store. He wanted to see happiness light her eyes and fill his heart. Surely her eyes wouldn't stay so sad. Surely she wouldn't always be so shy and wary around him. A woman who'd been treated the way she had needed time. He squared his shoulders, and steeled his spine, pleased to be the man to do that for her. To show her in the little ways and the larger ones that she was safe, she was cherished and already she was loved.

Up ahead light glimmered faintly through the darkness and storm, growing brighter with every step. Calvin rushed past the house, mantled in snow, on his way to the barn. Austin strained to see through the snowfall and inside the house. All he saw was a glimpse of the dancing firelight and the sofa, but not her. He hoped she'd been able to lie down and rest this afternoon and that she no longer felt poorly. He thought of how ill she'd been this morning and wished he could do something to make it better for her.

Calvin raced to the barn door and stopped, swishing his tail, head up, eager to be let in out of the cold. Austin hardly felt the bitter wind as he trudged through the snow to open the barn door. Calvin marched right in, relieved to be out of the storm, which was reaching blizzard strength. Austin followed him in and barred the door.

"It's all right, girl. You're someplace safe." He turned his attention to the quiet, sad-eyed mare still tied to the back of the wagon box. His fingers fumbled with the knot in the reins, too numb to feel the leather straps. Heck, he was colder than he'd thought. Thoughts of Willa had kept him from noticing. When he took a step, he couldn't feel his feet. He hadn't noticed that before, either.

"Guess I'd better show you to your new stall, girl," he crooned to the trembling mare.

Calvin lifted his head, pricked his ears and blew out his breath in a long, burdened sigh as if he had an opinion on the barn's new occupant.

"Don't worry, buddy." He led the mare down the aisle. "This little girl won't get your big corner stall."

Calvin blew out an answering huff. Rosie, the cow, poked her head over her stall gate, mooing a friendly hello. The little black mare said nothing in response. She kept her head down, breathing heavily, and her skin prickled with fear.

"It's okay, girl." He opened the gate of the stall he'd prepared for her yesterday. The straw crunched crisply beneath her hooves as she slowly stepped inside. She watched him as if expecting the worst as he unbuckled her bridle and slipped it off over her head. The moment she was free, she stayed braced as if waiting for a blow. Anxiety whistled in her fast, shallow breaths.

Poor thing.

Calvin's ears were pricked with a question when Austin stepped foot in the aisle again. With the latch secure, he headed toward his buddy.

"She's had a rough road," he explained to the pampered gelding as he brushed snow off forelock and mane. "Look at it this way. Won't it be nice to share your stable with another horse?"

Calvin snorted, stomping his back foot.

Austin laughed, amused as always by the gelding he'd raised from a foal. "Seems you and I both have a lot of adjusting to do."

It took time to rub down both horses, feed them and water them and give the cow the same attention. He noticed the milk bucket was missing, his first clue Willa had taken it upon herself to milk Rosie before he'd come home.

He didn't like her doing what he considered his job, but he remembered the set of her jaw last night over the dishes and how determined she'd been to finish cooking his breakfast. Showing him she had a good work ethic was important to her. He bid the animals good-night, grabbed the gunnysack full of Willa's wrapped purchases, secured the outside door and let the blizzard batter him. He trudged through the blinding snow—there were no signs of the house through the brutal storm.

It was the hope for the future that pulled him across the yard, that fueled his dogged steps through the drifting snow and bone-chilling bitterness. Hope that in time the fear he read in Willa's eyes would fade and a deep abiding love would take its place. That she would smile when he stepped foot inside the house and turn to him with the kind of adoration he'd seen on his mother's face every time she'd gazed upon Pa.

He stumbled in the darkness, striking the banister hard enough to rattle his teeth. He tromped up the snow-covered steps, his gait unwieldy. Every part of him that had been numb before was now frozen. His gloves slipped on the doorknob. He couldn't seem to turn it, but it opened for him. Willa stood in the fall of light, backing away to make room for him. The lamplight burned his eyes after the inky darkness of the storm. It was the dark, he told himself, and not emotion.

"I was starting to worry," she confessed, closing the door after him. "I didn't know if you would be safe coming all the way from town."

"I know every step of the way by heart." It touched him that she'd been concerned. The crinkle in her forehead and the way her eyes searched him as if to make sure he was all right touched him down deep. Feeling twisted to life in his chest in a painful coil.

There was hope for something special between them. He could feel it in his soul. He took comfort in that as he dropped the bag to the floor and unwound his scarf. Ice crackled, breaking apart in the warmth of the house.

"Here, let me help you." Her slender fingers plucked the scarf away from his face. "Goodness, your skin is so white. Almost bloodless. You've gotten too cold, Austin."

"I'm fine."

"No, you aren't." Concern wreathed her exquisite face, drawing little adorable tucks around her eyes and the soft corners of her mouth. Her blueberry eyes darkened a shade as she tugged off his gloves and covered his fingers with her much smaller ones.

He couldn't answer her. His throat closed right up. His tongue tied into knots. Her concern for him was about the loveliest thing he'd ever known. His chest filled with emotion.

"You're like ice." The song of her voice drew him after her. She didn't need to tug him along. Her voice held him captive as she waltzed ahead of him deeper into the room. He couldn't look away from the swirl of her skirts, the quiet pad of her shoes and the straight elegant line of her back. Her braid swished from side to side with her gait, drawing his attention. She was wearing her old calico work dress, not the new one he'd bought her. Not the new shoes he'd told her to get.

The woman had a stubborn streak, but he forgot to

be upset about it as she held his hands in hers. She was here, and that was all that mattered. When she reached the golden glow from the hearth she turned to him, releasing her grip to wrestle with his snow-caked coat buttons. But her hold on him remained, unbroken.

Please come to love me. The plea welled up within him with the power to blind him. With every tug of the fabric, every button that came free, his heart beat with the melody of what could be. He shrugged out of the coat, hardly aware of doing it or of the roar of the fire. Only her nearness mattered. The whisper of her movements, the sigh of her breath, the brush of her hair against his chin, as soft as silk.

He wanted to love her, too. With all the heart and devotion he had in him. He took his coat and gloves from her; she really shouldn't wait on him. "I always get cold like this. No need to fuss, but it's nice, Willa."

"I've got a cup of coffee poured for you. I'll go fetch it." Her gaze locked on his, as if searching to make sure he was all right, before she rustled away.

Definitely better coming home to a wife. Gratitude burned like a hot lump in his chest, chasing away some of the numbness. Chills set in as he thawed out. Pain streaked through his fingers and needled his toes.

The images of what could be spread out before him. A little babe napping in a basket, and Willa in that pretty blue dress turning from the counter with a cup in her hand and a contented smile lighting up her face. Love would shine in her eyes with the same brightness as in his heart.

That was his wish, all he'd ever wanted. And now

he wanted it with Willa. He'd never been so close to his dream before and she seemed to bring the hope of it with her as she breezed near.

"This should help warm you up." She held out the cup with careful fingers. A crinkle dug into her forehead as she watched him intently. "I put a little sugar in it. Do you w-want anything else?"

"No, Willa. You don't have to wait on me. That's not why I brought you here." He resisted the urge to cup the dear side of her face with his free hand, needing to touch her. But his skin was ice-cold and he would be too numb to feel the warm satin of her skin anyway. He read the anxiety shadowing her eyes, making those blueberry depths dark.

"Isn't that what a wife does?" She shrugged, swirling away with a flash of the faded dress. "I'll have supper on the table in a few minutes. Thank you for sending Evelyn over. She was very helpful today."

"Yes, she usually is," he drawled dryly. "Exactly what *helpful* information did she give you?"

"She told me you like roast beef and thick pan gravy." She padded into the kitchen to put a pot on the table. "Also that you like baked potatoes, but if there's gravy you like them mashed."

"And you went to the trouble of mashing them tonight?" He watched as she removed the lid, steam lifted and whipped potatoes sat, smooth and buttery in their pot.

"It was no trouble." She felt aware of every movement she made and of his eyes on her, watching. The fragrance made her stomach rumble. Thank goodness her nausea was faint and hardly noticeable as she gave the thickening gravy a final stir. A dash more pepper and she poured it into the gravy boat. "Supper is ready, if you're thawed out enough to eat, that is."

"Somehow I'll manage. Everything smells good. My mouth is watering from here." He hadn't said anything about the coffee he carried in one capable hand. Jed would have been in a rage by now, because sugar wasn't enough to flavor an evening cup of coffee. Whiskey was the best sweetener.

So far, she hadn't seen Austin drink. Just concentrate on the meal, she told herself. The meat had rested long enough, so she took up the meat fork and the knife and made the first slice.

"Let me." Austin's hand curled over hers, stopping her. His cold skin reminded her of how hard he'd worked through the day and of his frigid drive from town. His hand was steady, not the touch of a man who relaxed after work with a half pint of whiskey. His grip was gentle, almost a caress as he finessed the knife from her grasp. The solid wall of his chest pressed against her back, trapping her for a moment against him.

He felt even bigger than he looked, so solid he could have been made of iron. She felt small by comparison, and a bubble of panic caught in her chest and made her gasp. But he was already moving away, not a man meaning to trap her against him. At least not at this moment.

"Willa, did you polish the cabinets? And the floor?" He drew the platter near, intent on his carving. Rich, beefy aroma lifted in the air. Anyone watching him might think he was focused on the task, but she saw his gaze cut sideways to her. "What else did you do?"

"I know your sister did a light cleaning before I came, but I wanted to do something more thorough." She carried the basket of sliced johnnycake to the table. "I made a promise to you, Austin, one I intend to keep. I will be such a good wife you will not regret helping me. I need a home."

"I mean to keep my promises to you, too." He set down the knife, laid it aside and set the platter on the table beside her. Something darkened his eyes, something she did not recognize as he leaned in close. So close, his breath was a whisper against her ear. So close, she could see the texture of his day's stubble on his jaw. "As long as I'm alive, you will have a home. You won't be hungry. You're safe now, Willa. You don't need to work so hard to prove anything to me."

"I need to earn my way." She slipped away, but putting space between them didn't help. It was as if the walls of the house shrank and were closing in on her, and it felt as if all the air had been sucked out of the room. Her throat closed and she felt as if she were suffocating as she lifted the coffeepot from the stove. Its heat penetrated her hot pad, warming her hand as she set it on the trivet next to the gravy. "Besides, you hardly know me."

"True, but I feel like I've always known you." He brought his coffee cup to the table, sidling up beside her so that their arms touched. "When I read your advertisement, something in your words grabbed me and wouldn't let go. It was as if I knew how it would be between us."

"What do you mean?" How could her simple advertisement do that much? She darted away, breathing hard to draw in air. Her lungs felt crushed, her ribs unyielding, and she stumbled to Austin's chair. "They were just words."

"Maybe it was your voice in those words. It was brief but powerful." He set his cup down beside his plate, towering over her like a mountain. So big, it was him shrinking the room, she realized. His masculine power radiated with a tangible force that overwhelmed her. And his kindness? She knew better than to trust in it too much.

Her ribs wrenched hard, fighting off the memory of Jed hauling her by the roots of her hair, slamming her into the wall and tossing her to the ground. While she bled, he stood over her and set her straight on a wife's duties by day and by night.

Austin's approach may be different, but who was to say what lay beneath his gentle manner? He was a man. How could he be much different? She was his convenient wife, someone he'd shopped for out of a newspaper and chose sight unseen. He had expectations—probably not so different from Jed's—and so she wrapped her fingers around the top rail of the ladder-back chair and pulled it out for him.

"I had to pay by the word, that's all." She spoke of the advertisement, continuing to hold out his chair, waiting for him to sit into it. "I only had a few coins, so it had to be brief."

"Maybe, but it felt as if fate was guiding me." His hand covered hers and lifted it from the chair back. He stared at her callused fingers a moment, a muscle working along his jaw. He turned thoughtful. "When my mother died, she nearly took my father with her. In his grief, he could barely breathe without her beside him. They had a bond stronger than all the others I've seen. They each lived for the other. Ma wasn't whole unless Pa was in the room. Pa was not whole without her, and he's never stopped grieving her."

"It's a nice story." She knew that's all it could be. Men did not love like that. She didn't know if men loved at all. She'd had no father in her life. Jed had never loved anyone but himself and a bottle of his treasured whiskey.

"It's not make-believe and not embellished." Austin tugged her gently around the table, his shadow falling over her when he stepped in front of the lamp. "Happy marriages run in my family. It's a family trait. Maybe it's a rule written down somewhere long ago. That when a Dermot marries, love reigns."

He could not be serious, although he looked like he believed it as he pulled out her chair instead and eased her down into it. The edge of the cushion bumped against the back of her legs and she settled into the softness. Why was he helping her, when she should be holding his chair? Last night he'd been on his good behavior, but tonight? Wasn't it time for him to be himself? To show her the man who lurked beneath the mellowness?

He knelt beside her to gaze into her eyes. She read

his kindness there, nothing worse, and his quiet, un-spoken hope. The hope for happiness.

For love.

Her chin sank and her head bobbed down of its own accord, even though she tried to stop it. Austin wanted her love? It was worse than if he'd been a drunk like Jed. He'd picked the wrong woman. She rubbed the spot above her heart where love had never lived.

Where she knew it never could.

How did she break it to him? Did she let him continue to hope for the impossible? Or did she tell him the truth now so he could annul the marriage and find another bride who could give him the pretense he wanted?

Chapter Seven

"But our marriage is a convenient one." She lifted the basket of johnnycake with a tremble, careful not to look at him. The warm cornmeal scent drifted upward as she set a square of cake on the edge of her plate. She didn't look at him and her words had held no ring of emotion.

"That doesn't matter." Austin rose to his full height and circled to his chair. "You might be surprised to learn that my mother was a mail-order bride."

"No, how could that be?" Curiosity glimmered like blue promises when she raised her chin and studied him across the table. "She was a convenient wife."

"My pa tells the story better than I do." He picked up the platter near to him and forked several slabs of meat onto his plate. His stomach growled with hunger, but he was too hopeful to pay it any heed. He handed her the beef, not bothering to fight the glitters of affection threatening to take him over. She was stunning with the lamplight soft on her ivory complexion and burnishing her dark hair.

He thought about the bundle of purchases still in the entry she hadn't touched yet—she was more concerned with serving his supper than material things. He thought about the way she'd shivered in bed last night and how she'd tried to hold out his chair for him. He could see the shadows in her. He understood that sometimes it was hard to believe when hard times came to an end.

"My pa was living in the wilds of Minnesota working to save for his own land one day." He dug into the potatoes—boy, did they look creamy. The woman sure could cook. "He bought an advertisement, said he was looking for a wife who could tolerate a sense of humor in a man. Ma's was the first letter to arrive at the nearby trading post fifty miles away."

"I know how remote that lifestyle can be. Where I used to live wasn't much better. Is that why he wrote away for a bride?"

"Yes. No eligible ladies were anywhere nearby. Ma rode in a stagecoach all the way from Maine. Her parents had died, her older brother had gone bankrupt and lost the family home, so she had nowhere to go." He ladled thick gravy over his potatoes, thinking he'd never seen finer gravy. Looked as if he'd been as fortunate in a wife as his father had been.

"A stagecoach." Willa shook her head. "Your poor mother. It's such an antiquated way to travel. I'm so thankful for modern trains."

"I am, too. I only had to wait days for your arrival.

My pa waited months." He took a bite of roast. Juicy, flavorful, so good he nearly groaned. Willa had yet to eat, holding her fork in midair, watching him and waiting.

"She climbed out of the stagecoach at the trading post. She said she hadn't put her foot to the ground before two dozen bachelors swarmed her." He washed down his food with a gulp of coffee. "Every man vied for her attention, offering her proposals on the spot. A pretty young lady was a rarity in those parts and she could have had her choice of them. Truth was she'd been turning down proposals ever since she'd left Chicago."

"But she kept her promise to your pa?"

"Yes. Ma wasn't about to break her word to him. She confessed to us kids later that she was sweet on him long before she met him. His sense of humor had come through in his letters and that had hooked her. She wanted no other husband but him. They were married two months shy of twenty-one years and what had started out as a necessary marriage for her became something rare. We all knew Ma held on so long through her illness because her love was so strong she couldn't endure leaving Pa behind."

"I see." Willa turned quiet and bowed her head again. She took a small bite of mashed potato. That was it—she said nothing more. When he'd meant to encourage her, to reassure her that great affection could come out of a marriage between strangers, it seemed to do the opposite.

"Is that what you are hoping for?" She set down her

fork with a faint *clink* against the edge of her plate. "A strong and rare love?"

He heard the hollowness in her voice and the soft notes of distress. The light from the lamp caressed the crinkles of emotion carved into her forehead as she turned her wary, uncertain gaze on him. He swallowed hard, seeing he hadn't reassured her at all. "It's something to shoot for, don't you think? Wouldn't it be nice?"

"Austin, I have to tell you something." She swallowed visibly and drew herself up in her chair. "Do you know how my parents met?"

"No. You haven't told me anything about your father." Curious, he leaned forward across the small table, interested and hoping she was about to open up to him. His hopes dropped when he saw emotion gather in her eyes like tears of sorrow. He knew hers would not be a story like his, of true love.

"My father owned a prosperous hotel in Virginia City." She blew out a soft breath of air as if in pain. "He was married. He had a family. Two daughters and five sons. His wife belonged to all the social clubs in town and she was very handsome in her furs and jewels. They were very fine people."

"And how did he meet your mother?" Looking into Willa's eyes, which were stark with pain, it was easy to imagine all sorts of tragedies happening. Illness, accident, death. A widower needing to remarry.

"My mother was a new maid in his hotel." Willa broke her piece of johnnycake in two with nervous fingers. "One day Ma stayed late to help an elderly, wealthy lady settle into her room for the night. When she was hurrying down the stairs to leave for home, the owner pulled her into a vacant room and forced himself on her. She tried to fight, but she couldn't stop him. She screamed, but no one came. When she tried to tell what happened, no one but my grandmother believed her. Ma was fifteen."

"Fifteen," he repeated, shaking his head, not wanting to believe it. Not wanting to believe that Willa's mother had endured such brutality. One look at the tears standing in Willa's eyes punched the air from his chest. "Let me guess. She found out she was expecting you."

"Yes. A terrible scandal. She was a marked woman having a child out of wedlock. Shunned by polite society. Demoted from her job. The owner told of how she'd asked him for it, that she was a bad girl, and she lived with that shame. No one else would hire her with her reputation and her pregnancy."

"So she continued to work for the man who raped her?"

"Until he sold the hotel and moved his family to a more prosperous place. Ma works there still." She dipped the tip of her knife into the butter ball, her hands trembling along with her voice. Her chin went up, showing the steely strength within her.

"I'm sorry, Willa." He didn't know what else to say. "That's a terrible story. You must have lived your life an outcast."

"I was a bastard. A loose woman's daughter. I thought you should know." She set down the butter knife when her hand shook too hard to hold it.

"That makes no difference to me. You are just as

lovely to me now as you were when you stepped off the train."

"I'm afraid you want too much from me. You never mentioned love in your letter. It was never a condition of our marriage."

"Don't you want it to be? I mean one day, when we are no longer strangers?" He could feel her anguish and see the happy images he'd held for their future begin to fall. "Everyone wants a family, a place to belong. Someone to love and someone to love them. It's why I answered your letter. It's why I chose you."

"It's not what we agreed on." Panic and misery marked her, pulling down the corners of her mouth and painting hopelessness in shades of blue.

"I know," he agreed. "But don't you have hopes, too?"

"Hopes?" That stumped her. She certainly did not have the same type of expectations he did. "I came because of my condition. You know I need a roof over my head for the baby. I need a husband to provide for us, something I cannot possibly do on my own. That's the only reason I'm here. I thought you understood that."

"I do." Furrows crinkled his forehead. He looked amazing with the lamplight gleaming on his dark locks, making him more handsome than any one man had the right to be. "But I want you to understand that just because practical matters brought us together, it doesn't mean it can't be more. What I feel...well, I was hoping you might feel the start of something, too."

"You mean love." She swallowed hard, seeing her hopes crack around her, ready to fall in pieces to the ground. Her hopes were modest compared to his but they had held her up during the train journey and given her the strength to marry a stranger. She stared down at her hands, red from the soap she'd used to scrub the floor and from the wax that polished it. She had to be honest with him. "I don't believe in love. It isn't real."

"Sure it is." So smooth his voice, so certain he was right.

"I've never seen even a glimmer of it anywhere." She straightened her spine, squared her shoulders and drew up the courage to be honest. "I can work hard, I can keep my promise to be a good wife, but love? No, I can't promise that." She shook her head.

"This is my fault." His buttery baritone could tempt even her to believe. "I'm jumping the gun, as usual. I think it's important for you to know what I'm hoping for, but I don't expect these things now, Willa. We hardly know each other. You're right. I'm just trying to say life will get better for both of us. Having you here is the best thing that could happen to me."

"Because you're hoping in time I will come to love you?" She had to ask the question, she couldn't leave it alone and continue eating supper the way Austin did, as if nothing were wrong. She couldn't let him believe those things falsely. This man had rescued her, he'd sent her a train ticket with no questions asked and given her his home, the best she'd ever known. No one had treated her with such kindness.

No, she owed him the truth. Gazing across the table at him sitting straight and tall, it made her heart twist tight with an emotion she'd never felt before. Gratitude overwhelmed her for what he'd done. Leaving her to sleep last night without touching her, insisting she buy new clothes she didn't need and this fine meal from the plentiful food in the cellar and pantry. Why, he'd given her more than she'd ever had. Safety, security, and even if she did not know what lurked deep inside him, she did know on the surface he sought to be kind.

She owed him for that alone. She cleared her throat, but her voice came shaky and thin anyway, wobbling with emotion. "I don't even know if I can love my unborn child because I have no love in me. I know I never will."

She watched disappointment twist across his face but his square chin firmed, when she expected anger. A wince of pain tightened the corners of his mouth. His eyes remained fixed on her, glossy with emotions she didn't know how to read.

"You're right. Love wasn't part of our bargain." He blew out a gentle breath like someone trying to hide a wound. He cut into his meat, his knife scraping on the plate. Silence settled between them as the muscles in his jaw bunched and lines dug into his forehead.

He looked like a man thinking things over, and her stomach clamped up tight. He looked like a man debating the merits of staying married to her. Miserable, she choked down a bite of johnnycake, hoping the cornmeal would settle the sudden onset of nausea—from worry this time, not from the pregnancy. She washed it down with tea, waiting for the silence to end.

Now that he knew the truth, what if he changed his mind about wanting her for his wife? She set the glass on the table, careful to hide her shaky hand. The old panic returned. She didn't have a penny to her name. Where would she go? Where would she find work? After the baby came, who would care for the newborn while she made a living? How could she afford to pay someone to care for the babe? She did not want to go back to living out of an abandoned barn again.

She peered through her lashes, studying Austin's manner as he chased down a mouthful of beef with a swallow of coffee. With his eyebrows drawn together like that, he *could* be angry with her. He'd spent so much money on her—the train ticket and all those costly garments. What would his temper be like? Would he yell and throw things? Or would his rage be more horrible?

Bracing herself for the worst, she swallowed hard and lowered her gaze, staring at the food on her plate. She drew a forkful of potato through a puddle of gravy, forcing herself to eat for the baby's sake. She knew she was too thin. Echoes of Jed's rage played over and over in her ears. The terrible words he shouted and the things he called her seemed to reverberate in her mind like silence in the room.

"I brought a little mare home for you." When he finally spoke, there was no trace of anger in his words and no disappointment. No emotion of any kind. "I don't want you isolated out here when I take Calvin to work, and she will be easy to handle. I wasn't sure if you'd driven before."

"No." She shook her head, swallowing hard. Her

throat burned. So did the back of her eyes. "Jed didn't allow me to drive the horses."

"Well, I expect you to. You'll need to get out and get to town for groceries and the like." He didn't look at her as he picked up his knife to cut another bite of meat. "I picked the mare up at a sale a while back. She'd been so mishandled, scared of every little thing and had so many scars, I couldn't handle leaving her there. Who knew what would have come of her, so I bought her. She's been living at the livery for a while now, but she'll do better here in a quieter barn. She's gentle and she would be a good match for you."

"But I don't know how to drive." The words rasped out of her throat, each one painful against the rising tide of emotion she couldn't seem to hold down. It rose in an excruciating bubble, bringing tears to her eyes.

"It's easy to learn." He lifted his gaze to hers, letting her see the shadows and the disappointment. It didn't show in his voice, but she knew she'd hurt him.

Despair filled her, and she could say nothing more.

I have no love in me. I know I never will. Willa's confession haunted him as he added wood to the fire. The flames leapt and danced, greedily consuming the bark and moss on the outside of the log, snapping and popping. He straightened, aware of the rattle of the dishes as Willa dried them in the silence that had stretched from the rest of the meal and threatened to continue until sleep claimed him.

Not the evening he'd figured on, with her keeping to one side of the room and he to the other. It felt as if the Rocky Mountains separated them. The breach between them was so wide, he wasn't sure if anything could bridge it. Standing in the shadows of the room, hands on his hips, he watched Willa's slender form as she put away the dishes. The swish of her faded skirt, the curve of her arm, the desolation that clung to her.

He could not imagine her earlier life. He'd been the oldest boy, welcomed into a loving marriage. His childhood had been one of laughter and familial closeness. The only thing wrong was his luck in love.

It looked as if that hadn't changed any, either. He finally had a wife, but it seemed like love might always elude him. He'd picked the wrong gal, he thought, hating the loneliness that clung to him like shadows as he crossed the room. Snow had melted on the gunnysack still slumped in the entrance corner. He dusted off the slush and slung the sack over one shoulder.

"That is next on my list," she said. A final dish slipped into place on the stack. Uncertainty twisted the bow of her lips. "You shouldn't need to bother with that, Austin."

"I don't mind. I suppose you were going to put these things away." He couldn't say why anger knotted tight in his throat, but it did.

"That was my plan, unless—" She paused, turned fully toward him and straightened her slender shoulders. She looked fragile and determined not to be. She took an unsteady breath, remorse shimmering in shades of blue. "Unless you were planning on taking it all back to the store?"

"Now why would I want to do that?" He set the sack

down on the nearby end table and shoved a few things out of the way to make more room.

"Oh, maybe you've changed your mind about me and, Austin, if you have, I would understand." She lifted her chin, standing tall, but for all the good it did. She was petite, too thin and looked far too lonely. His chest warmed against his will, filling with feelings that had nothing to do with anger.

It was heartbreak. When he dug beneath the layer of burning emotions, he could feel his hopes breaking. It looked as if the happy family image he'd been holding on to for so long wouldn't come to pass. "You think I would send you away?"

"I'm not what you expected." She shrugged, her only explanation.

Another spear of anger threatened but he ignored it, seeing it for what it was. "I know you hardly know me, Willa, but I am not a man to break his word. I promised to take care of you and I will. Those vows I made at our wedding? I meant them."

Relief whispered out of her in a sigh. The way she clutched the edge of the table with a white-knuckled grip told him something of her fears of being abandoned and unwanted.

He swallowed hard, trying to hide his hurt. "You can't get rid of me that easily, pretty lady."

She almost smiled, but it wasn't humor that curved the corners of her mouth or eased away the tension in the dainty line of her jaw. She didn't speak, she didn't whisper, all she could do was to mouth the words *thank you* across the distance between them.

She really didn't understand what he wanted from her. He grimaced at the disappointment dragging him down. He worked the ties of the gunnysack free, his teeth clenched and jaw taut, at a loss what to do now. There would be no easy conversation between them from this point on. No good-natured moments, no sitting companionably together in front of the fire as the evening ticked by like he'd hoped.

"What are you doing?" The quite notes of alarm in her voice shook him out of his thoughts.

"Hanging up your new coat." He figured it was obvious.

"But my old coat is still usable." She rushed toward him in her patched shoes. "I was hoping to save the new one for good."

"No, this is for every day." He refused to hand over the rag. "Just like the dresses. You should be wearing them."

"To do work in? They are too fine for that. I could spill something on them and stain the fabric." She tried to grab the old coat out of his hands.

He let it go. "You may wear it to the barn. You may wear it outside if you're throwing out wash water or such. But that's it. And your dresses? Only to work in, Willa. Do you hear me?"

She swallowed hard, fisting her hands, clutching the patched wool garment as if it was all she had left in the world. Was it so hard to accept something from him, her husband?

He rasped out a breath, trying to wrestle his own hurts down and get them under control. Maybe he just couldn't grasp what was driving her. "I'm trying to make your life better, Willa. Will you let me do that for you?"

"Yes, of course. I'm thankful." She looked wistfully up at him, the light in her eyes fading to a silent plea for him to understand. "I'll put these things away. What else can I do for you this evening?"

How did he ask her to be what she could not? He would have been happy to start with being friends.

He shook his head, noticing how tired she appeared. Dark circles bruised the skin beneath her eyes. Remembering how bony she'd been against his hand, a painful thinness she worked to hide from him, he sighed heavily. He cared for her. So very much.

"Do you know what you can do?" He hefted the gunnysack to carry it into the bedroom for her. "Please enjoy hanging up your new things. I'm going to sit and read until bedtime."

"Oh. Okay." She must have felt the failure between them, too, because sadness clung to her the same way it did to him. She didn't seem to know how to fix it any more than he did. As her gaze met his, a connection he couldn't explain whipped into place, as if lassoing his heart to hers.

When she walked away, he'd never felt lonelier. He sat down with his volume of Shakespeare, but not even Hamlet's dilemma could make him forget that she was in the next room, or that the distance between them grew with every breath he took.

Chapter Eight

The blizzard woke her. It thrashed like a wild animal against the north wall of the bedroom, crazed as
if trying to get in. The air felt brutally icy against her
face, so she buried herself deeper into the soft pillow
and drew the edges of the covers up over her head. It
muffled but could not silence the eerie roar of the wind
bashing against the siding or the snow scratching like
sand against the windowpanes.

In the front room, the clock chimed faintly. It was
hard to hear through the layers of blankets, the wall
and the storm, but she counted four dongs. Four in the
morning. She rolled onto her side to stare at the man
asleep beside her. Austin's soft breath puffed in and out
in a peaceful rhythm. Unlike Jed, his wasn't the deep,
lost sleep of the drunk, measured by bouts of deafen-
ing snoring.

She did not know what to make of the man. Austin
wasn't like anyone she'd known before, at least no one

she'd been close to. He reminded her of the popular children when she'd been young and attended school, before her mother pulled her out to work in the hotel. She'd admired those classmates with their fine things and confident happiness, whose lives seemed golden and untouched by the shadows that filled hers.

In the dark, she could make out the high plain of his forehead and the tousled hair tumbling over it like thick silk. She took time studying the slope of his nose and the cut of his cheekbones. The carved crags chiseled into his cheeks remained, even in sleep. Powerful masculinity clung to him, strong enough to make her shiver. She dug her teeth into her bottom lip and had to wonder.

Why hadn't some woman set her bonnet for him long ago? She didn't believe for a moment that any lady would choose another man over him...unless there was a reason to do so. She kept coming back to the same conclusion. It frightened her because she hadn't seen that part of him yet.

Last night she'd caught a glimpse of his anger, but he'd kept it veiled and in control. Last night was another night he hadn't drank or tried to force himself on her. After he'd put his foot down about her new clothes, he'd retreated to read on the sofa. He held no grudge when she'd padded into the room with her mending. She'd sat on the far end of the cushion, stitching quietly, aware of how disappointed he must be in her. She'd gone to bed early, leaving him behind in the lamplight.

Now what did she do? Already her stomach quivered. She hated the morning sickness she had to fight.

She hated the condition that had pulled her back into a marriage when, for one brief moment standing sadly at Jed's graveside, she thought she had been free.

The minutes were ticking by and soon Austin would be up. She had to figure out what to do. She'd hurt him with her honesty last night. Guilt filled her and she rolled away to stare at the ceiling. Icy air burned the inside of her nose and turned the tip numb, so she ducked under the covers again. She'd never wanted to hurt him, only to set the record straight and keep him from expecting something she could never give.

Whatever his faults, whatever the side of Austin she did not yet know, he'd been good to her. Better than anyone ever had and she owed him much more than she could ever repay. But how could she begin to make this right for him? He'd kept her when she'd given him an out, a reason to end the marriage. She didn't know what else to do, except to try harder.

At least yer good for something, Jed's voice echoed through her memories. *Yer good for hard work but not much more.*

Willa tossed back the covers and sat up slowly, hoping her stomach cooperated. The little twist of sickness was nothing to worry about so she eased off the bed, careful not to jostle Austin awake. She pulled on her old housecoat, stepped into thick slippers she'd knitted long ago and crept from the dark room.

Cold pressed on her from every direction and she shivered all the way to the kitchen. She used the little shovel to uncover the ashes and the poker to stir the bed of embers kept warm through the night. As she added a handful of moss to the glowing coals, she planned her morning. First, she would get coffee boiling and then—

"What are you doing?" A booming voice startled her as it thundered around the kitchen like a storm. The poker slipped from her hand and crashed to the floor. Large stocking feet marched into view. She looked up the length of his legs to the man towering above her with fisted hands on his hips, anger lining his face.

Her hopes withered. Maybe there was no way to make things right with him. "I—I'm fixing coffee."

"But it's freezing out here." He grabbed her by the wrists and lifted her off the floor. "And so are you. What were you thinking?"

"That you might want a hot cup of coffee before you go out to the barn." His hands weren't bruising her exactly, but his grip held her captive. Fear beat behind her ribs. What would Austin's rage be like? She swallowed hard, still determined to do the right thing. "I thought you liked coffee in the morning, but I can make tea."

"Willa." The anger slid from him and he let her go. "Getting up and lighting the fires is my job. I don't want you doing my work."

"But I thought it would help." She felt foolish and ridiculous. As if she could ever make up for not being what he needed. Now what did she do?

Silent, he turned away from her, rescued the poker from the floor and knelt in front of the stove. She had to scoot back to make room for him and bumped against the table. It moved noisily a few inches and the sharp creak of wood on wood shot through the kitchen like a gunshot.

The moss had burned out, but Austin added kindling anyway, slivers of dry cedar that smoldered and caught on the red coals, burning hot and fast. He didn't say a word while he worked, adding small chunks of wood to the flames in the stove. Maybe he was thinking about what to do with her. The fire grew steadily, licking and snapping. Heat blew out like a wind and the frost on the side of the stove began to melt in quiet plops onto the hardwood floor. She resisted the urge to mop them up, not sure how Austin would react.

He closed the door, squared his mountain-strong shoulders and rose to his full height. She couldn't meet his gaze, so she stared at the top button of his flannel shirt and wished she understood him.

"From now on, you stay in bed until the house is warm." His tone brooked no argument, ringing above the droning blizzard and the greedy roar of the fire. "Do you understand? I don't want you catching a—"

Her stomach cramped, nausea rose and she clamped her hand over her mouth. *Oh, no.* She raced back to the bedroom and slammed the door, unable to hold back the illness that left her weak and slumping over the chamber pot.

"Not sure what I'm going to do about the woman," he confessed to Rosie as he stripped the last of the milk from her udder. Droplets splashed into the bucket, steaming in the early morning cold. "Do you have any insights on that? You're a female. Maybe you can give me advice on the way a woman thinks."

If Rosie had any wisdom to share, she kept it to

herself. She flicked her tail, watching him with silky brown eyes.

"Yeah, I figured you might stay silent on the subject." He winked, grabbed the pail by the handle and whipped the milking stool out of the stall. "I'm not surprised you females are sticking together."

Rosie ambled over and laid her chin on his shoulder. Nice girl.

"Yeah, don't try and be sweet to make up for it. I know where I stand," he quipped, giving her a rub on the nose before he latched the gate tight.

Calvin nickered, leaning over his gate, too. His black forelock tumbled into his eyes and his chestnut coat gleamed in the lantern light. Curious brown eyes met his, begging for attention, so Austin ambled over and rubbed his nose, too. "How's the grain tasting?"

The gelding rumbled deep in his throat, a contented sound as he offered his head for more petting. They were old friends and understood each other well. There was no need for words as they stood in silence, Calvin lipping Austin's woolen scarf with affection.

He couldn't get Willa out of his mind. The image of her kneeling on that icy floor, shivering in nothing but her housecoat, called up a protective fury strong enough to blind him.

Just calm down, he told himself, aware of the mare backing into the corner of her stall. She sensed his mood and he was frightening her. Much the same way as he'd done to Willa before she'd darted from the room, overcome with morning sickness.

What made a pregnant woman think to start a fire on

a bitterly cold morning, he didn't know. She'd wanted to make him coffee? Couldn't she see it was his concern for her that mattered? Frustration ate at him. Calvin blew out a like-sounding sigh, reaching over to grab Austin's hat brim. Perhaps trying to fix his master's mood.

"You are a good friend." He patted the horse, rescued his Stetson and shrugged off his frustration. Emotion like that never did anyone a lick of good. "You've got everything you need, buddy. A clean stall, a comfortable bed, enough water and food. You're set for the morning, right?"

Calvin looked over his shoulder to check on the grain in his trough.

"I'll be back to slip you some more around lunchtime before I hitch you up," he promised, then ruffled the gelding's forelock lovingly and turned in the aisle. The little mare watched him with cautious eyes, still in her corner. He'd been caring for her for three months and she still didn't trust him.

She reminded him a good deal of Willa.

He slipped through the door and barred it behind him. The storm blew hard, battering him as he started out and whipping his face. At least he could see the faint outline of the house through the veil of thickly tumbling snow. A glint of light from the front window guided his way. Would Willa be in the kitchen, forcing herself to work when she felt ill? He bowed his head into the wind and trudged through the drifts, not sure if he could make his bride understand.

Maybe she couldn't. Remembering last night, he

could still see her with that look of resignation, thinking he might want to end the marriage and send her away. She didn't understand who he was because of the man she'd been married to before, the one who must have broken every dream she'd ever had.

He didn't know how to fix that, but he intended to figure out a way. He reached the door, stomped snow off his boots and stumbled into the house. Warmth met him like a welcome friend as he hung up his wraps and tucked his boots in the corner. He listened to the sounds of her in the kitchen. The sizzle of the bacon, the scrape of a spatula against a fry pan and the clunk of a platter on the table.

He should have known she'd fix breakfast for him even when she felt queasy. His gait sounded on the floor, drawing her gaze. Pale as a sheet, she stood at the stove concentrating on her work. When she turned and saw him, a question quirked up her eyebrows. He remembered what she'd told him last night. *I can work hard, I can keep my promise to be a good wife.* That mattered to her. That was what drove her. Hope shone blue in her eyes as she watched him approach.

He should have known. He should have figured this out sooner. He raked a hand through his hair, frustrated at himself. He'd been a bachelor too long, maybe, or perhaps it simply wasn't easy learning to take another's outlook and needs in account at every turn. He curled his fingers around the top rung of his chair, taking in all she'd done for him. The napkins folded just so. The table set with care. His cup of coffee steaming on the table, waiting for him. Pancakes, bacon, eggs sunnyside up and some buttermilk biscuits that looked delicious. Even the butter was cut into little rosettes.

He swallowed down the first words that slid onto his tongue, words that hadn't worked before. No sense getting upset at all the work she'd done, when she had to be struggling to hold it together. Her hand trembled with the weakness of her condition as she reached out to take the pail of milk from him, the pail he'd forgotten he was holding. She captured his senses—the light on her hair, the fragrance of soap, the flash of her blue dress beneath the faded apron she wore.

"This is a very fine table you've prepared." He tried to keep his worry for her out of his voice and his appreciation in. It wasn't easy when he wanted to order her to lie down, to bring her a damp cloth to lay across her forehead and let her rest. But he knew what pride was like so he pushed his needs aside and thought of hers. "I don't think I've ever seen a finer breakfast."

"I'm glad." She lit up at his praise like a winter's dawn—slow and sweet and quietly spectacular. "Go ahead, sit down while the food is hot. On a morning as cold as this, things will cool off fast."

"You're looking better than you did yesterday about this time." He walked around the table to pull out her chair. He watched her struggle with indecision, perhaps thinking there was more work she wanted to do, before she quietly slipped onto the cushion.

"Your sister's tea made all the difference. My stomach is much calmer." She laid the napkin across her lap, still wearing her apron.

He hesitated a moment and gazed down at her, taking

in little details about her he'd missed before. Like the tiny curls of short hair at the base of her neck, swirling darkly against her ivory skin. Like the straight line of the part in her hair, somehow vulnerable. She brought out powerfully protective feelings he didn't know he had. He resisted the urge to curl his hands around her slender shoulders and squeeze gently, just to touch her, just to offer her some comfort. He'd never met anyone who needed it more.

It took all his willpower to step away.

"You won't need to worry about cooking the rest of the day." He sat down and dug in. Almost a shame to use the butter she'd prettied up, he thought, as he dug his knife into a rosette. When he broke apart a biscuit, the aroma nearly made him groan. One thing was for sure—the woman could cook.

"Why not? Will you be going to town?" Gingerly, Willa took a small bite of her dry toast, looking as if she were praying it would stay down. "It's Sunday, surely the livery is closed for business."

"It is, and I have a hired man who feeds and tends the horses and keeps an eye on things for me, so I have one whole day off in a week." The biscuit practically melted on his tongue. Delicious. "No, my brother Brant stopped by the livery last night. It seems Evelyn was taken with you and praised you so much, that everyone else can't wait to meet you. Pa has invited us over for dinner."

"Oh." She laid a hand on her stomach and cut her gaze to the door, looking a little green. "Then it's a good thing I'm wearing a new dress."

"Yes, it is." He watched as she poured a cup of tea and sipped it slowly. He wished he could do something for her, anything at all. "Are you sure you don't need to lie down?"

"No, I'm fine, thank you." Her chin came up, taking on that stubborn set he was staring to recognize.

That was the end to their conversation. He couldn't think of anything to say and she kept her attention on her teacup. Sure, he could entertain her with stories of his family, warn her about his brothers' wives, tell her tales about his pa, but he held back.

Willa didn't seem to be looking for a family, or else she would be interested in more than being a convenient wife. That weighed heavily on him as the silence stretched until he wondered if it would ever end.

"Willa, you look very nice." Austin's voice traveled across the length of the cabin, through the open bedroom door to where she stood fussing with her new woolen hood. She drew the ties snug beneath her chin, realizing the importance of the new clothes.

Of course, he would want her to look presentable for his sake. She couldn't very well do that in the garments she'd brought with her. Being the wife of a local business owner would take some getting used to. She hardly recognized herself in the mirror as she stepped away from it. "You look nice, too. I'm ready to go if you are."

"The fires are banked. I have the sleigh waiting outside the door and a few extra blankets." He lowered the lamp's wick until the flame went out. "I don't want you to get cold in your condition."

She didn't know what to do about the man. He made her feel inadequate. With every step she took toward him, she'd already failed him. What if his disappointment in her only continued to grow? She hated that notion, especially when she owed him so much. She ran her fingertips along the finely stitched edge of the sash at her waist, the fabric so soft she still couldn't believe it was hers. "The blizzard is pretty much blown out. I should be warm enough."

"Except for the mean wind that barreled in after it." The chiseled line of his mouth softened in the corners. He looked terribly fine in a blue flannel shirt and new denims. "You didn't need to bake anything to bring."

"I wanted to." She lifted the johnnycake which was well wrapped in a dishtowel, and wished she'd had more time to have made something fancier, like a frosted layer cake. "I wanted to contribute something to the meal."

"I'm sure my sisters-in-law will appreciate it." His hand brushed lightly against her shoulder, the faintest pressure seeing her out the door. He said nothing more, his tall, muscular body a big wall of heat a scant inch behind her. He stood so near, the hairs on her arms stood on end and prickled strangely.

Bitter air battered her as Austin bent to lock up. He moved beside her, blocking the wind. His hand caught her elbow. "Careful, there's ice on the steps I couldn't chip off."

"That's nice, but I'm not breakable." She didn't feel comfortable that he thought she was. "I know you're being a good husband, and I appreciate that, I truly do, but you don't have to do so much for me."

"It's my job and I intend to do it well." He winked at her and in the sheen of his deep blue eyes there was something more. An unspoken sadness that when tempered with his kindness, brought tears to her eyes.

She'd really hurt him last night, much more than she'd thought. She let him guide her down the steps, since it meant so much to him. Not that she needed his help, not that she wanted it. She was too independent, but it seemed the right concession to make. It seemed to make him happy, since the corners of his mouth turned up into the good-natured grin that came easily to him. She let him help her into the sleigh and even tuck the blankets around her.

What kind of man was this, she didn't know. She huddled on the chilly seat, shivering while the horse swished his tail, impatient to move. The warming iron tucked at the foot of the sleigh warmed her toes as she watched Austin lift the horse blanket from the back of the gelding, pat him with a kind word and circle to his seat.

Austin was the kind of man who blanketed his horse in the cold, who saw his wife across icy steps and tucked her in first. Looking at him in the gray daylight, framed by the evergreen forest in the background and the satin roll of silver clouds overhead, she saw him clearly as he tucked away the horse blanket. Not framed by her own fears or from her own expectations.

Austin Dermot wore a finely tailored black coat, fine leather driving gloves. His denims were crisp and new, just like his boats. His black Stetson crowned him, a finishing touch to the kind of successful, small-town businessman he was.

Willa swallowed, unable to hold back a curl of warmth in her chest for the man who settled down beside her. His steely arm pressed against her shoulder.

"Are you ready for this?" He gave the reins a snap, but the horse was already moving. Calvin had no fear of retribution as he took charge of their journey.

"My family is a lot to handle," Austin warned in his good-natured manner. "I'll do what I can to shield you."

"What do you mean?" Uncertainty whispered through her. "I've already met Evelyn. She was nice."

"And so you're thinking, how bad can they be?" Austin grinned, bringing out a hint of dimples. "Well, you are about to find out."

Chapter Nine

Her jaw dropped as the sleigh rounded a corner and a two-story house came into sight. The structure, with its gabled dormers and gingerbread trim, had a stately, faintly fairy-tale quality as it sat nestled in a field of snow and rimmed by majestic forests. Lemony lamplight glowed from the many windows and onto the covered wraparound porch, and when they approached the front door swept open.

"Austin!" A blond man wrapped a gray scarf around his neck as he bounded down the steps. "There you are. I had to be the first to get a look at your Willa."

"Charlie. Should have known. Evelyn made you promise to be the greeter, did she?" Beside her, Austin glanced up at the front door and she followed his gaze. A bunch of people clustered together, craning their necks for a better view of her.

Goodness. Heat scorched her face. Everyone was

staring and smiling at her. She wasn't used to being the object of attention, so she swallowed and willed her stomach to stay calm. She may be dressed in fine clothes, but she felt the same inside. She hadn't changed. What if Austin's family saw right through the fine dress to who she was? What if they didn't like her? How would that affect Austin?

"Charlie, this is Willa." Austin handed over the reins and stood, impressive at his full height. With the breaking sun behind him he looked larger than life, as if he could right any wrong. He knuckled back the brim of his Stetson to reveal his magnificent smile. "Thanks for taking Calvin for me. You remember how he likes his straw arranged?"

"I do, and there's never been a more spoiled horse than this one here." Charlie winked, clearly an amiable young man, as he patted Calvin's neck. The gelding stomped his hoof as if he were the one in charge. Charlie chuckled, amused. "It's good to meet you, Willa. Calvin, I suppose I have to warm your oats this time, too?"

The gelding nickered his opinion, clearly in the affirmative. She looked up as Austin caught her hand and helped her from the sleigh in one swift tug. His grip unsettled her. His touch was like magic. For a breathless moment she felt disoriented, not sure what was up or down, as if gravity lost its grip on her. Weightless, her heart stilled and all she knew was the steel of Austin's hand in hers and his blue eyes peering into her. She felt a snap of connection and a brand-new awareness she'd never known before. As if the distance yawning between them had swung closed and they were heart to heart.

Then her foot sank into the snow to touch the ground. Her pulse kicked to a start and the world came back into focus. Silent fields of snow, solemn evergreens, the gleam of lamplight on the shoveled steps. She blinked, unable to catch her breath. The connection between them remained. Not sure what had happened, she didn't seem able to move.

"Don't stand out there!" an older man called in a deep, smoky baritone. "Bring the girl in so we can get a look at her."

"I will, as long as you all agree to behave," Austin called out, chipper and happy sounding.

"We aren't promising anything," the man called out from above.

Dizzy, she stumbled forward as Austin gently led her. He tugged at her senses, making her aware of his hot palm against hers, the scent of wind and hay on his coat and the crunch of his step in the snow.

"Don't worry, they'll love you." His words rumbled low and buttery and just for her. He leaned in, his lips grazing her forehead. "They can be nosy, so I'll be right beside you until you settle in."

His words didn't seem to penetrate the fog of her brain. All she could feel was him. His arm pressed against hers, male-hard and reassuring as they took the steps together.

"We have been waiting a long time for this moment." The same man smiled. Austin's father. "We never thought he would marry. We feared no woman would have him."

"We all worried and drew the same conclusion." Evelyn's familiar voice penetrated the fog of Willa's brain, but only slightly. Austin dominated her senses. It was the knell of his boots she heard and the comforting squeeze of his fingers against hers she felt. He was all she could see—the dashing tilt of his Stetson, the jaunty grin snaring the corners of his mouth and the encouraging light as his gaze found hers. Looking into him made the world vanish again and her pulse slowed. Warmth ribboned through her chest.

What was happening? She'd never felt like this before.

"This is such a happy day." A woman's voice broke through and Willa shook her head, tearing her gaze away from Austin, disoriented again. The woman looked to be in her mid-twenties, with friendly green eyes and a lovely dress. "Austin has a bride. We're all so excited."

She felt shy, not used to being around so many strangers. She couldn't remember the last time she'd attended any social function. She was tongue-tied when she tried to say hello.

"We're so pleased you're here." Another woman reached out to draw Willa into the house where people crowded around her.

So many strangers, but they were Austin's family. She spotted tall, broad-shouldered men, who must be his brothers, and the pretty women they were married to. Everyone smiled at her as Austin joined her in the foyer, while thumps and laughter in the background spoke of children playing in another room.

Somehow she had to untie her tongue. She wanted to make a good impression, for Austin's sake. So he wouldn't be disappointed in her in front of his family, those who mattered most to him. She steeled her spine and battled down her shyness. "I'm pleased to be here, too. Thank you for having me. Here is something for the table."

"Hmm, it smells good." Evelyn snatched the bundle, her friendly smile helping Willa feel more at ease. "If Austin will let go of you so we can have you, come into the kitchen with us."

"Yes, come," the woman who'd drawn her into the house said. "We still have a bit of cooking left, but that's a good thing because we'll have you all to ourselves."

"We've been dying to meet you ever since Austin told us you'd accepted his proposal. I'm Berry, by the way." The woman with sparkling green eyes took off for the kitchen. "Come, we'll get you some tea to help you warm up. Austin, let go of the woman."

"I promised her I wouldn't leave her alone with the likes of you." His fingers remained locked in hers, his tone easygoing. He was the largest man in the room, taller than his father and the men who flanked him. His younger brothers, she realized, all had families of their own.

"Good decision, son." Austin's father had salt-and-pepper hair, Austin's shoulders and Austin's smile. He closed the door against the cold. "It's a real pleasure to meet you, Willa. Welcome to my home."

"Welcome to the family," one of the brothers offered with a single manly nod.

"Thanks for marrying our big brother, Willa." The other brother had Austin's smile, too. "We feared no one would ever have the courage."

"I'm more courageous than I look," she quipped, aware of the exact second when Austin's hand left hers. He moved behind her to help her off with her coat. She loosened the sash and fumbled with her buttons. "I was pleasantly surprised when I detrained here in town and discovered he wasn't all that bad."

His brothers roared with laughter. The women in the room chuckled merrily. Austin's smile outshone them all, something she could not see because he stood behind her, but felt in the air as his hands settled on her shoulders.

"That's a good one," Brant barked out.

"We like her, Austin." Derek nodded his approval while Pa watched over them, beaming approval.

"I got lucky when Willa answered my letter." He lifted the garment off her carefully, feeling how shaky she was. She'd spent the last two years almost entirely alone on a remote farm with only the company of an abusive husband. But she was doing well. Already his family adored her.

Who wouldn't? She was beauty personified with the rich tumble of her dark, silken hair and the wisps framing her porcelain face. She was slender grace and innocent sweetness. As lovely as she was on the outside, it was her gentleness shining through that made her striking. He swallowed hard, feeling.

Just feeling.

"No, I was the lucky one," she insisted, breaking into his thoughts as she slipped away. Evelyn and the sisters-in-law clustered around her, drawing her from him. Willa glanced over her shoulder and her brief smile let him know it was all right. She wanted to go with them.

"Don't worry, Austin." Evelyn laid a protective arm across Willa's slim shoulder. "We'll take good care of her."

"You'd better." He let her go, since it was what she wanted.

What surprised him was the tug of his heart when she left the room.

It wouldn't be wise to fall in love with her, keeping in mind what she'd told him last night.

"I didn't know mail-order brides looked like that." Brant lowered his voice and shook his head, as if he couldn't believe his eyes. "I've never seen a prettier woman. Where did she come from?"

"The better question is what is she doing with you?" Derek elbowed Austin in the arm. "I'm still in shock. That's your bride? You married her? Unbelievable."

"I know just what you mean." He would never forget his first view of Willa standing at the depot. Wisps of hair had framed her heart-shaped face, anxiety bowed her rosebud mouth and with such a slight, almost fragile quality to her she'd looked as if the wind could blow her away. "She wasn't what I was expecting, but I sure hope I can deserve her."

"She's awful young." Pa followed them into the library, where the faint trace of cigar smoke lingered in the room filled with leather furniture and lined with bookshelves. "I figured she'd be older, as a widow."

"She's old enough to be married twice." Austin slipped into one of the chairs, holding his hands out to the fire roaring in the river stone hearth. His real problem sat on his tongue, a problem he couldn't tell his family. How could he confess to his brothers, who'd made good matches, and his father, who'd found true love with his own mail-order bride, that Willa was not everything he'd hoped for?

"Pa!" a little boy's voice called out.

"Pa," another little voice echoed. Twin sets of feet thundered into the library. Three-year-old Arthur and four-year-old Stewart dashed to a breathless stop in front of Brant. "You gotta come see the train wreck we made with our train set. It's a big one this time."

"Sure, boys. I've got to see this." Brant ruffled his sons' heads, making them laugh, as he stood from his chair.

"You gotta come, too, Uncle Austin!" Stewart hopped in place, as cute as could be.

"Come and see." Arthur wore a wide, endearing smile and grabbed Austin by the hand.

"How can I say no to that? You know how I like trains." He launched to his feet, letting the child tug him along, talking excitedly.

That's what I want, he thought, not sure how it could be. Willa wanted a marriage of duty. That was far different from the large, happy family full of love and laughter he wanted. He shook his head. Nope, he couldn't see it working out now.

"Food is on the table." Berry poked her head into the parlor and winked. "Austin, I sure like Willa. She's a keeper."

"Yes, she is." No matter what, he would take care of her. The tie that had bound him to her from the first moment he'd read her plea in the territorial paper remained, unbreakable.

He inspected the train wreck and commented on the spectacular event to please his nephews, but he couldn't get beyond his feelings for Willa. She was his to keep, and the emotions he had for her went beyond duty and obligation. Analyzing them was best done at a later time.

"So there I was, four years old and stuck up in this tree." Brant wiped the last of his gravy with a piece of johnnycake. "All the big neighbor kids had swung over to the next tree, not even realizing I'd climbed up after them."

"I was stuck on the ground," Derek explained as he pushed back his chair to relax a little, done with his meal. "I couldn't go up after him, I was too small, but I didn't want to run home and tell Ma we'd disobeyed her."

"Who were you kidding?" Austin's coffee cup clinked to a rest in its saucer. "You were sitting there crying like a baby."

"Hey, I *was* a baby," Derek protested. "It was expected."

"My poor baby." Derek's wife, Delia, reached over to pat his cheeks like a two-year-old. Her eyes sparkled with amusement. "And here I thought you were a big tough guy."

"I was tough. For a two-year-old," Derek protested.

"Sure you were." Mr. Dermot chuckled.

"That's why you were sobbing so hard," Evelyn chimed in.

Willa took a sip of tea, intrigued by the merriment. She'd grown up in a solemn house where joy was as scarce as luxury. But in this home, joy beamed as freely as the lamplight on the table.

"Don't cry, Uncle Derek." Young Stewart scrunched his face up with concern.

"Then Austin saved the day." Brant went on with his story, taking time to reach out and cover his wife's hand with his. Berry gazed up at him happy, too.

"I didn't do much," Austin said with a casual shoulder shrug. "I climbed up and brought him down."

"You were a rock." Brant laughed easily. "I was so terrified I couldn't breathe. The only thing that scared me more was the chance of Ma looking out the window and spying me up in the tree where I wasn't supposed to be. I couldn't make my little fingers let go, so I just hung there the entire time it took for Austin to climb up the old maple tree. A wind kicked up and it was rocking me back and forth like a dead leaf."

"If I'd have seen it, I would have had an apoplexy." Austin's father leaned back in his chair with a cup of coffee in hand, his face crinkling in humor. "A four-year-old over thirty feet up in the air. What were you thinking, that's what I'd like to know."

"Nothing much," Brant quipped.

"At least that hasn't changed," Derek teased back.

"Sweat was pouring down my neck worrying Ma would catch us," Austin confessed as he set down his cup. He balled up his cloth napkin and tossed it beside his empty plate. "I knew I would be the one to get a whipping, because I should have been watching you better."

"So here I was, starting to slip because my hands were sweaty," Brant added. "The wind was knocking me back and forth along with the rest of the branches. I start to slip."

"Derek—the baby—is sobbing up a storm below me," Austin added picking up the story. "Brant is starting to cry above me."

"It wasn't crying," he denied staunchly. "I was more like squeaking since I was too scared to actually breathe. You have to breathe to be able to cry."

"It sounded like crying to me," Austin chuckled. "I'm two thirds up the tree, going as fast as I can because all the crying is bound to alert Ma at any moment. The branch Brant is holding begins to bend. Then *crack,* it gives way completely."

"I'm airborne, still clutching the branch for all I'm worth," Brant continued.

"I have visions of him knocking me off the limb I'm on and taking me down with him." Austin twisted in his chair to look at her. The lamplight burnished his hair and worshipped the chiseled planes of his face—straight sloping nose, high cheekbones and the strong cut of his jaw. Laughter looked good on him. It polished away all the sadness and disappointment, making him seem like a different man.

She'd never seen this side of Austin before.

"But all of a sudden I jerked to a stop." Brant shook his head, as if he couldn't believe his luck. "Something stopped my descent. I sat there, tears streaking down my face—"

"I thought you said you weren't crying," Derek interrupted to tease.

"—and when I looked up, I was still holding on to the broken limb. But it had gotten caught between a snag and another branch, and that's what stopped me. By the time Austin got to me, I couldn't let go of that stick. I clutched it all the way to the ground."

"I had to pry his little fingers off it before we went back in the house." Austin tipped back his head and laughed.

"Those are my boys," Mr. Dermot chuckled. "Nothing but trouble. Just wait until your sons are old enough to give you gray hair."

"Are you kidding? Berry and I are watching them like a pair of hawks." Brant laughed. "I know every trick in the book. No one's pulling the wool over my eyes or winding up stuck in a tree."

A baby's cry rose from the next room. "I'd better go check and see what our future troublemaker needs," Delia laughed as she slipped out of her seat.

The conversation turned to the chances that Evelyn's baby might be a boy, too, making for the fourth grandson in the family. The words blurred together as Willa sipped her cup of tea. Over the rim she watched her husband, relaxed and affable. Laugh lines looked at home on his face, tucked in with fine lines around his dazzling blue eyes.

He'd become even more handsome to her. A small gust of warmth returned to brush against her heart.

"Time to retire to the library, men." Mr. Dermot pushed back from the table. "You know what happened last time we lingered at the table."

"I drove you off, that's what." Evelyn bobbed out of her chair, bright with happiness. "Just stay out of our way and we *might* reward you with dried blueberry pie."

"Maybe," Berry chipped in mischievously, standing up to begin stacking plates. "We'll just have to see how you behave."

"That's a woman for you." Brant winked as he exchanged a smile with his wife. "They have all the power."

"And don't you forget it, mister." Berry laughed as the men rose from their chairs.

Willa set down her teacup, but before she could stand and help stack the dirty dishes, Austin circled behind her chair and pulled it out for her. Warm tingles skittered across her nape, knowing he was right behind her, so close she could feel the fan of his breath in her hair. She stood on wobbly knees, this time not from the morning sickness but from something she didn't understand.

"How are you feeling?" he asked, his voice resonate and low so that only she could hear.

"Better." Her worries felt lighter seeing this new side of him. His good humor went deeper than she'd dared to hope, and since he clearly wasn't a drinker like Jed, maybe she should stop expecting the worst of him.

"Just take it easy, okay?" His big hand landed on her shoulder to gently squeeze. What had been comforting and encouraging before, now felt like something more. She watched him join the men, his gait confident, his impressive shoulders straight and strong and his laughter ringing like deep-noted music.

He's a better man than I dared to hope for. She stacked her plate on top of his, staring as the brothers bumped shoulders, talking and jostling as they crossed through the parlor.

"I picked up a new brand of whiskey." Mr. Dermot's voice rose among all the others and carried back to her. "It's a quality label. I've been saving it for my boys."

"Then crack open the bottle," Brant called out.

"And haul out the cigars," Derek chimed in.

"That sounds good to me," Austin agreed, his tone light and jovial as he trailed out of her sight.

Whiskey. Willa's heart stopped beating. Just when she'd believed he didn't drink. Dread filled her as she listened to the faint rumble of men's voices in the distant room.

"Willa, are you all right?" Evelyn abandoned her stack of dishes and circled the table. "Do you need to lie down?"

"No, no. I'm all right." The warm curl next to her heart had vanished right along with her hopes. So, Austin did drink. She just hadn't seen it yet. She knew what that meant. Dejected, she lifted her chin and added Mr. Dermot's plate to her stack.

At least there would be no more guessing or wondering or waiting for the dark side of her husband to show up. She was about to get a good look at the real Austin. Her stomach twisted into a knot of worry as she lifted the stack of dishes and followed her sisters-in-law to the kitchen.

Chapter Ten

She couldn't stop imagining the worst as she set the dishes on the work counter alongside the other stacks. It looked as if a whirlwind had gone off in the kitchen. Empty dishes and bowls, cooking dishes and pans lay everywhere. Hard to know exactly where to start, so she grabbed the washbasins to fill with hot water from the stove's reservoir.

"No you don't, Willa dear." Berry swept in to grab the basin and gently nudged her out of the way. "I'll do the heavy lifting, as I'm not the one expecting. Yet."

"Although it's fun to try, isn't it?" Delia entered the room, carrying her babe in arms. The little bundle looked at them with curious blue eyes, before stuffing his fist into his mouth and letting out a wail.

"I'm holding out hopes for a girl next time." Berry turned the knob and steaming water poured into a basin. "How about you, Willa?"

"What?" She blinked, her gaze traveling across the

work table to where Evelyn dealt with the leftovers. It was hard to get her mind off of worrying about Austin and that whiskey bottle. She covered her stomach with her hands. "How did you all know?"

"I didn't say a word. Cross my heart." Evelyn covered the remaining biscuits and set them inside a hamper.

"It was the ginger tea," Berry explained. "It's a dead giveaway."

"We knew the moment Evelyn made the pot for you." Delia settled down in a corner chair to nurse. "How far along are you?"

"Almost three months." She forced her hands away from her stomach, watching the natural ease Delia had with her son. The woman paused to smile down at her baby nestled against her breast and ran a loving hand over his soft downy head.

"Nearly that far along? You'd never know it. You're such a wee thing." Berry hefted the basin onto the counter. "We know there's no way the child is Austin's."

"No, as we'd never met before our wedding day." Shame gripped her, tying up her tongue. Or maybe that had more to do with her fears about Austin and how much he intended to drink. She strained to hear anything coming from the library, but all she heard were the sounds of the children playing in the parlor, building worlds and adventures with their train set.

"I'm a w-widow," she blurted, before the Dermot women could think the worst of her.

"We know, but it wouldn't matter to us if you weren't." Berry smiled gently over the steaming water.

She grabbed up a bar of soap and shaved bits into the basin. "Austin did tell us that, but not much else."

"I don't think he knew much more, as my letter of acceptance to him was brief." She remembered how hard that letter had been to write, her hand shaking so hard she'd barely been able to hold a pen. She'd huddled behind the trading post building in the shelter of wind and snow, fearful of the future and relieved she had a home to go to. Never would she have imagined in less than two weeks' time she would be here, standing in a beautiful kitchen in a gracious home surrounded by kind women. Women she was now related to.

"What are you hoping for?" Evelyn closed the hamper's lid. "A boy or a girl?"

"Gee, I haven't thought that far." Her knees weakened. She'd tried not to think of the babe at all, as someone she could fail. What did she know about family? Jed's family had disowned him. She could never rightly call what she grew up in a family. She shrugged, not knowing how to explain what she felt. Her mind was too preoccupied with other worries. *What about that whiskey bottle?* It haunted her as she spied a dish towel hanging on a hook and snapped it up. What would Austin be like drunk?

"If it's a girl, you'll be the most popular one here," Berry quipped as she plunged the glassware into the soapy water. "Pop wants a granddaughter. He's so funny. When I first learned I was pregnant with Stewart, he told me he was putting in an order for a boy. He wanted a grandson."

"Then by the time I was carrying Kyle, Pop had his

fingers crossed for a little girl." Delia laughed sweetly. "Of course, when Kyle came along, Pop wasn't disappointed. What he truly wanted was a healthy, happy grandchild. I told him we'll see what we can do next time around."

"Now it's Willa's turn." Berry slipped a handful of silverware into the rinse water. "We're real glad you're here, by the way. Austin deserves a good wife. He's a nice man."

"He is nice." Every little thing he'd done for her weighed on her now. She was so, so grateful but the fear wouldn't leave her. "I couldn't believe my eyes when I stepped off the train and saw him."

"I imagine he felt the same way." Evelyn swept over to take charge of the forks Willa had dried and put them away in a drawer. "You are clearly the best thing that could have happened to my brother."

"Oh, I don't know about that." She thought of how she'd hurt him with her honesty last night. But wouldn't being dishonest have hurt worse in the end?

"We do. He's had such a hard time finding himself a wife," Delia added from the corner. "Of course, living in this small of a town so far from everywhere else, there just aren't a lot of unmarried women to choose from."

"He had a steady girlfriend in school. He was serious about her," Berry added. "I happen to know he was planning on marrying her."

"But she up and left town after graduation. Wanted to get a job in New York," Evelyn explained. "She worried if she married Austin, her life would be too small."

"She broke his heart." Berry's face crinkled in sympathy, shaking her head as if remembering that sad time. "It took him a while to recover from that and by then, his friends from school were getting married. Everyone was already paired up. It's as if he lost his chance."

"And he hasn't gotten another one." Delia shook her head, too. "We all watched every pretty woman who came to town look him over and choose another."

"When Savannah Knowles arrived—well, Savannah Brooks now—she had the pick of all the bachelors around these parts." Evelyn leaned against the counter. "It broke my heart when she up and married someone else."

"Same with Clara Woodrow and every new lady schoolteacher who stepped foot in this town," Berry agreed. "It was heartbreaking to watch him put on his best suit and try to win the lady's attention, only to be passed over."

"He's been looking for a wife for eight years," Delia explained. "Eight long years. He watched his younger brothers marry and have families and still, no one chose him."

"Why?" Willa swiped the knives carefully. Now was her chance to find out what she'd worried about from the moment the postmaster had handed her Austin's first letter.

"Who knows? He's certainly handsome enough." Evelyn snapped up the knives the instant they were dried. "He makes a fine living. He's as good as a man comes. He's been longing for a wife and family for so long. It just hasn't happened for him before you, Willa."

"There's not one thing wrong with Austin. My guess is that he's just never been the one to turn a lady's head," Berry said. "You know how it is. When a man looks at you, your heart just clicks like a key turning a lock and you know he's the one."

"I do," Delia agreed. "It's a powerful thing. The moment that happened to me, I couldn't see anyone but Derek. How does a man compete with something like that?"

"He can't. He just has to wait until that click happens for him." Evelyn stopped to give Willa's hand a squeeze.

She didn't know what the women were talking about. What click? And how could something like that matter so much in the choice of a husband? Maybe things had been different for them, they had the luxury of waiting to marry and of finding the best man they could.

"We can all tell he's taken with you." Berry started on the plates next, swiping quickly but effectively and slipping them with a plop into the rinse basin. "The way he looks at you."

"His eyes soften. His whole big tough attitude softens." Delia nodded in approval. "That's the way it should be."

"He cares for you, Willa." Evelyn took a dried plate and slid it into a shelf. "Which is why we adore you so much. Austin has been lonely a long time. He deserves someone nice like you to love."

"I don't know if I'm all that nice." She shrugged, wishing she could see the world the way these women did. She hated that she could never be what they thought she was. "I'm sure trying hard to be a good wife to him."

"We know. He might not know how to thank you—" Berry began, dropping the final plate into the basin.

"Being that he's a man," Delia said, continuing the thought.

"But we appreciate you, Willa," Evelyn concluded. "Delia, is Kyle asleep?"

"Yes, thankfully. I'm going to go put him down and check on the men. My guess is they'll be in the mood for pie about now."

"You know it's true. The Dermot men have a notorious sweet tooth." Berry leaned in as she scrubbed a pot. "For your future reference. If Austin is ever in a bad mood, just whip him up something sweet to eat. It works wonders every time."

"It's a good thing I love to bake." Willa carefully dried the pot Berry slipped into the rinse water, not quite sure why everyone laughed. Apparently they all thought she'd made a joke. She smiled, shaking her head as she handed Evelyn the pot.

"See? You're perfect for Austin." Evelyn beamed. "I knew it the moment I saw you."

"You are his best hope for happiness." Delia rose from the chair with her sleeping son in her arms. "You have no notion how grateful we all are to you."

"To me?" She plucked a fry pan out of the rinse water.

"Yes, we all love Austin so much." Sincerity shone

richly in Berry's smile as she reached out and took Willa's hand.

The contact was surprising and sisterly—something she'd never known before. The ever-present walls around her heart slid down a notch. Emotion pressed against the back of her throat. "I didn't do anything but marry him."

"Exactly." Delia hesitated at the doorway, cradling her child. "Do you hear that? Those men of ours must be having a rip-roaring time."

"I do hear that. Laughter." Evelyn tilted her head. "I like it. Come on, Willa, put that pan down and we'll take them the dessert we promised."

The pan clunked against the counter and she listened to the bark of male laughter muffled through the walls of the house. Her stomach clenched up tight, fighting the common-day images that rose up from her memory. Jed and his buddies drinking in the yard, the hot summer wind swirling around them while the wheat stood too long in the fields, unharvested. Jed rising up on wobbly feet, his fist bunched to strike her as he demanded she fetch another whiskey bottle out of the cellar. Jed hung-over the next morning, taking his belt to her because there was no more alcohol in the cellar.

Those were the days she'd walked the two miles to town and wished with all the depth of her being that she could simply keep on walking. But she knew better. Jed would have hunted her down. He never would have let her go.

"Oh, I think May will surprise us all." Delia's voice cut into Willa's thoughts as deftly as the knife she used to slice the fragrant pie. "Just when you think winter will never end, when it's at its meanest, that's when the season has turned. The best springs always follow a hard winter."

"You are an eternal optimist, my dear," Berry called over her shoulder, scrubbing at the last of the pots. "I'm afraid this winter will go on forever. Whatever start spring got before this cold spell is gone."

"It just feels that way." Evelyn took down a stack of dessert plates from the carved oak cabinets and set them on the work table. "Winter always ends. I'm voting for a warm May. I've been in the mood for a picnic. I can almost feel the bright sun on my face."

The conversation resumed and Willa tried to pay attention as she held the dishes one by one for Delia to fill with thick slabs of blueberry pie. Willa couldn't stop worrying about what she was going to find in the library. Austin loud. Austin mean. Austin cruel. She simply couldn't envision it. She couldn't stand to try.

"There. That's enough. Let's go serve them. C'mon, Willa." Delia scooped up half the plates and apparently expected her to do the same.

Tension had twisted up her muscles in so many knots it was a wonder she could shuffle her feet forward. The plates wobbled in her hands as she took one uncertain step after another. Somehow she put one shoe in front of the other to trail Delia through the house.

She smiled at the children's merriment as the train crashed spectacularly—again—in the parlor. The crystal lamp covers rattled as she passed through the dining room and her heart struggled against her rib cage like a trapped bird desperate to get out.

She smelled the cigar smoke before she saw it curling in the air. She stepped into the male territory of the library and braced for the worst. Willa didn't dare lift her gaze to search for him as she followed Delia's skirt into the room.

Austin. She could feel his gaze on her, as tangible as a touch to the side of her face. His presence pulled on her, but she kept her eyes down. The last thing she wanted to see was her husband with a drink in his hand and alcohol glazing his eyes. She was stiff with tension she could barely lower a plate to hand it to Mr. Dermot. It wobbled while she waited for him to take it.

"Why, this looks as delicious as it smells." Austin's father laid his cigar to rest in an ashtray. "Delia, you've outdone yourself. This is a treat."

"That's the last of my dried berries. I can't wait for summer." Delia's voice came as if from miles away. "Willa, we'll have to show you all our favorite wild berry-picking spots. In fact, I'm going to team up with Berry and Evelyn and we'll bring you plantings for your own blueberries, strawberries and raspberries. We all get together and make jam."

"That sounds nice." Her lips felt numb, and her voice felt strained. It didn't sound like her own. She was aware of Austin with every breath she took. She could see the tip of his shoes at the edge of her vision, so close she could reach out and touch him.

"This is fine, thank you, Willa." Mr. Dermot took

charge of his plate. "You ladies spoil us more than we deserve."

"You're right about that," Delia teased easily.

Willa could smell the whiskey as she turned toward Austin with his plate. Her pulse thundered in her ears with thick, hollow beats. Disappointment rocked through her so hard, her hand trembled with every thud of her heartbeat as she held out his plate to him.

"Hey there." His rich baritone rang low and intimate, only for her. He didn't sound drunk at all. "I hope Evelyn and the girls aren't overwhelming you."

"They've been wonderful." His voice tempted her to look up at him, but she had to resist. She kept her chin down, staring at the shine of his boots and the machine-made stitches hemming his denims. She saw his strong, well-shaped hand catch the rim of the plate, so she let go. Swallowing hard against her rising hopelessness, she took a step back, bobbed her head and whirled away.

His other hand snared her wrist, manacling her to him, refusing to let her go. Trapping her, using his greater strength against her. She should have known. Her chin slipped down lower, the conversations around the room were indistinguishable buzzes. She wasn't aware of anyone else when Austin rose from his chair.

Her heart stopped beating and she froze, trapped. His massive granite form towered over her, so close she could feel the fan of his breath against her nape. He gave a little tug, spinning her around to face him, so strong she could not stop him.

"Hey." His thumb brushed the underside of her jaw,

tilting her chin gently up to bring her gaze to his. "Are you all right?"

She stared into his blue depths, realizing they were still just as clear as she'd ever seen them. Kind, filled with concern, he searched her face as if he thought he could read what was wrong there. On the small table next to his armchair sat a snifter of alcohol a few inches deep. Apparently Austin did not drink his whiskey in one long gulp. She took in the rest of the room, noticing other glasses mostly untouched and cigars sat smoking away. The men were talking about some upcoming horse race. Mr. Dermot dug into his pie and the other men were too busy talking to eat.

This was nothing like what she expected. Air rushed out of her lungs, breath she hadn't realized she'd been holding. This was a different scene than Jed holding his tin cup sloshing over with cheap alcohol and arguing with his buddies who were doing the same, the lot of them guzzling until they were too drunk to stand up on their own.

"Is the morning sickness troubling you?" His thumb trailed along the line of her jaw, a slow and steady stroke that left a blaze of sensation across her skin and warmed away her fears.

"No, I just need a little more tea, that's all." She couldn't help leaning into his touch, just a little, so grateful for this man. So thankful he was more than she could ever expect.

Far more than she ever deserved.

Austin Dermot wasn't the type of man to drink until he was drunk. She should have known. She swallowed hard, hoping her voice sounded normal when she spoke. "I'm sure all I need is a slice of that pie."

"It does look good enough to fix any ailment." Austin's hand curled around her neck, gently cradling her. It was a kind touch and caring.

She didn't know a touch could feel that way.

"You say the word and we can leave anytime." He leaned in, speaking against the shell of her ear. "I know you may need to lie down and rest. If you don't feel comfortable doing it here, I'll be glad to drive you home."

"Oh, I don't want to take you away from your family." Her hand seemed to lift of its own accord and land on the center of his chest. Not to push him away or to act as a barrier between them, but simply to touch him. "I'd like to stay."

"You sure?"

She nodded. It was hard not to be tempted by the kindness of his face and mellow note in his voice— tempted to believe in fairy tales. If she were a different woman, maybe as sheltered as Evelyn had been or as confident as Delia and Berry, it would be easy to spin romances out of a man's steady kindness.

But she could not.

Whatever this was that she felt, it had to be relief. Relief that Austin was a man who could handle his whiskey. Relief that his closeness and his touch no longer frightened her. Relief that she hadn't disappointed him in front of his family, as she'd sworn not to do. *That* was what mattered, and not the warm tingle of sensation gathering beneath the press of his palm to her neck.

"When Berry learned that I liked to knit, she promised to show me a new stitch, something I've always wanted to learn how to do." She didn't lift her hand from his chest and stayed in his shadow. His heart thudded reliably. She could count the beats. It was an intimate thing, to feel those metered *thu-thumps* that made the moment between them real and changing. Austin was no longer a stranger, but a man she wanted to know.

Chapter Eleven

"That's a real pretty gal you married." Pa knelt to give the harness buckle a tug. Cold wind sailed through the barn doors, but nothing could erase the fatherly pride on the man's face as he straightened. "You did real fine, son."

"I got lucky." He tried to keep his grin in place as his gaze drifted across the snowy yard to the light spilling from the house's windows. He turned away, downhearted. What would his father think if he knew the truth? Pressure built behind his ribs as he took charge of Calvin's reins and did his best to keep his disappointments hidden.

"You sure did, you big oaf," Brant teased, leading his horse and sleigh toward the open double doors. "What a lady like that was doing advertising for a husband is anyone's guess."

"She must have been real desperate." Derek joined in

jovially, backing his gelding into his sleigh's traces. "At least now he can commiserate with us married men."

"Yep, the old ball and chain is watching." Brant laughed as a distant voice called out to him.

"I heard that, buddy, and if you want a hot supper tonight you'll rephrase that." Berry must be on her way with the kids.

"Pa! Pa!" Two little boys tumbled into sight.

"Do we getta drive Milton?" Stewart asked.

"Can we?" Arthur pleaded.

"That depends if you picked up all your toys for grandpa." Brant swooped each son off the ground, one in each arm.

"We did!" Stewart wrapped his arms around Brant's neck.

"We did," Arthur echoed, his brow serious.

"They did a fine job picking up." Berry carried a small basket, leftovers from the noon meal. She slipped it onto the floorboards and waited while her husband settled the boys on the seat. Love shone on her face, and love answered in Brant's eyes when he helped his wife into the sleigh.

Don't think about what you haven't got, Austin told himself firmly. No sense in imagining he might have the same one day. That he would be taking his own firstborn in his arms, the way Derek had done when his children entered the barn. The sense of unity among Brant's family was so strong and the connection so unbreakable that it changed the air in the barn and chased the cold from the wind.

"Willa." Her name cracked across his tongue. She

seemed alone somehow, walking up by herself as the families settled into their sleighs. The little boys talked in high, sweet voices and the babe gave a squall before falling back to sleep.

She came to him like a shadow, but it wasn't sadness she brought with her. Life sparkled in the solemn blue eyes that met his. The curve of her mouth looked natural and easy, as if she'd smiled a lot with the other women. He held her elbow to help her into the sleigh and the distance between them wasn't as great when she gazed up at him.

"Did you have a good time with your brothers?" she asked. "We could hear you men laughing all the way into the parlor."

He nodded, leaned in to tuck the driving robes around her. The ride home was bound to be chilly. "How did your knitting go?"

"Wonderful. I'm so glad I kept a few of my knitting needles instead of selling them when I was h-hungry." Her voice lowered over that word. "I'm itching to start a new project."

"It might be fun for you to pick out what you need at the mercantile, next time you're in town."

"Maybe."

There wasn't much he could do for her. He couldn't lean down and kiss her rosebud lips. He couldn't lay a hand on her shoulder in reassurance. He couldn't heal what had been wounded in her. But knitting supplies? That he could afford. "If it wasn't so cold out, I'd take you and the mare out for a driving lesson."

"This weather won't last forever."

Was that hope in her voice? He tucked the edges of the robe around her more tightly, taking care of her in this small way. He straightened, hating to step away from her even if it was only to circle around to the other side of the sleigh.

"Warm weather will be here in no time," he agreed. "We'll get you a light little buggy, one that will be easy for you to hitch up yourself."

She didn't answer, but her smile was answer enough. Almost a real smile. One that curved her mouth into a thing of splendor and painted her eyes so blue, his throat ached at the sight.

This isn't longing for her, he told himself, rubbing the heel of his hand above his hurting heart. Probably it's just indigestion. At least that's what he wanted to believe.

"So long!" Brant called out as the little family pulled away. Merry goodbyes rang in answer, echoing inside the high-ceilinged barn. The little family made a nice picture driving away in the sleigh, with both little boys on their father's lap, tucked in his arms. Each child held the end of one rein, while Brant gave the leather straps a snap and nosed the gelding toward home.

In a couple of years he would have Willa's child—now his, too—to hold on his lap as he drove away. And if the baby were a girl… He shook his head at that. He didn't know much about little girls, but he would do his best to learn. Maybe the child would draw them closer together, he reasoned as he slipped onto the seat beside his bride and took up Calvin's reins.

The gelding stood at the ready, leaning into his harness with his ears pricked, and then swiveled to take in the conversation. No sense in disappointing the horse, so Austin snapped the reins.

"See you all soon," he called out as the runners squeaked against the straw and then whispered against snow. "Have a good evening, Pa."

"You, too, son. Goodbye, Willa."

"Goodbye." Her dulcet alto moved through him like his own breath, and he couldn't get her out of his system as Calvin trotted down the tree-lined driveway. The world blurred, not from the speed but because his eyes filled with emotion too confusing to untangle and name. He was married, but unlike his father's marriage he didn't think there was a chance this would be a union built on love.

Heck, that was the risk he'd taken in choosing a mail-order bride. But he *had* a bride—that was the important point. He was no longer as alone as he'd been, and today among his family had shown him something. He still had the chance to be a father. By this time next year, he'd have a little child to help Willa raise. A son to teach about horses, or a little daughter to…well, he didn't exactly know about that, but he knew it would all work out.

"Your family is wonderful." Willa broke the silence, twisting toward him in the sleigh. The brush of happiness still animated her adorable face and resonated in her sparkling eyes. "I had the best time. I like them so much."

"They liked you, too." He couldn't resist leaning a little closer to her. When he breathed in her light rose scent, his chest hitched harder than he would have liked. "You ladies had a good time."

"I've never had a better one. Oh, we talked about sewing and knitting and the children...." She paused as a crook of worry dug in above the bridge of her nose. "I'm sorry, going on like that. I—"

"It's all right," he interrupted before she could stop and before her brightness could fade. "I hear Berry is an expert knitter. She made this scarf for me."

"I should have known." Willa reached out on impulse. With an intake of her breath, she froze midway to touching him. Her eyebrows arched, her mouth dropped into a sweet little *O* when she realized what she'd been about to do.

"Go on. It's okay." He one-handed the reins so he could pull the end of the scarf from beneath his coat for her to look at. "It was my Christmas present."

"I've been so worried about everything I didn't even notice before. It's a lovely scarf." She ducked her head lightly, her gaze centered on the scarf she held.

The twist in his chest rung tighter. He was torn between wanting her and knowing if he reached out to her he would frighten her away. So he sat still, barely daring to breathe and letting Calvin worry about turning onto the country road that would take them home. The horse knew where they were going, but this single moment with Willa needed his attention more. This one instant in time mattered more than anything.

"Berry really is very talented." She let go up the scarf, ending the moment as she leaned back against the seat-back. "I'm sure I could never be as good of a knitter, but I'd like to try. I've always wanted to learn to do cables but I could never figure them out quite right on my own."

"I imagine you will need to knit all sorts of things to have on hand when the baby comes."

"I haven't thought that far ahead." She lifted her chin to meet his gaze, hers a timid blue. "Today seeing Delia's baby made it more real."

"I imagine it's something a new widow would dread thinking about when the future was uncertain." He reached over to tuck the robes more tightly around her where they had come loose with her movements. He couldn't help wanting to take care of her. "That's not the case now. Your life here is secure. I'm here to make sure of it."

"That means a lot to me, Austin." Her hand lighted on his arm, the sweetest of touches.

"I'm glad to do it for you, Willa." His throat ached with emotions he shouldn't be feeling, and if he were smart, he never would. "You're my bride."

"You're a good man, Austin." She seemed at ease being this close to him, and he was thankful for the change as he gave the blanket a final tuck around her, bringing him dangerously close to her. He breathed in roses and the warm, sweet scent that was hers alone. A wisp of her hair blew against his cheek as gentle as a caress.

Don't let your heart flutter, he told himself even though he was pretty sure it did anyway.

"I'm going to try to do my best by you, Willa." It broke something inside him to ease back against the seat. A knot of longing tugged hard behind his ribs, wanting to stay close.

But Willa didn't want that kind of relationship.

"I was real scared when I saw you with that glass of whiskey." Her confession came so quietly, it could barely be heard over the wind whirring by like a whistle in his ears. Her hand on his forearm remained, a tentative link between them. "It was my greatest fear that you would turn out to be a drunk, someone who couldn't be in control of it."

"My pa brings out a bottle now and then, but we sip more than we glug."

"I noticed." That hint of a smile returned, just as he'd hoped it would. "Is it true you've waited eight years for a wife?"

"I see the ladies were filling your head with stories about me." He noticed she was shivering. As thick as the robes were, the temperatures were dropping rapidly. He started to shiver, too. "Not sure what else they said about me, but that much is true."

"I see." Her teeth clattered. Her forehead furrowed in thought. "I think I see why you chose me."

"Why?" he asked, curious to know what she thought, because she couldn't possibly know the reason.

"The baby." Chills began to wrack her and she looked so fragile sitting there, shaking hard, so sweet and petite he couldn't help sidling up closer. He moved slowly so as not to scare her. She didn't gasp when he lifted his arm to lay it across her shoulders. She only stiffened slightly as he drew her against his side.

"This will help keep you warm," he said. "Is that better?"

"Yes." Her teeth stopped clacking. "You chose me because you want a family. By harvest time, you will have one."

"That's true enough." He wasn't going to think about his disappointment, which seemed to make the wind harsher. He hadn't expected Willa to understand. But he did want a family. More than that, he wanted a bride to love.

Since it was too cold to talk, they fell silent as Calvin pulled them home.

Calvin's nicker of excitement sailed back on the bitter wind. Willa gave a sigh of relief at the sight of their little house tucked beneath a twilight sky. The first evening stars hung crisp and bright, twinkling with promise.

"We're home. Finally." Austin set down his reins as Calvin came to an impatient stop. "I'll get you inside, stir the fires and then I'll get Calvin in the barn."

"No, the wind's too cold for him to stand. I'll come to the barn with you and we can walk to the house together. It's not far, and I'd like to see the mare."

"And I'd like to show her to you." He gave the reins a snap, but Calvin was already moving across the yard toward the closed barn door. "Have you thought of a name yet?"

"No, but I'm working on it." She was a little breathless. His body's warmth seemed to flow through her. The man was as good as a crackling fire for heat.

When Austin climbed out of the sleigh, cold wrapped around her from all sides, making her miss him. She couldn't help noticing the fine figure he made as the gathering dusk closed around him. Imposing height, manly shoulders and masculine grace. He powered the door open and led Calvin inside the small barn. A cow's moo greeted them.

"I know, Rosie. Sorry, girl. I'm late with your milking," he called out, tossing Willa a sheepish grin. "She's a sweet girl but a bit temperamental."

Brown ears pricked up as two chocolate eyes studied them over the top of her stall. Even in the shadows Rosie looked adorable with a wide forehead, a sloping nose and a soft velvet muzzle that mooed a protest.

"See what I mean?" Austin's chuckle rolled through the dark, pushing back the shadows. Or maybe it just seemed that way as the doors closed and a match flared to life. Light grew on the lantern's wick, tossing orange-tinted light across the man's face.

She thought of the stories Evelyn and the girls had told her in the parlor this afternoon of Austin, both as a boy and as a bachelor wishing for a bride. "I think Rosie is a dear. Would you like me to milk her? It was always my job on the farm."

"It's far too cold and it's not your job here." Austin's hand, as reliable as iron, gripped hers and she felt a strange tingle move through her as she stepped to the ground. He leaned in, his smile contagious. "Not unless it's your most favorite thing in the world to do the milking."

"I wouldn't say that, but I like cows." She didn't

know why she felt a sting of loss when Austin released her hand. "I'd never been close to a cow before the day Jed marched me into the barn to teach me to milk her. I was terrified of her because she was so big, but she was as gentle as a lamb. I never sobbed so hard as the day the bank took her."

"I'm sorry to hear that." Something hard crossed Austin's face, an expression she'd seen before.

Maybe he didn't like to hear about her life with another man. She bit her bottom lip, determined to try and remember that. "I guess the point of the story is that I rather liked the cow."

"I don't want to stand in the way of a friendship between you and Rosie." Austin knelt to release Calvin from his traces. "But let me milk her when the weather is like this."

"Fine." She wanted to argue that she could be milking while he unhitched and rubbed down the horse, but she was trying to be a good wife. A good wife didn't argue with her husband. She didn't give him cause to be irritated. If he wanted to milk the cow, then that was his call. Not that that was an easy thing, but she didn't want to disappoint him again. She had to figure out a way to stop doing that.

Maybe it would be okay if she petted Rosie. How could anyone resist those pleading eyes? Her hand reached out, the cow leaned over the gate and a pink tongue snagged her new coat's sash.

"Oh!" Surprised, she reacted too late. A good six inches of the sash was in the cow's mouth. "Rosie, let go of that, sweet girl."

Big brown eyes blinked, rimmed by long curly lashes, and gave her a mutinous look. Rosie gripped the sash tighter, refusing to let go. Trouble danced in her eyes as she blinked again.

"You are a funny girl. Guess you've got me held captive, don't you?" Delight trickled through her as she gave the cow lots of extra pets. Pleased, Rosie leaned in for more attention.

What a good day she'd had, she thought. She'd never before had such a day as a wife. The memories of that sad, sparse time where life was grim and bleak with unending work faded for a moment. Its power was not as strong as her happiness.

A movement caught her attention in the next stall, a disturbance in the shadows. Straw rustled as the shadows became a small black horse with fathomless eyes and a splash of white on her forehead. A star, Willa realized when the mare stopped several feet from her gate, safely out of reach.

She's mine. The thought filled her with a strange swirl of joy. Her own mare. She couldn't believe it. With a horse, she could go anywhere. She was free.

Austin's footsteps padded behind her, accompanied by the clomp of Calvin's hooves. The little mare lifted her head, watching the man cautiously with her skin flickering in fear.

"Is she all right?" Willa held out her hand, but the mare shied back, sank into the shadows and disappeared from sight.

"She's just afraid to trust us." Calvin's gate whispered shut. Straw rustled as the big horse crossed to his trough and dug into his grain. Willa felt her nape tingle as the man drew near. "She's a pretty little thing, isn't she?"

"Yes. So dainty. Such a beautiful face." She wished the mare would come closer. She wanted to make friends. She leaned against the gate longingly, afraid of the excitement building inside her.

Don't go counting on this, Willa. She thought of all the things that could happen. Austin could change his mind. The mare might be too afraid to be a good driving horse. Someone might offer Austin good money for her, and she'd be gone. Good things didn't last, so it was best not to count on them. She'd learned that lesson the hard way.

But she couldn't helping hoping—just a little. Austin planted his feet beside hers, reached over her shoulder and gently tried to tug the sash from Rosie's mouth.

"Let go, sweet girl, c'mon," his smoky baritone rumbled softly.

Hard not to be affected by that voice. It rolled through her in a slow sweep of vibrations. She shivered, but not from the chilly air. No, she didn't notice the wintry cold as she watched Austin and the cow. What did she notice? His gentle heart and his gentle hands.

"That's it, funny girl. I'll be in to milk you as soon as I get the fires going for Willa. How's that?" He stroked the cow's poll with a familiarity that had Rosie sighing and pressing up into his touch. "You know what that means? You get grain when I come back. Lots and lots of it. Do we have a deal?"

Rosie gave a besotted sigh, let go of the sash and Willa's heart tumbled a full inch.

She gave a little sigh, too.

Chapter Twelve

He didn't like how chilly Willa looked as he shouldered through the front door. To make matters worse, the house radiated iciness. Frosty nails in the floor crunched beneath his boots as he led her to the sofa.

"Leave your wraps on until I have this place warm." He hated leaving her side to stir the embers in the hearth, but he needed to get her warm. As he knelt before the hearth, he remained aware of her...of her quiet breath in the stillness, the rustle of her clothes as she shifted her weight from one foot to the other, the clack of her teeth chattering in the icy air. It didn't feel like April, almost May. He added moss to the embers, and flames snapped to life, tossing more light into the room.

He glanced over his shoulder. Willa had wrapped her arms around herself. It was too cold for her. Maybe he should have bundled her up in a blanket or two. He worried about her frailty. Regular meals in this house had done her good, her face had lost that too-thin look, but he still worried.

He added kindling and wood to the blaze, remembering how proud he'd been to show her off to his family. Nothing could be finer than the feeling of sitting at the family dinner table with her at his side. Only unless it was the ride home in the sleigh, with her snug against his side. Her body had felt warm and soft against his. Her rose fragrance still clung to him—faintly, but it was there—and every time he breathed in, warmth kicked into his blood. Desire for his bride.

The bride who did not desire him. Chances were good she never would. That was a secret he'd kept from his family, a failure he didn't know how to fix.

"Things should start warming up now." He stood, his knees cracking from the cold. "I'll put the leftovers Berry sent with us in the kitchen, but I want you to stay put until the house is warm. No kitchen work, at least until I get back from milking."

"But I'm fine." Her chin came up, a show of strength. A plea whisked across her face, a silent question he couldn't understand or guess at, but his feelings strengthened, just like the fire in the hearth. "I'll get supper warming. It's hardly effort at all."

"I know, but I worry." Emotions he couldn't stop or name. He resisted the urge to lean forward and plant a kiss on her forehead. She would never know how hard it was to take a step backward when everything within him wanted to draw her close and be a part of her.

"You have to take extra care of yourself," he said instead. "Think of the baby."

"Yes, but I'm not going to sit around. I'm not so good at that." Clear eyes met his, brimming with sincerity. "I want to have supper waiting when you come in. You've got to be cold and hungry."

"Let's worry about you this time." He couldn't help reaching out to cup her finely carved chin in his hand. More heat spilled into his blood when he felt her satin-soft skin against his own, coarse and callused. Caring surged through him with an intensity he had to fight to deny.

What was he going to do about her? *I have no love in me. I know I never will.* Her words haunted him and he was still at a loss. If love would never come to their marriage, then what did they have? He didn't know, but she didn't pull away from his touch.

She gazed up at him with her top teeth digging into her bottom lip. The cold didn't feel as overpowering here, standing near to her, her body a few scant inches from his. His heart lurched in his chest, wanting her and wanting to take care of her.

"Supper can wait a few minutes. You didn't get a chance to nap today." He tried to keep his feelings out of his voice, but he wasn't sure how much he succeeded. "Remember that lecture my sisters gave me? Now that they've met you, they are going to be watching me like hawks. I don't want to slack off, or they will be after me in no time."

"Yes, I noticed how they made big, strong you quake in your boots."

"I'm easily intimidated by women," he joked, just to watch her smile. Just to see the splash of humor light her up. There went his heart again, lurching against his will.

"If that's true, then I should be the one telling you what to do." Her smile grew until it was real, dominating her face and reaching her eyes.

He stared down at the bow of her mouth upturned in a tantalizing curve. The need to kiss her whipped up in him like a sudden blizzard. It hit him with enough force to rattle his bones and make blood surge in his veins. What would her lips feel like, feather-soft against his? Caring roared through him, stronger than the need to kiss her.

What was he going to do about his feelings for her? Not acknowledging them wasn't working. They rose up anyway, refusing to be ignored or to pay heed to the fact that this wasn't a real marriage.

Just one in name only.

"Austin?" Her voice penetrated his thoughts and he realized she'd been asking him something.

"Maybe you'd better say that again. I'm a man. I'm easily distracted." He used humor again because it seemed to wipe the worry twisting her forehead.

"I said Rosie is waiting for you." She gave a little head bob, a dear movement against the palm of his hand.

"Yep, I'd best get back out there." He couldn't bring himself to step away. "I'm sure she's anxious, wondering what's keeping me. She really loves her grain."

"Oh, I don't think it's the grain." She gazed up at him, and for a second—just one brief instant—something that looked like caring shone within her. It was gone too quickly for him to be sure.

Hope licked through him. When he took a step away from her, regret speared between his ribs, arrowing deep, and he knew it for the sign it was. He didn't want to leave her side. His emotions ran deeper than he thought.

Not sure what to do about that, he checked the fire—which was burning steadily and brightly—before backing away. Willa made a pretty picture standing in the fall of firelight, with her windswept hair and unguarded eyes.

She hated the exhaustion that dragged on her like lead weights as she put warmed leftovers on the table, but she stayed silent. She didn't want Austin to know. She could feel him watching her as she slid the platter from the rack, set it on the table's center and turned to close the oven door.

"I'll get the rest. You look asleep on your feet." He set the milk pail on the counter.

"I'm almost done."

"Yes, you are." He held out her chair and gestured toward the cushion. "I can handle the rest. Please."

"I—" She wanted to argue, but the low silky notes of his words tempted her. She could see how much this meant to him. He was genuine in his concern for her, and it touched her. She knew it was concern for the child she carried, but it was nice all the same. "Thank you."

"Good." His breath stirred her hair as she sat. "I should have realized how much you need a daily nap."

"I didn't, either. The pregnancy is starting to have a bigger effect on me."

"That's to be expected. Did I tell you the doctor is coming by tomorrow? I wanted him to check you over and make sure everything is progressing all right."

"A doctor?" She couldn't help gasping a little. "They're expensive."

"But necessary. When I spoke to Doc Wetherbee yesterday when I repaired a shoe for his horse, he said he'd be glad to drop by in the afternoon to check on you. He's a kind man. You'll like him."

"I would feel relieved to know everything is fine." Another luxury her child would have. Good medical care.

"It's settled, then." His nearness skidded across her skin in little pleasant tingles as he helped her to scoot in her chair. Was it her imagination or did she feel especially warm?

Perhaps it was from the steam of the tea and the food on the table in front of her. Heat radiated off the nearby stove, but that didn't seem to be the source of her problem. She couldn't think what was wrong with her—her breath came in quick little gasps, too—as she watched him carry the basket of warm rolls to the table.

What a fine-looking man he was. She noticed it more keenly than ever before. She bit her lip, appreciating the masculine way he moved, the muscles in his arms and how they rippled beneath his shirt when he set his coffee on the table.

"Home always seemed incredibly quiet and calm after a visit with the family." His chair scraped against the floor as he settled in at the table.

"It does. It was chaos. But pleasant," she emphasized.

"I don't know what I would do without them all. It must have been lonely for you growing up an only child." He grabbed the serving spoon and filled it, lifting one eyebrow in a silent question asking for her plate.

It was another courtesy he showed her, serving her first. Those courtesies kept adding up. She held out her plate for him and watched it fill with chicken and dumplings. How could she ever do enough for him to make up for his kindnesses?

"Yes, it was a bit lonely but I didn't know the difference." The sad, one-room shanty she'd grown up in seemed so far away, it could have been a dream. "I couldn't help notice how well you and your brothers and sister get along. You're close. I can't imagine what that must have been like growing up."

"Trouble, that's what. Also very loud and obnoxious." He filled his plate to the brim and dug in. "I didn't have a moment alone to myself until the day I moved out to live on my own."

"I see that twinkle in your eyes. It wasn't all that bad."

"No, it was very, very good." He took a bite and washed it down with coffee. "You saw my brothers. We're a big strapping bunch. Between the three of us, we nearly drove Ma crazy. I can still hear her shouting from the kitchen. 'If I have to come out there and separate you boys, then mark my words you will be sorry.'"

"Were you ever sorry?"

"Sometimes." Laughter bracketed his mouth, teasing out his handsome dimples. "Brant would poke his tongue out at me and I'd try to grab it and the next thing you know the three of us were wrestling around on the floor, knocking something over. A lamp would break and we'd be in for a licking."

"And you were the older brother. You should have known better."

"Exactly Ma's reasoning. She never understood how aggravating younger brothers could be. I tried to explain how it wasn't my fault. She never saw my side of things." The humor glinting in his eyes said differently. "If my brothers weren't so aggravating, I wouldn't have had to make them stop."

"You were simply the innocent bystander."

"Just minding my own business. Evelyn was the worst. By the time she hit school age, she figured out that our folks thought she could do no wrong. Their little angelic girl, compared to the three of us, always fighting, rolling around in the dirt and climbing trees."

"It wouldn't be hard to see why they might have thought that," she said wryly. Why couldn't she stop looking at his dimples? Dimples had never affected her like this before.

"To this day, Pa doesn't believe us." Austin cut open a dinner roll. "Evelyn would do things to purposely get us into trouble. Like sneaking into the parlor and quietly turning over the coffee table and making it look like we'd been fighting in there. Ma would come in from her garden, take one look and we'd be banished to our rooms with no supper. Evelyn would be as sweet as could be. 'I tried to stop them, Ma', she would practically sing. 'But they wouldn't listen to me.'"

"Personally, I'm taking Evelyn's side." The joke crossed her lips and she was laughing, just a little. "I'm sure you boys were guilty about something."

"We used to play ball inside the house—not supposed to—but sometimes it just happened." He swiped butter on his roll and took a bite. "One day we were fighting for the ball on our way out the door, I gave Derek a shove and he tumbled backward and landed bottom first in Ma's Christmas cactus. She'd inherited that plant from her mother, who'd passed away, and boy, did we get into trouble for that. I can still see eight-year-old Derek with his backside in the planter, stuck. It took all of us pulling on him and holding on to the planter to get him free."

"You're making that up." She set down her fork she was laughing so hard. "That can't be what happened."

"I swear it. Ma was yelling, Derek refused to give up the ball and Brant was tattling on how I was the one who gave Derek the push. After we got him out, the plant was never the same. Leaves had torn off. Stems had broken off. It didn't bloom when the next Christmas rolled around. Boy, we were in trouble. We weren't allowed anywhere near that plant under threat of thrashing. Ma meant business."

"Something tells me the story doesn't end there."

"Not by a long shot. This is where Evelyn comes in.

My parents' sweet, innocent, never-did-a-single-thing-wrong daughter." He set down his fork, transformed in the light. No longer the stranger he'd been, but the man she knew. The man who made her lean a little closer, caught by his story.

"One day, Ma finds a stem broken off the cactus for no apparent reason. It's just laying on the floor. She hunts us down, hauls us off our ponies and marches us into the parlor. 'Look at that,' she says, shaking us by our collars. 'Which of you did this? Confess now or else.' And since none of us knew what had happened, that's what we said. Big mistake."

"It was Evelyn?"

"Absolutely. Evelyn who smiled at us in triumph, standing where Ma couldn't see her. I saw that smug look. I saw her mouth, 'Ha, ha, I got you.' I knew why we were sent to bed hungry that night."

"I'm sure you deserved it in principle." She reached for her tea. "You probably got into trouble somewhere and your ma never knew about it."

"Likely, but Evelyn was rewarded by success and it didn't stop. Whenever she wanted to torment us, she would pluck a stem off the plant, make it look like we'd been roughhousing in the parlor and Ma never questioned it. Even when I tried to make her see the truth. Nope, not precious, angelic Evelyn. She would never do anything like that."

"I'm starting to like her even more now." She stirred sugar into her cup. "It sounds like growing up in your family was wonderful, except for the cactus incident."

"Wonderful? That's a word. Lucky is another." He

polished off the last of his chicken. His plate empty, he shoved it away and reached for the last of his coffee. "What about you? You're still looking pale. Let me guess. You should go lie down."

"It's not long until bedtime." She took a sip of tea, determined to hide the truth. Her arms felt heavy and weak, just like the rest of her. Lifting the teacup felt like an effort, but one she was determined to hide.

"You look ready to fall out of that chair." He pushed from the table and circled close. He stole her cup, seized her hand and helped her to her feet. Once again he stood so close she could feel his body's heat. His masculine scent was somehow comforting, just like his hand that folded around hers. "Let's get you to bed, okay? A good night's sleep is what you need."

"No. The dishes need to be done. The kitchen needs to be tidied. I didn't even get a chance to do the day's sweeping."

"The sweeping and tidying can wait." He tugged her along, his strength greater than hers, and there was nothing she could do to stop him. She stumbled forward, shivering as he leaned in to speak against her ear. "I'll do the dishes. Being sent to my room wasn't the only way I was punished. Ma would put me on kitchen cleanup when I got into trouble."

"So, you're saying you have a lot of dishwashing experience?"

"I tended to get into trouble a lot, but I never meant to. Honest."

There went his dimples, luring her again. Her heart skipped a beat. She didn't know how she'd been so lucky to get this man for her husband, but she wasn't going to disappoint him. Not anymore. Not ever again.

Gratitude for him filled her up so much, she couldn't speak. She let him lead her into their bedroom where he lit the lamp for her, set her teacup on her bedside table and left her alone. The image of his handsome smile lingered like a treasure in the silence as she sat on the edge of the bed in the room where she was safe.

Where she would always be safe.

A storm set in around bedtime. Austin marked his page, put aside his book and knelt to bank the fire. As he listened to the wind beat against the west side of the house and echo in the room, he realized even sitting by himself he didn't feel as lonely. Something had changed during supper. The ice between them melted and Willa's guard inched down just enough for him to see a hint of the woman she was meant to be.

One day that careful hint of her smile would blossom into the real thing. One day she would laugh fully out loud, and he couldn't wait to hear that sound or see her face wreathed in an all-out smile, her eyes sparkling without a single shadow in them. Hope lifted him as he stood, hung the shovel on its hook and turned out the lamp. After tonight, he had to believe that in time she would at least come to care for him.

Snow pelted the house. It sounded like they were in for a serious blow. The blizzard's wail drowned out the rhythm of his gait as he crossed the dark room and eased open the door. His eyes adjusted to the dark and he waited until he could make out her sleeping form.

She lay on her side, her dark hair fanning out behind her, her hands folded on her pillow as dainty as could be. She hardly made a shape under the covers. He worried about how thin she was. What about the babe? It was husbandly concern that drove him to pick up the afghan folded on the chest at the foot of the bed. Concern—not caring.

Not the first seeds of love.

He shook out the length of wool his mother had crocheted long ago in his youth, and laid it gently over Willa's sleeping form. Ma would have loved her, he thought, as he tucked the edge carefully into place below her chin. Ma would have fussed over her like there was no tomorrow.

Willa gave a little sigh in her sleep, an endearing sound that wrapped around his heart. She lay peacefully, and he couldn't help drinking in the sight of her— her porcelain profile, her perfect sloping nose and her mouth lush and tempting relaxed into the perfect shape for kissing.

Hold it there, Austin. You're thinking about kissing her way too much. He was lucky she'd let him hold her hand. He gave the covers a slight tug to bring them up around her chin so no chilly air could slip in. He had to accept facts. Willa had come to him out of desperation, not because she wanted a husband to love. He'd taken that risk the moment he'd slipped a train ticket and ten dollars for meals into the envelope along with his written proposal.

He'd gotten himself a fine woman. Pa had been the first to mention it when they'd broken out the whiskey. A man's duty to his wife was the most important thing. He'd waited eight long years for his own bride. He didn't dare be disappointed by Willa and her confession that she didn't believe in love.

He took a step back in the dark room and sat down on the nearby chair. The cushion squeaked, but the sound was swallowed up by the blizzard beating against the wallboards like a wild animal fighting to get in. He tugged off his boots, watching Willa sleep, breathing in and out, so very vulnerable.

Devotion filled him up. Maybe she couldn't love him, but something had happened between them tonight at the supper table. It made him see what could be. There could be something between them—not what he'd hoped for and far less than what he needed, but it was a great deal more than he'd had as a bachelor.

He would consider it a privilege to be as close to her as she would let him.

Chapter Thirteen

The sound in the wind was the reason Willa looked up from her work. The heavy storm took on a musical sound, and the snow that had been thudding against the windows changed to a *splat*. Rain. It fell in gray sheets, making watery sounds against the side of the house. She abandoned the fabric spread out on the table to wander to the window. Maybe this storm was the change she'd been waiting for. Spring in these mountains would be beautiful.

The clock chimed four times, drawing her attention. She tapped across the freshly polished floor, lifted the lid from the kettle and stirred the fragrant bean-and-beef soup. It had been a specialty of the hotel where she'd worked when her ma lived, before her sad marriage to Jed. She considered the dish one of her best. She hoped Austin would think so, too, she thought, as she added a handful of chopped dried parsley and replaced the lid. That would be fine simmering away while she was in the barn. But just to be sure, she knelt to open the stove door. A few turns with the shovel to bank part of the fire, and she was ready to go.

Her muscles ached pleasantly from a day of satisfying work. The furniture shone with new polish, the windows glinted without a streak and her only regret was that she'd run out of time to do more than cut the material for every window in the house. Tonight would get a start on sewing them. She slipped out of her new shoes and into her old ones before pulling on her old coat and hood. It would take not take much time at all to hem the fabric and sew on a ruffled edge. Thinking how cheerful the house would be put a smile on her face as she shouldered out into the storm.

Icy rain blew in her face and slapped against her coat as she sloshed and slid across the yard. Snow hung on the miles of forest surrounding the yard, weighing heavily on branches. Low clouds and a heavy rain veil obscured all view of the valley below and the mountains beyond. She swiped rivulets out of her eyes, wrenched open the stubborn barn door enough to slip in. Whoops. She had to hold in her breath to squeeze through. Her stomach wasn't as flat as it had been.

The baby was showing. Her heart stuttered as she laid a hand there, where the faintest bump made real the child's existence. She thought of Austin's nephews—*her* nephews now—and for the first time let herself wonder about the new life. A little bundle to cradle in her arms, who would grin up at her the way Delia's baby had, who would grow up to run and play like the older nephews, so sweet in his or her own unique way.

Emotion ached behind her eyes, feelings she didn't understand. As she gave the door a harder push, she wondered if she could ever be the kind of mother Delia was, so loving and happy. Or if she could ever be as patient and warm as Berry.

Rosie lowed in welcome. Big brown eyes peeked over the top of her stall, ears pricked forward. The cow danced in place, happy to have company.

"How have you ladies been?" she asked, also glancing at the mare, which was nothing but a shadow in the far corner.

Rosie mooed cheerfully in a very long answer, perhaps a bovine comment on her day.

Amused, Willa heaved the door closed behind her and hurried to light the lantern hung on the closest post. "How about you, little mare?"

The shadow in the back stall didn't move. Her wary eyes blinked.

"I know the feeling." The match flared, the wick caught and she shook the match's flame out carefully. "Austin told me you had a hard experience before you came here, but you don't need to be afraid of me."

The mare froze, her eyes wide with uncertainty. The poor little thing. Willa grabbed the three-legged stool from the corner and the clean milk pail from its hook and hauled both into the aisle.

"Moo!" Rosie leaned her chin against the top of the gate and lifted her eyebrows in censure.

"Yes, yes, I won't forget the grain. And I can see if I did, you would remind me." She couldn't exactly say why she was so merry, but today everything felt lighter.

Even spring dared to show its face and an old familiar emotion lifted her up—a feeling she hadn't experienced in a long time.

Hope. She pried open the barrel lid, and the creak it made drowned out all other noise. She startled when a cool wind puffed against her, swirling her skirts.

"Allow me." A big gloved hand caught the lid and held it.

Austin. Raindrops glistened on his hat brim and glittered across the line of his shoulders. Her breath caught and his nearness washed over her like heat from a warm and cozy fire. Her stomach felt strange and floaty, like a soap bubble about to pop.

"You're home early." Her voice caught, sounding thin and not at all like her own.

"I wanted to have time to give you a driving lesson before it got too dark, but halfway home it started to rain. It's tough going out there." The low notes he spoke wrapped around her like a warm blanket, snug and comfortable and she couldn't step away. He unhooked a small pail from the wall and held it for her.

"Another time then."

"I promise. Do you want me to take the scoop?"

"What? Oh, no." She blinked, realizing her hand was still in the barrel holding the grain scoop. She'd been so absorbed by him she'd forgotten what she was doing. It was a mystery how he grabbed her attention. Her gaze stayed centered on him and refused to go anywhere else, which made filling the pail tricky. It was even harder pretending she wasn't affected by him.

"That's a lot of grain," he commented, taking a peek at the bucket.

"I'm trying to make friends with her. With the mare." What was wrong with her? She could seem to make her mouth work, either. "I thought grain would help."

"Grain always helps."

Rosie mooed, as if that were her opinion, too, but it sounded far away, miles away. Everything did—everything except Austin.

Concentrate, Willa, she told herself for all the good it did. The scoop sank into the grain but she couldn't tell how much was in it when she aimed for the pail. The rush of kernels spilling into the bucket told her she'd hit her mark, but all she could see was Austin half-in and half-out of the shadows, with a day's growth stubbling his jaw and caring softening his granite face.

This was very disconcerting. What was the matter with her? It had to be gratitude. That's what she was feeling, that's all and nothing else. What else could it be?

Mystery solved. Relieved, she left the scoop in the barrel, hoping she had enough in her pail. Austin didn't say anything, so maybe she did. Something else filled her—longing—as she eased around his big frame. He stole the oxygen from the air, making it hard to breathe, and her knees wobbled as she walked away. Best to ignore it.

"I stopped by the mercantile on my way home." He turned to heft the door shut against the battering wind. "I remembered what you said about knitting. I had Mrs.

Pole choose some yarn for you, something to make for the baby."

"You did that?" Surprise crept across her face as she clutched the grain pail in her arms.

"Sure. There's no reason you shouldn't have picked out what you wanted, but I did it on impulse. If I'd planned it, I would have asked what you wanted over breakfast." He patted Calvin's neck. "Mrs. Pole said you can always trade it in if you don't like it. I just thought you might want to get started. Time's a wastin'."

Whew, that was a long explanation, he told himself. Maybe he was trying to pretend what he felt for her was casual and that he wasn't all wrapped up in her. That he didn't spend nearly every waking hour of the day thinking of her. Calvin gave a snort and grabbed at the Stetson's brim. He lifted his muzzle high, intentionally keeping the hat out of Austin's reach.

Funny guy. He made an unsuccessful grab at the hat and the gelding preened with delight. It was hard to notice, what with watching Willa the way he did. He couldn't look away. He didn't even want to blink. She held him spellbound simply standing in the aisle. Dark wisps framing her face caressed the sides of her cheeks the way his fingers ached to.

"I would love to get started on a project." Happiness swept across her, upturning the corners of her mouth and animating her eyes in a way he'd never seen before. "Berry, Delia and Evelyn promised to write down their favorite baby patterns for me."

"Good." He bent to unhitch the horse, his fingers

working quickly. He liked knowing that she could see his gesture for what it was. He'd wanted to do something for her, that was all. There was always the chance a knitting project could distract her from her determination to excel at every aspect of housekeeping.

"I'm starting to realize how much I need to get done." Willa didn't seem to notice as Rosie leaned against her stall door and dipped her nose into the grain bucket. Jowls worked and grain disappeared and Willa didn't respond. Her gaze stayed on his, shrinking the distance between them.

"The next six months will zip by before you know it." He released Calvin from his collar, hardly aware of anything but the woman holding the pail. During his day at work, he'd missed her presence, the melody of her voice and the way his pulse caught when her honest blue eyes met his.

"I thought I had plenty of time until Evelyn told me all the things she's already made. I don't have a single piece of clothing ready, not even a blanket. I don't want to get caught short come October. I want to be a good mother and have what the baby will need."

"We'll make sure to be ready for him. Or her," he added, giving Calvin a pat before sweeping the wrapped bundle of yawn from the sleigh seat. "You're not alone in this, right? I'm here to help you."

"I know, Austin. Thank you. You have no notion how much I appreciate you." She tilted her head back to look at him. Soft little tendrils stroked her face again, tempting him even more to do the same. He swallowed hard, holding back the urge to kiss the worry away from the corner of her lips.

There he went, thinking about kissing her again, this convenient bride of his. He reached over to take the bucket before Rosie ate more than her share. In the corner, the little mare watched them, her nose up to scent the grain, but she didn't come close.

"Just doin' my job as a husband," he drawled, once again trying to be casual when what he felt wasn't casual at all. He leaned over the mare's stall and poured grain into her trough. The animal watched him with wary eyes, keeping her distance. At least Willa was comfortable letting him close to her. She didn't stiffen in the relatively close quarters of the aisle when he brushed close. "I wouldn't want you to decide I wasn't good enough, annul this marriage and find a better man."

"I can't see that happening." She ran a careful finger across the soft skeins of lightweight yarn peeking out of their package. "Then again, I haven't met any of the eligible men in town yet. Berry made it a point to let me know you are one of many men around these parts who couldn't find a wife."

"Yes, but unlike me, those other men all have something lacking." He winked, petted Rosie's nose and emptied the bucket in her trough. "Those other men aren't worth even a look."

"Is that so?"

"Absolutely."

"Then it's a good thing you found me." Laughter

twinkled like blue dreams in her eyes. Nothing could be more exquisite. She tilted her head to one side, studying him through the thick dark curls of her lashes. "I guess I'd better stick with you."

"Guess so." He moved away with the empty bucket, or at least he meant to. Funny how his feet didn't carry him away from her like he told them to. He seemed stuck in place, unable to step away from the dazzle of her smile, breathing in her rose-and-woman scent until his lungs threatened to burst. Tenderness welled up too strong to hold back. He swallowed hard, but it clung to his voice, vibrating in the low notes, revealed. "Do you like the yarn?"

"It's beautiful. It's perfect." She was luminous, gleaming with emotions soft and gentle, something that could be the start of caring. Her gaze boldly met his, unafraid, no longer reserved, filled with what looked like trust.

"Mrs. Pole said you'd want something neutral, that could go with either a boy or a girl." The words stuttered out of him, not sounding like his normal easygoing self. Then again, his heart thundered in his ears so loudly, he couldn't hear well enough to tell.

"The yellow is a beautiful shade, lemony and cheerful. It's soft."

"Yes, soft." He swallowed hard, staring at her mouth again, trying hard to concentrate on the yarn when all he could see was the satin of her lips, slightly parted.

"I'm going to start with little socks." Unaware, she ran her fingertip over the fragile strand of wool. "Socks are practical."

"Good idea." He felt Rosie nudge him square in the middle of his back, but he didn't budge. Out of the corner of his eye he saw Calvin in the aisle, waiting to be rubbed down. The gelding gave a toss of his head, his teeth still gripped on the brim of the Stetson. The black mare stayed in the shadows, her dark gaze silently watching.

"I can't tell you what this means, Austin. What you've already given this baby is enough."

"What do you mean?" He hadn't done so much. Not yet, anyway. "There isn't much I can do until October. I know a little about rocking babies. I'm an uncle three times over, you know."

"Oh, I know." Willa dared to reach out and lay a hand on his chest, right above the rapid-fire beat of his heart. He covered her hand with his, keeping her trapped there. Could she feel what she did to him? How she made him react to her? Hard to tell. Looking down at her with emotion tucked into the corners of her face, so real and earnest he'd never seen the like.

"Such a nice house to live in. Plenty of good food on the table. Medical care. The doctor's visit went well today. Everything is fine as long as I gain more weight." She smiled up at him. Such a beautiful smile. "But this life you're able to give him—or her. Fine warm things to wear, a real family. He—or she—will have aunts, uncles, a grandfather, cousins and you. The baby will have you."

With the way she gazed up at him as if he'd hung the moon, maybe he'd better make things real clear. "I was teasing you before about all those other men. I'm not sure how I compare. I'm not all that you seem to think I am."

"I think you are." She went up on tiptoe, so sweet she made his eyes burn. She leaned in, the tendrils of her hair tickling his chin and catching on his day's stubble. The tenderness rising up inside him threatened to take over as the warm satin of her lips brushed his cheek.

Hell, he was hooked. There was no going backward. There was nothing to be done about it. *I love you,* he thought as she slipped away, the yarn skeins in her arms. She set them on top of the grain barrel.

He could deny it no longer. He was in love with a woman who could never love him.

How was this all going to work out? He didn't know, but judging by the hurt already in his heart, not well.

Perched on the wooden stool, Willa leaned her forehead against Rosie's warm side. Milk zinged into the pail as she gently squeezed. The cow stood patiently eating away at the fresh hay in her feeder.

She couldn't see Austin from behind Rosie, but her ears had fine-tuned themselves to his every sound. The rustle of his movements in the straw as he readied Calvin's stall for the night, the low murmur of his voice as he spoke to his horse or the timid little mare and the pad of his boots in the aisle, it all moved through her like a beloved song.

She listened, ears straining for his next sounds as she stripped the last of the milk from Rosie's udder.

She heard the jingle of the harness as he put it away, the metallic clink as he stowed Calvin's grooming tools and the creak as a stall gate opened.

"I was going to come in here and finish up, but you beat me to it." Straw crackled as his big black boots came into sight. "Let me get that. I have to make myself useful somewhere."

"Uh—" She didn't exactly know why her tongue tied up in an unexpected knot. As the lingering effects of his rumbling baritone moved through her, she looked up the long length of his denim-encased legs, up his muscled torso to the wide set of his shoulders. My, but he was a terribly well-built man. That truth had never quite struck her like this before. His manly strength seemed so overpowering her fingers itched to settle on him and feel once again his iron strength.

Goodness, what was wrong with her? She stood up slowly, laying both hands on Rosie's flank for support. Perhaps she was light-headed from leaning over for so long. Yes, that had to be it because her knees definitely felt weak as he ambled closer. His masculine heat seemed to sizzle across her skin as he leaned so close to her she could see the raindrops still damp in his thick dark hair. A cowlick sat at the crown of his head in a swirl. Her fingertips yearned to reach out and smooth down that whirl of hair.

"That's a good girl," he crooned, talking low to Rosie. "Your water tub is full. You're all ready for the night."

The cow looked over her shoulder at him, mooing

gently in return. Those big chocolate-brown eyes shone with adoration as the cow gazed at Austin.

Willa didn't blame her one bit. It was hard not to admire him as he swept the stool away and turned to her with an intense focus. She felt like the only woman in the world.

"Whew, listen to it rain." Austin tipped his head, listening to the drumbeat battering the roof. Tinkling sounds rang everywhere as the snow began to melt. Water dripped off the eaves and plopped on the snowy ground, and the music of it serenaded her as she stumbled through the gate and into the aisle.

The black mare watched with unblinking eyes, poised as if ready to leap away at any danger.

"Good night, girl." She gripped the top rail, breathless as the man sidled up behind her. The steely wall of his chest wasn't exactly touching her back but she felt as if it were. Heat swirled down her spine and left her dizzy.

Maybe she should have taken a longer nap this afternoon, she thought. Then she couldn't think anymore, as her entire mind went blank because Austin leaned closer. His chest pressed against her right shoulder blade and when he spoke, his words vibrated through her from her fingertips to her toes.

"Good night, little mare." Kindness layered his voice, so rich and deep it was impossible to ignore. Curls of emotion came to life around her heart—her heart that remained worn and lifeless, scarred and empty.

The mare didn't move, watching them from the shadows where she felt safe.

Willa knew how that felt. Lantern light licked over her as Austin moved away.

"C'mon." His easygoing drawl hooked her and she turned toward him.

"Let's go in," he said. "I'm starving. That lunch you packed me didn't help one bit. It was so tasty, I kept thinking, hmm, I wonder what she's making for supper?"

"It was just a roast beef sandwich." Honestly, the man could flatter.

"I'm not sure all you did to make it taste good and I don't care, as long as you do it again tomorrow." He swung the milking stool into place and set the milk pail down next to her package of yarn. "The cornbread, the cookies, the leftover pie from Sunday. I thought I'd died and gone to heaven."

"Unlikely." She tugged her hood into place, giving the ties a yank.

"I could be there right now, for all I know." He took his Stetson from Calvin, who offered it with mischief in his eyes. Austin smoothed the teeth marks from the brim, donned it and gave his gelding a friendly nose rub. "All afternoon long I kept thinking of those biscuits you made. I got to hoping you'd made them for tonight and maybe a stew, something to warm me up on a cold spring day."

"Well, you never know. Something even better might be on tonight's menu," she told him, scooping up her yarn.

"Good news. This afternoon around three-thirty I was looking forward to more of your cooking so much that I was hungry enough to eat my own shoe." He grabbed the milk bucket and heaved open the door. "I've been like to die of starvation ever since. It was all I could do not to dive into the pickle barrel when I stopped by the mercantile. I kept eyeing all the food so hard, I gave Mrs. Pole a scare. As if any moment she feared I'd lose control and dive into her food stocks with my bare hands."

"Now you're just exaggerating." Clutching the yarn in one arm she moved toward the doorway, but she didn't get by him unaffected. More tingles erupted on her skin and skidded down her arms as she brushed so close to him, she could smell the hay on his coat and see the individual whiskers shadowing his jaw.

It has to be gratitude, she told herself, at a loss for another way to explain what was happening to her. No one had ever done so much for her. No one had ever shown her kindness the way he had. Of course she would feel strongly for him, for this man who was her husband.

"Seriously, Mrs. Pole swiped the sweat off her brow and blew out a sigh of great relief when I left her store." He wedged the door shut and joined her in the blustery wind. "My stomach growled so hard, I could have been a bear standing at her counter."

"Austin, honestly." Just like a man, she supposed, prone to exaggeration. "I'm sure Mrs. Pole couldn't hear your stomach."

"Don't be too sure. I swore I heard it echo in the store a few times as she was tallying up your yarn." He splashed in a puddle beside her, his mouth crooked with humor.

"If that's true, then I shall be far too embarrassed to step foot inside the mercantile again." Rain cuffed her cheek as she turned into the wind, she took a step and her right shoe slid on the water pooled on top of the hard-packed snow. She took a step to correct it and her left shoe slid in a different direction.

"Hold on to me." Austin's arm wrapped around her waist, catching her before she could fall and using the ice to glide her firmly against him. Tucked into his side, her slipping shoe bumped against the side of his and slid no farther.

"That was close. Thanks." Breathless, she tried not to let her feelings show as the fiery band of his arm burned through her clothing, a heat she could not deny. She took a tentative step, one shoe went out from under her and she was off balance and falling.

But did she? No. Again, Austin's strength held her up even when her feet could find no purchase. Rainwater sloshed beneath her old shoes; the tread had been worn away years ago. It rained so hard and water pooled quickly, she doubted the path to the house would get any easier. She held on to him, curling her fingers into his coat.

"Try skating," he quipped. He seemed as steadfast as one of the mountains spearing up into the rolling clouds. Twilight hovered in the edges of the sky, darkening the rain that glistened like dewdrops on his Stetson's brim and the magnificent plane of his chest. "I'll hold you up. I'd never let you fall."

Her shoes were slipping everywhere—behind her,

in front of her, off to the side. Was she afraid of smashing to the ground?

Not a chance. Austin's arm held her secure, the good husband he was, and more gratitude filled her. The appreciation for him simply did not stop. He was the kind of man a woman could lean on and depend on. A man who tried never to let anyone down.

"That's it, you're getting it." His words were cut to shreds by the worsening wind. Cold bullets shot down from the sky hard enough to ping off the hard-packed ice.

Suddenly, she slid again. This time she gave a little push away from Austin's hold and glided. For a few moments, rain pelted her face and the wind billowed her skirts and she was free, skimming along. Sailing along as light as a feather.

"Oh, my, I can't believe I did that." She grabbed the banister with her free hand. Joy sailed through her, as freely as the late April breeze. "I guess my old shoes are good for something."

"I can see you're glad you kept them." He splashed up to her, his big shadow falling across her. "You put them to good use."

"It was fun." She hopped onto the first step.

"Good. Doesn't sound like you've had a lot of fun in your life. It's time to make up for that." His boots splashed to a stop in front of her, the milk pail swinging in one hand. His gaze roamed her face, pink and glowing. Happiness looked amazing on her, intensifying her natural beauty and combining to make her more stunning than a simple man like him could take. Overwhelmed, he swallowed to find his throat dry. "You look a little different. Like a sunny May day. I don't know how else to say it."

"I know what you mean. I *feel* like a May day. That it will be blue skies ahead any moment now." Raindrops clung to her hood and the wet locks of hair curled adorably around her dear face. They glittered like diamonds, making her look like a lost princess in a peasant's coat. Looking at her could make a man believe.

"Spring is already here. That's what this rain is." He realized he'd leaned in closer to her, his gaze watching every little movement of her mouth. Those perfect lips, lush and flawless and satin-soft, mesmerized him more than anything had in his entire life.

"Austin, I wasn't talking about the weather."

"I know. I'm just bad at metaphors." His brain wasn't working one whit. All he could see was the dazzle inside her—her joy, her sweetness and her bright spirit. Love filled his chest with a painful ache, the growing pains of a heart expanding.

"I've yet to see anything you're bad at," she argued, chin up with a new mischievous gleam. He couldn't help leaning closer, watching her mouth form those words and stretch into a soft smile. "You're good at everything."

"I'm not so good at embroidery," he quipped, but the humor never reached his words. It died away at a much stronger emotion that had him tipping slowly closer.

He watched her eyes widen when she realized what he wanted. Her soft lips grew softer. He knew kissing her would be heaven as he cupped her chin in his free hand, letting raindrops tumble over them like promises. He thought about slanting his lips over hers. Everything within him wanted her kiss. He needed it more than words could say.

Chapter Fourteen

Her laughter died as she watched him lean in closer, his pupils dilating to full black. She shivered involuntarily—not cold and not afraid. Austin stared so hard at her mouth he didn't even seem to breathe. Her first thought was no, she wasn't ready for this. She considered darting away and escaping into the house. Panic shot through her, but she didn't move. She would have to be blind not to see how intent Austin was as he hesitated, a silent question in his eyes asking her if he could proceed.

He was asking—not doing what he wanted and forcing her to his will. How could she say no to him? He towered above her with longing written in shades of blue in his eyes. She braced as the inches separating them became an inch, until her breath mingled with his and she could see so far into him, she saw his soul. A strange sympathy filled her, one so strong it was as if she could feel the intensity of his longing for one single kiss.

The first brush of his mouth to hers surprised her with its softness. Just one feather-light stroke across the surface of her lips and it left a tingle behind.

That was a kiss? She blinked, dazed, confused by the simple beauty of an act she'd dreaded—one she knew for a fact was unpleasant. Emotion wrapped around her so tightly she could not breathe as Austin slanted his lips over hers a second time, intending to make this one last.

Sensation spread across the surface of her lips, both sweet and heated in the same moment, both gentle and ardent. Her hand curled into the fabric of his coat, holding on because it felt as if her feet had left the step. The world began to twirl, and the only thing steady and certain was Austin. His kiss balanced her. His lips caressed hers in slow, measured strokes that made her knees weak and tugged hurtfully at the edges of her guarded heart.

When he lifted his mouth from hers, they were both breathless, staring into each other's eyes as if nothing else existed. What did he see when he looked at her? The woman who could never love him? Or the one he hoped would?

Her pulse pounded so hard in her ears, it drowned out all else—the strike of wind, the music of rain and the exhale of her own breath as she realized what she'd done. In accepting his kiss, then Austin would expect more. She swallowed hard, panic building as she thought of his weight trapping her on the mattress, of how she'd have to hold back her tears of pain and shame and count the minutes until he was done. Panic lodged in her throat and she vaguely heard him say her name, but it was hard to focus on with her pulse thundering in her ears.

"Willa." His hand at her jawline was the gentlest touch she'd ever known. Caring telegraphed through him and into her, a force she wanted to deny and couldn't. Austin wanted something from her she didn't know how to give him, and the thought of it frightened her more than the notion of lying beneath him in their bed.

"We're getting rained on." Mellow humor layered his voice, his tone intimate and rich, and he leaned in closer to her as if a barricade between them had been lowered. His forehead brushed hers. She couldn't exactly say why it felt tender and intimate, as if he'd taken a step closer to her emotionally. He gazed into her eyes, which resonated with an emotion she didn't recognize. It was the most beautiful thing she'd ever seen.

"C'mon, I don't want you to catch a chill." His smile could make her forget the cold and damp and maybe even her panic. His fingers laced through hers as he tugged her up the steps. "We have to take extra care of you in your condition."

"Right." Relief ticked through her as she slipped through the door he held for her.

She set down her bundle and struggled to get her buttons through the wet wool buttonholes as Austin stepped behind her to help her. His body heat radiated through her and her breath caught. She was aware of every movement he made—the weight of his hands on her shoulders, holding her dripping coat so she could slip out of it, and the fan of his breath against her nape before she swirled away.

Why was she breathless? Why couldn't she seem to see straight as she circled around the sofa? She caught the end of the yellow material spread out on the kitchen table and started folding. The tingles remained on her lips, apparently burned there like a brand from his kiss.

That kiss. She shook her head, her fingers fumbling as she flipped the fold of calico over and over on itself until the table was clear. Austin's kiss was like nothing she'd ever felt. No whiskey breath, no drunken harshness, no painful crush of his lips to hers—no, Austin's kiss was as sweet as a fairy tale.

"Willa, you've been busy." Austin stayed in the shadows of the room, taking his time removing his boots, a hulking darkness at the edge of her vision. "What did you do today, polish every bit of wood in the house?"

"It didn't take long. I haven't polished the other rooms yet." She kept her back to him as she checked on the soup. The instant she lifted the lid, steam wafted up at her, spicy and fragrant and rich, bubbling perfectly. Why couldn't she stop being aware of him? Every pad of his step, every rustle of his clothes and the measured softness of his breathing?

She didn't want this. She wanted to go back to the blissful distance that used to stretch between them. Panic beat through her blood as she stirred the soup, watching the soft beans and chunks of roast beef swirl in the kettle. Don't think about him, she told herself. Just forget his kiss.

That kiss. If only she could forget it.

"I thought we talked about this." The poker clinked against the grate as he added more wood. The whoosh of the fire, the snap and crackle of bark burning and the nearness of Austin's presence put her teeth on edge. She never should have allowed him to kiss her. She gripped a bowl to fill, her hand trembling just enough she had to worry about spilling as she ladled soup. What was happening to her? How did she make it stop?

"I don't want you working so hard, Willa." More wood clunked onto the grate. "I'm not going to say it again."

She bit her lip, holding words inside. She wanted to tell him he didn't own her. Memories swirled up, bringing Jed's words into her thoughts. *You're my property, woman. When I tell you to do something, you'd damn well better do it or I'll make you sorry you didn't.*

Austin wasn't like that, but wasn't that what lay beneath his words? The reminder that his word was law in this house? Her hand trembled as she carried the full bowls to the table, nearly sloshing soup over the rims. Utensils clinked terribly when she set knives, spoons and forks into place. She was so upset with the ghost of his kiss still imprinted on her lips, that the basket of rolls slammed against the table with surprising force. That's how angry she was.

"Hey." Austin came from behind, his footsteps measured and unhurried, his stride confident, a man in his domain. He didn't bow to what she wanted. He did just what he pleased, bringing her expensive yarn and watching her skate across the ice and kissing her like he was a prince in a storybook, something that could not possibly be true.

The teapot slammed against the table with a hard *clank*. That was her doing, too.

"Willa." His hands curled over her shoulders, just touching her because it was what he wanted to do, because he had that right. Did he ask her permission? No. He just did it, towering behind her, dominating her with his superior strength and awesome good looks and all she could do was to hope he didn't try to kiss her again because she didn't think she could take it.

"You seem awfully upset."

"You think so?" She whirled from his touch to plop the tea ball into the pot. "I hope you like bean soup. I didn't get your permission before I decided on tonight's meal."

"It smells good. It's like I've died and gone to heaven." He reached over to grab a dish towel and lifted the rumbling teakettle from the stove. He ignored her huff of frustration as he went ahead and filled the teapot for her. "It's a good night for soup. All that damp and cold out there. It's just what I was hoping for. It'll warm us right up."

"I'm glad you approve." The butter dish landed on the table with a hard *clunk*. The lid jumped straight up and landed a little askew, but she didn't seem to notice as she marched toward him, jaw tight, lips in a no-nonsense straight line and her eyes flashing fire.

Maybe it was best to try another compliment. The

woman looked like she could use one. "The rolls smell good, too. Is that my mother's recipe."

"Evelyn gave it to me on Sunday." She shouldered past him, grabbed the teapot and stalked the few feet to the table, her back straight, her shoulders braced, her movements quick and harsh. Anger rose off her like steam from the soup as the teapot landed next to her plate.

Interesting. He had to bite the inside of his mouth to keep from smiling. He wasn't sure what had happened to his reserved and meek bride, but this side of her interested him. He never would have guessed it was there. Curious. Looked like it was time for another compliment. "It was good of you. I like soup."

"Isn't that what we agreed to? That I would cook your meals and keep your house?"

"That we did." He rushed to grab her chair and pull it out for her. His actions earned him a disparaging look, as if he were the last thing she wanted to set eyes on. How dear she looked with her gaze sizzling and raindrops crowning her hair like jewels.

"Not once did we discuss kissing." Sparks snapped as she focused on him.

"That's true." He couldn't deny it.

"Kissing has nothing to do with my work around here." She slipped onto the cushion, looking as if she didn't much like his hand on her chair within close proximity to her. She must have had no notion how funny she was or how dear. It just made him love her more.

"Right. I got that." He went to help her scoot her chair

in but she jerked it forward out of his hands. The loud thump echoed in the kitchen but it didn't trouble him. "Kissing was not mentioned in your advertisement."

"It wasn't mentioned as a condition of our marriage either, and I'll thank you not to forget it." She gave her napkin a hard snap. "You just can't go around doing whatever you want."

"Right. Got it." He had to step on his toe to keep from laughing. His chest swelled up with a mixture of amusement and affection that left him half choking and half struggling for words. "Next time I want to kiss you, I'll ask you first."

"Yes, you do that." She took a roll from the basket and broke it open, her pretty mouth pursed up kissably. "It's the least you can do."

"The very least," he agreed, having learned long ago not to argue with a mad woman. He settled into his chair and picked up his spoon. The only thing that looked more delicious than the meal in front of him was his bride glaring at him.

"I don't think you're taking me seriously. Is that a grin on your face?"

"No. It's appreciation for the meal. It looks mighty good." What was wrong with him that he wanted to reach across the table and capture her lips in a much less gentle kiss? "Thanks for going to all the trouble today to fix it."

"I learned to make it at the hotel where I used to work before I married." Her chin went up and her tone softened, but the look she tossed him did not. Daggers would be less dangerous than the stare she fixed on him. "It was the house specialty. Folks would come from miles to order it. Travelers new to the area would ask for it by name."

"That's where you learned to cook so well." He blew on his spoon to cool it before taking a bite. Flavors exploded on his tongue. He could honestly say he'd never tasted anything as good. "You've done a real fine job, Willa. I couldn't have found a better cook. I'm glad the woman who stepped off the train to marry me was you."

"Don't try and sweet-talk me out of my mood." She arched one brow, taking a dainty bite of her roll. "Maybe I've had just about enough of you."

"So I see." He didn't comment on the faint tug of amusement he spotted at the corners of her mouth. "I'll try to be less maddening from now on."

"That would be a big help."

"I'll do my best, but as a man I'm naturally maddening to a woman. The sisters-in-law explained this to me before your arrival." He took another bite of tasty soup. "You'll have to help me out by letting me know when I'm particularly irritating to you."

"Count on it." She dug into her soup, too. "And another thing. Stop telling me what to do."

"I've been doing that?" His poor heart gave a painful thud as he watched the lamplight caress the curves of her ivory face...like he longed to do. Boldly and without fear of frightening her, and his fingers ached to trace the contour of her full bottom lip. Their kiss lingered in his memory, warming him from the inside out. "It seems to me I've mostly been telling you *not* to do things."

"You know what I mean." Her brows arched higher. "I'm not going to spend the rest of our marriage jumping to do what you say."

"Okay, I won't expect you to." He filled his spoon and blew on it again.

"I've already done that with one man, and it wasn't right." She took a sip of her tea. "I was miserable. There was just no end to his bossing me around, and I won't have it again."

"Right." His easygoing agreement didn't hold a single note of anger. He shrugged his big shoulders, in a this-is-not-a-big-deal gesture. "I never meant to order you around, Willa. I'm concerned about you is all."

"I'm fine." Her anger ran out of steam seeing his caring. He exuded it just as he exuded an overpowering masculinity. It was impossible to miss, written everywhere in the tone of his voice, in the cut of his face and the gleam of his blue eyes. "Let's just eat our meal."

"Whatever you say." A hint of amusement lingered on his lips, on those lips that had felt like a dream on hers. Like something she used to imagine up as a young girl in a loveless home and in a childhood filled with hard work. One day, she'd dreamed a handsome man would fall in love and marry her and his kisses would be like stardust, so pure and true she could feel how much he loved her.

Grown up now, she knew that love didn't exist. So why did the dreams she'd thought long dead come alive with hope? Caring wasn't love, she told herself. Caring was a natural result of duty to another human being. She set down her cup, determined to avoid looking at him. Her bowl of soup held all of her attention, not the man across from her. She did not want to care about him because it terrified her. Just like his kiss had.

Had she really talked to him like that? She seized her spoon with white-knuckled force. Shame burned her face as she took a small sip. What had come over her? She thought of everything she'd said to him—every little thing—and the way she'd said it, scolding him like a shrew.

He'd taken every word amiably. He'd let her talk, he'd let her say those things to him and he hadn't burst into an insulted rage. Jed would have beaten her terribly. Mortified, she dared to watch her new husband through her lashes, spooning up soup, eating rolls and sipping coffee with a sort of habitual rhythm that spoke of a man used to eating his suppers alone and without conversation.

Disgrace filled her and her head bobbed down of its own accord. The man had waited so long for a bride. Why did it have to be her? She was going to fail him. Worse, she feared after tonight she already had. Anyone could see he deserved more than she could ever give.

After Willa's little outburst, Austin figured a smart man wouldn't push away from the table and lend a hand with the dishes where it wasn't welcomed. His sisters had warned him to be gentle because a lady's emotions were closer to the surface during pregnancy, not that he'd needed the warning. He had a new appreciation for his bride as he added wood to the fires while she cleared the table. Who knew she had a temper, and a cute one, to boot? She did the dishes, gathered up her sewing and settled down on the sofa while he watched her over the top of his volume of Shakespeare, wondering what other sides of her he had yet to see.

She sat with her head bent over her work, her needle darting in and out of the cheerful yellow fabric with quick precision. The click of the needle's tip against her thimble added a pleasant rhythm to his reading. He turned the page, where the ghost of Hamlet's father haunted the battlements, and yet his eyes couldn't fix on the text. Willa drew his attention with dark tendrils fallings around her face in artful curls. Her lips pursed in concentration.

Those lips. Desire kicked through him, remembering how her lips had felt beneath his. The memory of their kiss gripped him, refusing to let go. Willa sure had been worked up over that kiss.

But she hadn't said there wouldn't be another.

He pondered that as the clock ticked the passing hours on the mantel, the logs in the grate crumbled with a thud and he pushed out of his chair to tend to the flying embers. No, she hadn't forbidden him to kiss her when she'd been very clear about what she would and would not put up with around here. He hid his smile from her as he knelt at the hearth.

It's nearly bedtime, I'll just bank the fire, he *almost* said and caught himself. Perhaps in Willa's present mood, she would see that as bossy so he rephrased. "Willa, it's almost bedtime. Do you think I should bank the fire or were you going to stay up a little later?"

"No, go ahead and put down the fire." She looked up

from her sewing, her voice soft, but she avoided looking at him. "I'm going to bed."

"Okay."

He did as he was told, his senses staying attuned to her. Firelight danced in his eyes and fanned his face, but it was Willa who he envisioned folding up her sewing for the night. Willa, whose skirts rustled as she stood. He knew the beat of her step as she circled around the sofa. He listened to the tinkle of the china chimney, watched darkness descend as the lamp winked out and even in the darkness he could recognize the hint of her slender shape and her graceful lines. His heart thundered hopefully in the silence between them.

"Good night." Her words sounded humble, hardly more than a whisper as her silhouette moved away.

"'Night." He gripped the handle tightly, swallowing hard as she walked from the room. The shadows clung to her, trying to swallow her up and steal her from his sight. He knelt back to his work, but the small shovel banged against the grate because he wasn't paying close enough attention to what he was doing. She held his senses captive, even as she closed the bedroom door. Although he could no longer see her, she held him.

He fought images of her undressing alone in the dark, of standing there vulnerable and beautiful before she slipped her nightgown over her head. Tenderness surged through him like an ocean wave, obliterating everything else inside him—his wants, his needs, his dreams. All that mattered was Willa's wants and Willa's needs. Her dreams had become everything to him.

After he banked the coals to keep them warm

through the night, he rose to his feet. He took his time checking the locks on both front and kitchen doors before heading toward their room. Probably it would be best to give her plenty of time to crawl in bed before he opened the door. Remembering her earlier admonishments, he rapped his knuckles on the door in warning before easing into the silent room. A single lamp glowed, the wink turned low, giving barely enough light to see the slight bump beneath the covers that Willa made on her side of the bed.

Willa. More tenderness for her just kept rising up, made new every time he thought of her. She was turned on her side away from him, facing the wall, breathing so quietly she may already be asleep. He moved quietly, shrugging out of his clothes and hanging them with care. He didn't want Willa to find them on the floor come morning. Grinning at the memory of her temper, he padded across the floor to his side of the bed in his long underwear. He turned out the lamp, eased onto the mattress and stretched out beside his bride.

She was sleeping. He eased up on one elbow to study her. Soft breath, sweet woman. He breathed in her faint rose scent and his chest squeezed tight. He didn't know what the future would bring, but as he settled onto his pillow and on his side watching her, hope lingered, even in the dark. She'd said she would never love him, that she didn't believe in that rare affection, but she'd reacted quite strongly to his kiss. He'd looked into her eyes and saw her gentle caring spirit. Maybe all she needed was time.

He let his eyes drift shut and felt her stir in her sleep.

She rolled over, so close a lock of her hair caught on his whiskery chin. He didn't dare move, he didn't even breathe as she snuggled in against his chest. With a little sigh, she continued sleeping. When he carefully eased his arms around her, his heart sang.

Chapter Fifteen

Willa came slowly awake, warm and contented, and as sleep faded her awareness returned. Comfortable bed, the covers tucked beneath her chin and strong arms held her loosely. She opened her eyes in the still-dark room, realizing something was amiss. Something was out of sorts. Austin's body heat seeped into her, where he pressed up against her in the center of their bed.

Had he tugged her over in his sleep, or had she migrated over in hers? That question rattled her heart against her ribs as she gasped, fully awake. Austin's relaxed and rhythmic breathing assured her he still slept, that he wasn't cognizant of her predicament. The weight of his arm pressed on her heavily—not unpleasantly so—but still, it trapped her where she lay.

The threat of memories trying to surface had her breathing slow and deep to fight them back. She wasn't going to panic. Austin wouldn't hurt her; she knew that for sure after the way she'd treated him last night. The mortification rushed back with renewed force. She would be lucky if he didn't march her to the train and send her away this morning. They had not consummated their marriage so nothing truly held her here. As soon as she thought it, she knew Austin would never treat anyone that way, even a woman who had given him a piece of her mind.

What had she been thinking? That question tortured her again as she gingerly lifted his arm off her just enough to slip away. Without his heat, she instantly felt the chill of the early morning. Goose bumps raced across her skin, but she wasn't entirely sure it was from the cool air. And why was she breathing so quick and hard? The man affected her far more than she realized.

She sat up on her side of the bed, careful not to jostle the mattress. Her head swam, her stomach swam and she closed her eyes, praying the dizziness would pass. She needed a clear head to think. She had to figure out what to do after last night. How was she going to react to him? How was she going to forget about their kiss?

His kiss was a dream and it stirred up longings within her she didn't understand. It made her want to kiss him back. It made her want to believe that those stories she'd believed in as a girl—the ones of true love and happily-ever-after—weren't all lies. That maybe somewhere in this world true love really happened to an ordinary woman like her.

That was dangerous thinking. Her head stopped spinning and her stomach remained relatively still, for the moment, so she opened her eyes. The twitter of birds outside the window told her that sunup was not far away. Austin's deep and even breathing remained unbroken.

Memories surfaced from years ago as a first-time bride, when she'd been naive in the ways of men. She remembered lying on the floor of her shanty, pain drilling through her head and light burning her eyes. She hadn't known how long she'd been unconscious, but the blood that had been running freely down her face had dried on her skin and stained her dress and the dirt floor. Everything hurt so fiercely she didn't think she could move until Jed kicked her in the stomach. *Get up and don't back talk to me again.*

She blinked hard to erase that memory of her second hour in their shanty as Jed's bride. Emotions greater than thankfulness ached within her now.

Very hazardous emotions.

Don't look at Austin, she told herself. *Just turn your back on him and get out of bed.* But did her eyes listen?

Not a chance. They slid against her will to study him. He lay on his side, big and relaxed, taking up half the bed. Tousled dark hair tumbled over his forehead and a cowlick stood up at the crown of his head.

Emotion curled within her so achingly sweet she had to catch her breath and steady herself against the headboard. Nothing had hurt quite like the sensation she felt—a pain that wasn't a pain but more like a deep wrenching within her. As if a room opened up in the vicinity of her heart, making space where there had never been before.

What was the man doing to her?

"Good morning." He opened his eyes, deep inky pools in the darkness. He stretched lazily, looking comfortable and at home beside her. "You're awake early."

"I guess it was the rain." And the fact that she'd been in his arms, tucked close against him. How long had she slept like that? A few minutes? Hours? All night?

"Looks like spring may be here to stay. I think we've had our last winter squall." He eased up on one elbow and sat up in bed, looking harmless and completely safe.

Safe? No, she'd been wrong about that, judging by her body's reaction. She wasn't safe with him. He tied her up in knots. He confused her. And watching him sleep—tousled and rugged—well, it did something to her she couldn't define.

"How did you sleep?" He yawned, stretching his arms again, looking like a man content with himself. "Good?"

"All right." That seemed a harmless answer, because she really did feel rested. Her gaze trailed to his chest and she clearly remembered how hard and hot he'd felt tucked in behind her.

Goodness, what was wrong with her? Heat flamed across her face. At least it was still dark so he couldn't tell. The last thing she wanted was for him to catch her staring at his chest. Her only saving grace was that he didn't know she'd been in his arms.

"I'm surprised to see you sitting up. How's your morning sickness?" Friendliness danced in his morning-rough voice. "Shouldn't you be lying down?"

"Maybe." Her head began to spin again and she slipped down onto her pillow.

"That's right, take it easy." He held the covers for her. Once she was settled he tucked them around her. Was it her imagination, or was he still grinning? He straightened away from her but didn't move away completely. "You stay warm. I'll start the fires and bring you some tea."

"No, don't go to the trouble." She tried to sit up, but her stomach protested so she stayed where she was, willing it to settle. The last thing she wanted to do was to be sick in front of Austin.

"Just rest." His hand caressed her forehead, a light brush of his fingertips across her skin. Perhaps the touch was meant to be reassuring, but it blazed a trail of heat that seared long after he moved away.

She listened to the door creak open and his footsteps echo in the main room. She was alone, but she didn't feel alone. Awareness of him remained like his touch on her skin. Her stomach roiled, threatening to send her dashing to the chamber pot.

Just lay quiet, she told herself. It will pass. But it didn't. Her stomach clenched in a hard spasm, she flung back the covers and raced to the corner. Just in time. She leaned over the copper bowl, abdomen heaving, tears running down her face she wretched so hard.

When it was over, she sank onto her knees. No sense leaving in case she had need of the pot again. She closed her eyes to keep the room from swirling and took short, measured breaths.

Austin's footsteps padded closer and only then did

she realize the door was open. He'd clearly heard everything. Embarrassment added to her misery as she listened to him come closer.

"Hey, are you okay?" He knelt beside her, one hand settling on her back. Another dangerous touch that sparked heat along her skin where his wide palm rested. He smelled good, like pine and wood smoke. "Let's get you back to bed."

"Not yet." She shook her head once, then groaned because the room began to spin again. Worse, her stomach coiled up uncontrollably and she heaved again—in front of him. There wasn't one thing she could do to stop it. Could this be any more embarrassing? She leaned over the chamber pot, gasping, hoping the agony would come to an end.

"What a tough morning you're having." His baritone rumbled low and his voice was so full of affection she could no longer deny it was there. It rang in the notes of his voice, lingering in the still room.

Only then did she realize he'd been holding her hair back for her. He handed her a damp washcloth for her face. Lamplight tumbled in from the front room and highlighted the concern carved into his features.

"I've got water heating." He slipped his arm beneath her knees and lifted her against his chest, standing easily as if she weighed nothing at all. He carried her without any effort across the room. "You don't weigh much more than a sack of grain."

"A big sack of grain," she corrected, so weary she couldn't help letting her cheek fall against his shoulder.

"You are much prettier than any sack of grain and much more important to me." He eased her onto the bed, and did it gently, for so strong of a man. She stared up in wonder at him, framed by the dark. Not even the shadows could hide the emotion on his face. The honest, deep affection that shone so brightly for her.

The affection she could not give him in return. She searched for it in the void of her heart, but no feeling came. No fondness, no tenderness, no affection. She wanted to feel those things. Feeling inadequate, she collapsed onto her side of the bed.

"I hope you don't think I'm being bossy, but I'm bringing your tea and that's the way it is. If you want to stop me, now's your chance."

"I don't think I can," she murmured, weak against the pillow.

"I know and I'm taking advantage of it." He tucked the covers around her and brushed a lock of hair out of her eyes. The way he gazed down at her made her feel if she wasn't plain old Willa but someone more, someone special to him.

It's the baby, she thought. He's doing this because of the child she carried. That's how much he wanted to be a father.

"I'll be back with your tea. Just rest, Willa." His voice lingered on her name, low and intimate, and shivers broke out on her skin. He disappeared through the door, a better man than she'd ever imagined and one she knew she didn't deserve.

But how she wanted to try.

* * *

Austin poured a cup of tea from the pot. He couldn't hear Willa moving around. That was good. He hated to see her sick like that. He left the bacon in the warmer and made his way to their room.

She lay in the shadows, eyes closed and as pale as the sheet. It was impossible to keep his affections hidden as he padded across the room. The cup clinked in its saucer as he slipped it onto her bedside table. Last night holding her in his arms had been sweet. Sweetness clung to him now as he straightened, watching her lie there, his bride.

All she needed was time. Certainty filled him as he watched her eyes flutter open and focus on him. For a split second, in the unguarded moment before her shield went back up, he could see how vulnerable she was. It vanished as her chin lifted. Tension jumped along her delicate jawline as she tried levering herself up in bed.

"Let me help you with your pillow." He reached across her to grab his and tucked it behind her, aware of the tiny sigh she made as she accepted his help. Funny how she kept her gaze from meeting his. He gave the final pillow a pat, then all was in place and she leaned into the stack with a sigh. At least he'd helped to make her more comfortable.

"Thank you." She accepted the cup he held out for her, still not meeting his gaze. She sipped tentatively, her rosebud lips against the cup brim.

It was not at all hard to remember how those lips had felt on his. Affection surged through him with a force so strong it felt like that's all he was or all he could be.

He eased onto the edge of the mattress. "We need to schedule your first driving lesson."

"That would be good." She took another sip and seemed to relax a little, as if her stomach was starting to settle.

"Would you like to do it this afternoon?" His arms felt empty as he sat on the edge of the bed, aching to hold her. The few feet separating them seemed to stretch like a country mile. He resisted the need to gather her up in his arms. "I can get off work early."

"I appreciate that, Austin. It's good of you."

"If that's what you want to think. But the truth is you're going to need to pick up groceries soon. The supply in the pantry can't last forever. I could do that for you, but you'd probably be happier doing it yourself. What if I pick up the wrong thing? I'd like to avoid your temper." He winked, so she knew he really was kidding. He wasn't quite sure how to say what he meant. How he wanted everything to be right for her and as good as he could make it. She'd changed his life for the better. She'd changed his heart. He needed to give her all he possibly could.

"Oh, Austin, I'm so sorry about last night." Remorse shone in her eyes that locked on his, a shock to his soul. It was easy to read how badly she felt. Her chin wobbled. "I don't know what came over me. I've never said such things to anyone before."

"It's all right." He took her cup because it was empty, intending to refill it for her. "You have nothing to apologize for."

"But I do." Her hand lighted on his arm. "This baby needs you. I do, too."

"Maybe I need you, too," he confessed. Her touch seared through his shirtsleeve to the skin and bone beneath. Desire shot through him, desire he had to ignore. He shrugged. "Besides, it looks like I might need someone around to let me know when I step out of line. You seem fairly good at the job."

They smiled together and it felt good, as if something had been resolved he didn't understand. The air was cleared between them and so was the chagrin in her eyes. With a sigh, she sank a little farther into her pillows.

"I'll fetch you another cup," he told her. "Just close your eyes and rest. Breakfast will be in the warmer whenever you're up for it."

Her fingers squeezed his arm in a silent message of thanks. When he stood, he knew down deep that everything between them was going to be all right. His future with her was going to be just what he'd hoped for.

Perfect.

Willa stepped from the chair and onto the floor, liking the new curtain she'd hung on the front window next to the door. The merry fabric added cheer to the sunshine streaming through the panes. She grabbed the tiebacks she'd hemmed while in bed this morning, gathered the material in an artful bunch and tied a pretty bow. She took a step back to consider her work, gave the bow a tug and gathered back the curtain adorning the other side of the window.

Austin. She couldn't seem to get out of her mind all the little things about him she liked. The timbre of his voice, the comfort of his touch and how wonderful it had felt to awaken in his arms. Even in memory, her body responded warmly. And the way he'd settled her pillows for her, brought her tea and even held her hair while she'd been sick, made her appreciate him even more.

The remembered rhythm of his gait lingered like a favorite song in her mind as she pulled the chair away from the window, tucked it into place at the table where it belonged. Was it wrong that she missed him so much? Or that she'd enjoyed his kiss?

That's what really upset you last night, you may as well admit it, Willa. Worse, something else currently upset her as she grabbed another pinned curtain panel and headed to the sofa to work on it. As if the kiss weren't bad enough, the sensation of waking in his arms kept haunting her. Probably because she wanted to do it again. Somehow she had to erase it from her memory. Austin must have reached for her, because no way would she turn to anyone, especially a man, even in sleep.

Or would she? She needed to be strong. She may have been his wife, but she'd learned a long time ago to stand on her own feet. It was better not to need anyone.

Isn't it a little too late for that, Willa? She plopped onto the cushion and grabbed her needle and thread. The house felt empty and lonely instead of calm and still with only her in it. Since when had she started missing Austin?

Since today, she realized, threading her needle. Since his kiss. She missed his humor and the crook of his smile. She missed his steady companionship and his way of making her feel as if everything was going to be all right. The fire crackled in the grate, tossing heat into the room. It didn't seem to warm her the way Austin had, when she'd been cozy in his arms.

No doubt about it. She had a weakness for her husband. A smart woman would figure out a way to fight it. She thumbed on her thimble and poked her needle through the edge of the fabric. A knock rapped on the door a second before it swung open. The needle flew from her fingers as she jumped, startled.

"Thought I'd better knock." Austin filled the doorway, pure might and male strength. "Didn't want to startle you."

Too late for that. She couldn't catch her breath, and surely being startled was the reason—not the man. And where did her needle go? She couldn't think clearly enough to search for it. "You're back early."

"Isn't that what we agreed to this morning?" He ambled in, bringing the outside damp with him. "The snow is melting fast out there. There's just enough packed on the roads to make driving a bit of a challenge."

"And that's supposed to make me feel better?"

"Yes, as it will be harder when it all turns to mud. We could wait until the roads are better, but you'd probably be happier able to come and go as you please." He knelt down at the hearth to tend to the fire. "The curtain looks good. I'm surprised you aren't working on baby things, though."

"I wanted to get the house settled first." She thought of other touches she'd like for the rooms—doilies and tableclothes and pillows to match the curtains, but she had to be practical. There would be time for those things later, maybe between baby projects. "I planned to start knitting the yarn you gave me as soon as I finish curtains for all the rooms."

"Great." He lowered the damper with a clang. "Evelyn dropped by the livery this morning. She wanted to warn me that they were already planning another Sunday dinner. They liked spending time with you."

"And I need warning because?"

"I'm afraid spending too much time with my family might give you a poor opinion of me." He winked, standing full height and offering her his hand. "I worry about what they say to you when you ladies are all together."

"They have been telling me all your secrets." She laid her hand in his. A little charge snapped across her skin and dug deeper, almost painfully, burrowing in. She whooshed to her feet too fast, feeling dizzy. Or maybe that was just Austin's nearness. The man affected her more and more each day.

"Oh, no, I'm in big trouble now." His chuckle vibrated through her as if it were her own. She hardly noticed crossing the room at his side. He was all she saw. Powerful man, big heart and her future as his wife.

It would be so easy to lean on him, to let herself believe in lies. That he would always be there for her. That he would always be like this. That true love could exist.

She had to be careful not to be drawn in by false wishes.

"I've got your little mare hitched. She handles real nice. She'll drive easily for you." He held out her coat for her. As she stepped near to him quicksilvers of sensation lashed through her.

It was his chest, she realized, as she slipped her arms into the sleeves. The memory of being against his chest was a powerful thing. It clearly affected even a woman like her, one who knew better.

You can't believe, Willa. She ducked her head, stepping away from him. Torn between her wishes and her beliefs, she concentrated on buttoning up so she didn't have to see the caring shining brightly in his gaze.

"I hope you've got a name picked out." Austin opened the door and the damp cold air rushed over her. "We're going to have to call that sweet little thing something."

She stepped out into the day, surprised at the transformation around her. The melting snow dripped from rooftop and treetop, plopped from branches and puddled in low places to reveal a brand-new world. The white and gray of winter retreated and green emerged. Spring hinted in the tight buds of the trees and in the peep of early wildflowers budding through the thaw.

Snow had covered all this? Everywhere she looked, she saw color. Blue soaring mountains, robin's-egg sky, deep evergreen forests and splashes of purple and yellow as wildflowers fought to bloom. Hope surged through her with a force she'd never felt before as Austin's arm draped her shoulder.

"That one last winter storm blew in hard, but as hard as it was, it didn't last. Winter never does." His words held a deeper meaning, as if he understood at least some of her struggles. She'd never felt so close to another human being as he assisted her down the slick steps, careful of her and of the babe she carried.

Chapter Sixteen

The little mare shivered in her traces, perhaps not knowing what to expect. Austin felt for the frightened animal as the horse watched Willa approach, shying at the outstretched hand. When it didn't strike her, the horse studied the woman more carefully but didn't reach out for a human touch.

Maybe in time, he thought.

Looking at his bride was like a first glimpse of May after a long winter. He untied the tether from the banister post, careful to move slow and steady so as not to frighten the mare further.

"Will she be okay to drive?" Willa patiently waited, her hand still out to pet the mare's nose. But the animal stayed back as far as her collar and harnessing would allow. "She's skittish, poor thing."

"The only thing she's scared of is a human." He'd spent a lot of time trying to win the mare's trust and had failed every time. "I think she was whipped pretty badly by at least one owner, maybe by more than one. All she needs is time."

"She's beautiful. I wish I could pet her, but I don't want to scare her." Willa sighed longingly, the spring winds battering the wisps that never seemed to stay in her braid. "I've named her Star, because it's hopeful. Like a twinkle of light in the dark sky."

"I like it." The name suited the mare, with her coat as black as midnight and the white star on her forehead. The timid mustang watched him as he came nearer, perhaps expecting the worst. He knew how that could be. Enough bad things happen to you, and you begin to expect it.

"Let's get you up in the driver's seat." He clasped Willa's slender elbow, making sure she didn't slip in the slush. Memories of her settling against him in bed last night put vigor in his step as he helped her onto the running board. Her rose scent tempted him to ask for another kiss and when she smiled a thank-you to him, her perfect Cupid's-bow mouth was pure torment.

"Are you sure you want to trust me with the reins?" she quipped, as he reached to gather them from the dash.

"I'm fearless," he teased in return, offering her the leather straps. "A woman driver doesn't scare me."

"I guess we'll see about that. I keep having visions of driving off the road, getting stuck in the ditch or causing enough damage in a crash that you won't trust me with a horse again."

"Not going to happen, although I have to admit I

worried about the same things when Pa handed me my first set of reins. All I could think was, 'Don't wreck the family buckboard, Austin.'" He circled around the back of the vehicle, his boots splashing in the slush. "I repeated it to myself for the first couple of miles."

"I haven't heard this story before." She tilted her head back to look at him, pure splendor in the sunshine. The light worshipped her, doting on her finely carved face, luminous blue eyes and her innocent femininity that no canvas could do justice to. "Tell me."

"Maybe there's nothing left to tell." He settled in beside her, fighting the urge to draw her into his arms. He wanted to kiss her until neither of them could think straight. "I drove the family to town. End of story."

"I don't believe that for a second." She sparkled up at him, sitting prim and polite on the seat, clutching the reins in her slender hands. "The story of the tree-climbing incident comes to mind. I know there's more to the tale than you're admitting."

"Sheesh. I'm trying to hold on to my dignity here." He leaned back against the seat and chuckled, shook his head and caught his hat brim before a blast of cool breeze could steal it. "I don't want my bride to see me in a bad light."

"Too late for that," she joked, her shy chuckle tinkling like quiet music. The notes stuck with him and he laughed, too.

"I knew I shouldn't have introduced you to my family. Now you'll never see me in a good light, especially if I tell you the learning-to-drive tale." He knew that would only pique her curiosity, and he didn't mind.

Having her beside him, bright and merry and different from the withdrawn, sad-eyed woman who'd met him on the train platform was boon enough. His ego could survive the humiliation of a retelling of the story as long as it made her smile.

"You have to tell it to me now." She adjusted her grip on the reins. "Am I doing this right?"

"You're just fine." Somehow he was going to have to figure out a way to keep his pulse from leaping into a full-out gallop whenever she focused her wide blue eyes on him. "Star is a dependable horse and she responds best to a light bit. That means not too much pressure, so be sure and keep the reins slack so they aren't pulling on the bit."

"I was careful to watch you drive, so I would be ready for this. Now that I'm holding the reins, I'm not so sure." She swallowed once, blew out a cute little breath and straightened her spine. "I don't want to make a mistake."

"That's why I'm here. Go ahead and give the reins a light snap, just enough so she can feel it. That's right." In response, the mare stepped out, her steel shoes clanking on the hard-packed ice. "You have a nice light touch."

"I can't believe it. I'm really driving." Elation nearly lifted her off the edge of her seat. "I'm doing it."

"Yes, you are. A fine job, too."

"Oh, this is amazing. How do I turn?" She felt flustered when he leaned in to give the right rein a small tug, to head the mare a little southward. She should have known to do that, it was just overwhelming.

"When in doubt, you can just pull back on both reins. It doesn't hurt a thing to stop in the middle of the driveway." He towered beside her on the seat looking as invincible as those mountains. He shook his head, as if trying to ward off a memory. "If you get flustered, just stop, get your bearings and start up again when you're ready."

"Sure." She concentrated on the driveway up ahead, where ice gleamed in the sun and led the way into the shadowy forest. Star's ears perked up, swiveled as if to listen in on the human conversation. Willa tugged on the rein again. "Is this right? I want to keep the runners on the good patch of ice."

"That's it. You always have to think ahead of the horse, where she'll be and where you will be." He eased back, not a drop of nervousness showed. He appeared to have complete confidence in her. "It will become first nature, once you get the hang of it."

"I'm waiting to hear that story of yours." She gave the left rein enough tug to bring the mare on a straight course toward the forest. "What will it take to get you to tell it?"

"Some more of that bean soup for supper."

"You know we're having it leftover for tonight anyway."

"Then I guess I have no choice, but I warn you. It is a tale full of woe." Humor crinkled across his face. Laugh lines framed his eyes, dimples bracketed his grin and his chuckle rang warm enough to chase winter away for good.

"It can't be too woeful, since you and your family

managed to survive." She felt light-hearted and not at all like herself. More like a brand-new Willa, one with the wind in her face and tangling her hair, driving her own horse toward town. "No one seems scarred or maimed."

"Fortunately, not for the long term," he quipped. When he smiled into her eyes it felt as if he went all the way in, all the way down to the barriers around her heart where no one had been before. So close, she longed to nestle a little nearer to him on the seat. She ached to feel the comfort of his arms around her.

"I was moseying along just like you are doing now." The shadows made by the forest cloaked him, hinting only at the straight cut of his profile, the curve of his mouth and the set of his shoulders as he tugged down his hat brim against the wind. "I was twelve years old, around the time a boy ought to learn how to handle a team of horses. I loved the feel of the horses' mouths traveling up the leather straps. I loved the wind in my face and the feel of freedom. Like I could go anywhere."

"Yes, that's how I feel, too." There her eyes went, sliding toward him instead of staying firmly on the road ahead. She craved the sight of him. She had to see the flash of his dimples. She yearned for the sweetness she felt when their gazes met and his smile touched her deep within.

What was wrong with her? She blinked, but the road ahead didn't come into focus. The blur of trees in the shadowy forest seemed background to the man who made her pulse leap. The man who stirred something sweet and aching within her. Why did her gaze center on his lips? His lips could curve into a smile or into a hard granite line when he concentrated, and when he kissed...

Stop right there, Willa. She couldn't keep going like this. This was dangerous thinking. She forced her attention on the road, where melting water splashed on the surface of the hard-packed snow, making a musical sound beneath Star's hooves.

Thank goodness he continued with his story, unaware of her problem.

"I was nervous at first," he explained. "I didn't want anything to go wrong. If I made a mistake, my brothers would never let me live it down."

"I've noticed that about your brothers."

"So there I was, doing my best. Pa had just finished praising me and Ma had stopped Brant from mimicking me behind my back so all was well when it happened. Out of the blue, a snake slithered out of the grasses and onto the road in front of the team. Apparently, he didn't look both ways before he crossed, because we surprised him, too. The ten-foot-long snake coiled up and rattled its tail. One horse reared in terror, while the other lunged off the road, leaped across the ditch and landed in a field, dragging all of us along with him."

"That wasn't your fault," she sympathized, making a mental note to keep an eye out for snakes.

"No, but my reaction was. Instead of working to calm the horses and anticipate their reactions, I gave a whoop of terror, too. I'm not overly fond of snakes."

"A big strong man like you?"

"They put me in a sweat and I was sweating plenty seeing that big huge snake coiled up ready to strike. I sat there panicking, watching the horse rear up in front of me, his big broad back getting closer and closer. Pa tried to get hold of the reins, but I was frozen. I couldn't make my fingers let go and suddenly we were in the ditch, I was airborne and landed face first in a patch of blackberry bushes."

"Austin, you were hurt."

"Full of prickers and stained with berry juice. That wasn't the worst indignity. I broke my leg. There I was purple-black, bleeding from the stickers and hopping on one leg back to the others. Pa had gone airborne, too, but he landed in the field. He was fine. The buckboard wasn't so lucky. It was stuck in the ditch, pitched at an angle with a wheel and axel broken. My brothers laughed up a storm."

"And Evelyn?"

"Laughing with them. I can still see them, pointing their fingers at me. I had blackberries oozing off the top of my head. 'Well, son,' Pa said in that deep low baritone of his. 'I never thought you'd wreck the family vehicle your first time out while we were still in the driveway.'"

"Hey, I'm still in the driveway. I don't appreciate that story. It gives me a sense of doom."

"Sorry." His laughter burrowed into her, drawing her somehow closer to him although she hadn't moved an inch on the seat. It was as if her entire being leaned in to him, aching to be closer. The emotional longing became physical, as if every cell in her body yearned for his nearness. What was going on?

It was the weakness she had for him, she realized,

the softness he made her feel. Her mouth tingled once again with the memory of his kiss. It was impossible to forget. She feared she would be stuck reliving the memory of it over and over, never being able to stop. When he moved closer to lay his hands over hers on the reins, the snap of his touch went straight to her soul. The deepest places within her—both emotional and physical—tingled the way her lips had from his kiss.

"Perhaps I should have saved that story for a little later," he joked again, his breath fanning her ear and the side of her face. "Fortunately for us, it's not snake weather."

"Lucky me." The words came out thick and strained, as if not her own. "We're almost at the end of the driveway. So far I've done better than you on my first time out."

"Darlin', anyone could do better than my first time out. It was humiliating." His cheek rested against the side of her head, but it was more than a simple touch. Much more. The simple contact dug deep within her and stayed, as if it were a part of her. Peace filled her with a powerful sweep, way beyond any feeling she'd experienced before. Overcome, she wanted to lean into him, too, to draw in more of this feeling, this wonderful feeling.

"The county road is coming up." His words caressed her temple, almost a kiss against her skin. "You want to learn to judge how much of a tug, because that tells your mare how much of a turn you want her to make. Like this."

His left hand guided hers, showing her the pressure

to use on the rein. But all she could feel was him as the mare turned perfectly onto the road and into the sunlight. The brightness stung her eyes and her wish for him lit up her entire being. Everything within her yearned for him as he released his hold on her hands.

"You did that perfectly. You didn't need my help at all." He straightened up but he didn't move away.

"So far so good." She flashed him a smile. "I'm relieved not to have a disaster story to tell, the way you do."

"That's my brothers. They never let me live down a single mistake." He shook his head, not able to find the right words to describe Brant and Derek. Troublesome. Pesky. The best brothers a man could have.

"Oh? I have to hear more about all of those mistakes." She tilted her head to one side, studying him through her long lashes. "I'll beg Evelyn for more stories the next time I see her."

"I'm in big trouble," he chuckled. "I'm never going to have your good opinion after that."

"Oh, I don't know. My opinion of you might be so high those stories couldn't begin to lower it."

"Good to know." He'd been right. Love between them was only a matter of time. With every passing moment, he could feel her guard coming down. He ached, needing to be close to her, as close as he could get. He couldn't help letting his cheek come to rest against the top of her head.

Please love me, he wished with all his might. *Please, feel for me what I feel for you.*

The sun chose that moment to brighten, casting

spring's heat onto them as they flew toward town. The snow melted like a promise, giving way to a world lush and green.

"Here, let me help you down." Austin reached up for her in the shadow of the barn. The drive was done, her lesson was over and she was officially able to handle the mare on her own. She wasn't aware of her shoes touching the ground, only the connection she felt to Austin as she stepped from the seat. Her connection to him held her fast, refusing to let go even when her hand left his.

He reached to unbuckle the harness and free the mare. The late-afternoon light hung low on the horizon, skimming the tops of the evergreens and skimming over him. His hat brim, the line of his back and his muscled arms were bathed in light.

What a sight, she thought with a little sigh.

"That's it, Star. You did a fine job today." He worked slowly around the wary mare, keeping his voice calm as he spoke to her. He seemed aware of the horse's fear and did everything he could to reassure her.

Willa liked that about him. She liked so many things about Austin she couldn't begin to list them all. She felt buoyant as she followed him into the barn, so happy from the successful lesson and her life on this land that the spring wind was likely to lift her up and blow her away.

"Since you know how to hitch and unhitch, I won't make you take notes." Dimples framed his smile as he lifted Star's collar off her neck. Even from halfway across the barn his dimples had a hazardous effect. Her pulse skipped three beats and she couldn't look away.

Maybe it was time to admit this exhilaration she felt wasn't from the excitement of the drive. It came from something deeper. "Fine by me. I don't mind letting you do the heavy work."

"I'm a blacksmith." He hung up the horse collar. "I'm good at doing heavy work."

Rosie mooed for attention. Calvin poked his nose into the aisle and made a grab for Austin's hat, but the man didn't notice. His eyes remained on her, a smile touched his lips and her heart lurched crazily, missing three more beats. She ducked her chin, breaking the connection.

She felt too close to him and it frightened her because she trusted him so much. With every breath she took, she trusted him more. As she listened to the pad of his boots marching closer, she knew he would never lift a hand to hurt her. He would never say an unkind word. He would always be the stalwart, decent man he'd shown himself to be.

"Do you think Star will always be afraid of us?" she found herself asking instead, saying the first thing that came into her head because she didn't want to think about her past or their future. She didn't want to build up hopes for a future as his bride that might not come true.

"I don't know." Austin raised his hand slowly, but the mare sidestepped, mistrustful. "When I bought her, I had hoped she would eventually understand that she's safe."

"But she's still so afraid." Willa could feel the animal's anxiety in the air. "I hate to think how she's been treated."

"I do, too. The truth is, she may never overcome it completely. Sometimes the heart is too broken to trust again." He knelt to towel down the mare's long, lean legs. "I hope that's not the case with her. We just have to give her time."

Austin's words stuck with her. She knew what it was like to have a heart like that—too broken to trust again, too scarred to love.

After Jed, she'd told herself the fairy tales she'd grown up with as a child were lies. That the happy bonds she'd witnessed as a little girl in the mercantile, as parents drove their children to the schoolhouse and newlyweds walked past her grandmother's shanty hand in hand, were just people making the best of a bad situation, that was all. Finding the good where they could.

Now she wasn't so sure. A pressure built like a bubble in her chest, expanding painfully with every breath. She grabbed a brush from the shelf and approached the mare. "I'm going to groom you. Is that all right, Star?"

The mare's eyes darted from Austin to her. Her velvety muzzle sniffed the bristles and sighed. Her tether held her captive, a condition she could never escape. Hopelessness radiated from the animal, an emotion Willa understood too well.

"I won't hurt you, girl. I promise." She stroked her fingertips down Star's velvet-soft nose, but the horse merely continued to shiver in fine quakes.

"I thought she might do better with a lady. She's less

afraid of you." Austin continued his gentle work. "She handled very well for you on the drive."

"She was a dream. So very obedient. She's a good girl and I want her to feel happy here." She began brushing the mare's mane, going up on her tiptoes to brush the coarse tufts of sleek hair. "Thank you for the driving lesson."

"No problem." He rose to his full height to rub down the horse's flanks. "I tried to point out places in town I thought you might like. The bakery. The bookshop. Evelyn's house. You were concentrating on driving so I wasn't sure how much you heard."

"I just didn't want to crash into anyone on the street. Imagine the story that would make." She watched him circle around Star's backside, working his way closer. With his head bent to his task and dark hair tumbling into his eyes, he looked like her dream with the sunlight cast over him.

He was too far away. The few feet of distance between them felt like a mile. Against her will, she inched toward him, breathless and aching for him in a way she didn't understand. She wanted to be wrapped in his arms and pressed against his chest. She wanted his kisses tingling across her lips.

What are you thinking, Willa? Shimmery heat spilled into her veins and she blushed, staring hard at Star's mane. She started brushing again in gentle little strokes. There seemed to be no end to her weakness for her husband.

Simply the sight of his face filled her up. The glow she'd experienced before expanded until it felt as sustaining as the sun. When she spoke, her voice sounded thick and strained. "I'm trying to avoid doing anything that will result in a funny family story about me."

"Is that right? Well, then you owe me a story."

"What?" Everything vanished except for him and the burning light within her. "I don't have anything to tell."

"Hey, I revealed an incident from my past." He moved around her, rubbing the horse in short, quick strokes. "You ought to at least do the same."

"I've certainly never embarrassed myself the way you have." Mischief chimed in her playful tone.

"I have more dignified stories, but they aren't nearly as funny." He gave the towel a toss, his pupils dilating to black. No distance stood between them now. She reached to lay her hand on the flat of his chest, feeling his strength and his tenderness surge into her. Perhaps that was why her pulse skipped another string of beats when he leaned in, adjusted his hat and whispered softly.

"You made it clear I'd best ask for permission." Merriment tugged up the corners of his mouth and he looked like a man who was perfectly aware of his dimples' effect on a woman. "May I have another kiss?"

Yes. The answer rose up from her heart like a fairytale wish even as her common sense tried to stop it. He must have read the weakness on her face because he closed in, his mouth slanted over hers, and his kiss brushed pure heat across her lips. This time there was no tingle—no, there was nothing so mild as that. Tendrils of heat spiraled through her until her toes curled.

Nothing had ever been as consuming as his kiss.

The slow caress of his lips, the tantalizing stroke of his tongue and the gasp of his breath told her he was as surprised as she by the power of their kiss. Her head reeled, her blood stalled in her veins and when she looked up at him, clutching his coat, his gaze collided with hers. It was as if she could feel him within her. As if the connection between them had strengthened into steel and hooked into her soul so deeply nothing could remove it. She felt forever linked to him.

He said everything with a look. Endless caring shone in him, affection he held for her so strongly she could feel it. She could see everything within him. She could feel his love for her. His love shone down on her as if she were the most special woman on earth.

No way could that be true, but he seemed to believe it. That amazing love ebbed into her from him, bridging the distance between them. The shimmering, glowing emotion filled every part of her.

Every part, that is, except her scarred and broken heart.

Chapter Seventeen

How did she tell him? Willa stood at the counter washing dishes and listened to the pad of his steps draw nearer. Her husband carried an armload of heavy split cedar chunks like they weighed nothing. Raindrops shimmered in his dark hair and danced along the line of his shoulders. The glow within her remained faint but still there, intensifying as she watched him toss her an easygoing smile.

"I'm going to have to dig you a garden patch." He filled the wood box, working quickly, wood hitting the steel sides of the box with muted clangs. "I never did bother with one. So you'll have to tell me where you want it and I'll get to digging. Maybe this weekend?"

"Maybe." She plunked the pot she'd used to warm up the soup into the rinse water and gave it a good swish. "What will it take for you to dig out a flower bed, too?"

"Why, that's an easy one. I'll dig as many flower

beds as you want. The only thing I'll charge you is a kiss."

"Maybe that's too steep of a price."

"How about a peck on the cheek, then?"

"We'll see." Holding back laughter, she set the pot on a dishtowel to dry. "I want to see the flower beds first."

He laughed, brushing pieces of moss and bark from his sleeve into the box. "So, you want to see the type of work I do before payment?"

"Exactly. Got to make sure I'm getting my money's worth. Well, in this case, my kiss's worth."

"Then I'll do an exceptional job and hope for a bonus." Dimples framed his smile as he ambled closer.

Longing tripped through her blood, maple-syrup sweet and thick with heat. Her weakness for the man had grown. The only thing she wanted was to be enfolded in his arms and kiss him in the dark of night. She wanted to rest her cheek on his chest and feel how safe it was to be held by him. But did she have that right?

"Looks like you've got more curtains finished." He moved over to her sewing, which was folded neatly on the sofa cushion. "They're real pretty. I like what you've done."

"Yellow is my favorite color." She put the pot away. "It's like sunshine."

"I know you're independent and like to do things for yourself, but will you let me hang these for you? I'd like to do something for my beautiful bride."

"I should refuse since you have a tendency to fib. Beautiful? I don't think so." She blushed. Austin had a bad habit of using that word to describe her, something that could not possibly be true. But it made the glow inside her shine more brightly. How could anyone not come to care about this man? What was wrong with her that she could not?

"It's no fib. You're beautiful to me, Willa. I'll say that as many times as it takes for you to believe it." He swept up the panels of curtains, hauled over a chair and parked it in front of their biggest window. He tossed the panels over his shoulder and climbed up.

"I'm not sure what I'm going to do with you, Austin Dermot." Other than wanting to keep him forever. Shaking her head, she hung up the damp dishtowel and reached for the washbasins. She looked into the soapy, soiled water and saw no answer to her dilemma there. Austin was everything she needed and she wanted to be the same for him, but that was already impossible. How did you will a broken heart to mend? What if it was too damaged to ever mend?

"Please leave those basins alone." Austin watched her from his stance on the chair. "I'll carry the water. And before you say it's your job, come over here and advise me on the curtain hanging."

"You're hoping to distract me and empty out the basins when I'm not looking. Oh, I'm definitely wise to your ways."

He laughed, not bothering to deny it. "Fine, take the dishwater out. But don't say a single word if I don't hang these curtains the way you want them."

She blew out a sigh of resignation. Honestly, the man had a knack for getting his way. She untied her apron, hung it beside the towel and circled around the table. "All right, let's see these curtain-hanging skills of yours."

"Why do you say that as if you expect them to be lacking?" The humor in his smoky, familiar baritone did wonderful things to her. Things best not thought about.

He threaded her curtains onto the little rope that used to hold the limp, sad-looking sheets. The wide spread of his grin matched hers.

I'm happy, she thought. *This is what happiness feels like. To be so full up that you can't imagine it getting any better. Then it does.*

"There. I don't think I've got them centered." He tugged a little, bringing the ruffles snugly together. "What you do think?"

"It's just like I'd hoped." *This is a fairy tale,* she realized, watching him climb down from the chair. This wasn't something real enough to last.

A knock rapped on the front door, echoing through the house like a gunshot. It dragged her out of her thoughts as Austin hopped to the floor.

"It's probably one of my brothers." He gave the chair a shove and it slid into place at the table. "They are always coming over and bothering me. I can't believe they waited this long. I hope you don't mind."

"Of course not." Her pulse galloped, thumping against her ribs as if she'd run five miles as Austin swept by her. The man affected her more every time she was close to him. She could not deny the bond she felt to him, but her silent heart sat sadly still in the center of her chest as he crossed the room and opened the door.

"Berry wanted to see Willa, so I thought we'd come on by." Brant shouldered into the entry.

"Uncle Austin!" two little boys called out, wrenching free from their father's grip to run toward him.

"Hey there, buddies." The big man knelt down to wrap them both in a hug. "What have you two been up to?"

"Gettin' muddy," Stewart explained. "We got a big mud puddle in our yard."

"Real big," Arthur added.

"We splashed all through it."

"Until I caught them in the act." Berry swept in with a laugh and smiled to her husband, who closed the door behind her. "They were head-to-toe mud. I took my eyes off them for one minute. That was it."

"I remember the appeal of a mud puddle." Austin gave his nephews another hug before he stood. The boys stayed at his side. He reached down and ruffled their hair. "We have a real good mud puddle out front."

"Really?" Stewart perked up, eyes excited.

"But I don't reckon your ma would appreciate you playing in it." Austin's gentle ease with the boys tugged at Willa's heart. He would make such a good father.

Her hand slipped to her stomach, still so small but noticeable. At least she had this baby to give him. She couldn't make her heart feel; she didn't know how to bring it to life. Love wasn't a gift she could give him. But she could make him a father. Wasn't that the bond between them? Wasn't that why he did all this for her—because it was for the baby? That was why he gazed at her with loving affection.

"Willa." Berry shrugged out of the coat her husband held for her and touched his arm gently in silent thanks. She tossed her boys a smile as she left them in their uncle's care. "I copied off those patterns like I promised. Oh, I love the curtains. They brighten up the room. A serious improvement. You should have seen this place after he first built it. He had gunnysacks up before those old sheets."

"Why am I not surprised?"

"Men." She shook her head, casting a long-suffering look across the room. "They would live in a cave if they could get away with it. How are you feeling? Your color is good."

"I'm better." She knelt to add a bit of wood to the cook stove. "I'll have tea water ready in a moment, unless you would like coffee?"

"Tea is perfect. I brought you something." She reached into her reticule and pulled out several knitted garments in neat folds. Baby clothes. "I wanted to make sure I remembered the pattern right, so I sat down and knitted up these little things. That way you have something to follow if you need it and you already have a start on your preparations."

"Oh, Berry. They're so lovely. I can't believe you did this." She ran her fingertips over the exquisite garments. A little red cap and a snowy white shirt, both as soft as lamb's wool. A pair of wee yellow socks and light blue booties knitted for the tiniest feet. A fuzzy green sweater with flawless cables and pebbled edging. "I'd never imagined my baby would have anything so fine."

"We will help make sure you have plenty of lovely

things for him or her." Berry set the gifts on the table so they could admire them. "Delia made the sweater. Evelyn's making a baby afghan for you."

"I don't know how to thank you all." Those words seemed inadequate. She'd never expected anything like this. Suddenly the baby seemed real.

But did her heart warm with tenderness? No, and it shamed her. She swallowed hard, wishing she could be the woman she wanted to be, the woman Austin needed her to be.

"We're sisters now. This is what we do for each other." Berry swirled around to grab up a hot pad and whisked the bubbling teakettle off the stove. She glanced at her sons and merriment sparkled in her eyes. "Stewart? What did I say before we stepped through the door?"

"No running." Big blue eyes looked innocent in his round button face.

"And what were you doing?"

"Walking really, really fast."

Both boys stood frozen in place, two little owls side by side. Willa had never seen anything as cute.

"Please walk more slowly." Berry bit her lip to keep from laughing. They launched off at a sedate pace, chasing each other around the sofa. Joy danced in her eyes and she filled the teapot. "They keep me on my toes. You'll see once your child arrives. What are you doing tomorrow?"

"Laundry."

"Goodness, that will simply get in the way of the plans we've made for you." Berry set the kettle on a trivet, glancing across the kitchen to check on her sons…who were now rolling on the floor laughing. "Austin can wait another day for clean shirts. We are planning a Dermot girls get-together at Evelyn's house."

I guess that's me, too, she thought. She was now Willa Dermot. Funny how she'd never really thought of that before. Austin's laughter caught her ear, pulling her gaze to the tall man standing alongside his brother watching the boys on the floor. Lamplight polished him with a flawless luster she'd never seen before. First he'd been the stranger she'd come to marry, then the man she expected the worst of and finally the husband she was getting to know.

Around his family, he shone. His confidence, his manliness and his kindness blended together and stole her breath away. She could not move, she could not blink and as for breathing…? Forget it. She could only stare at the man who poked his nose into the air.

"Hmm. I'm hungry." He sniffed. "I'm scenting something on the wind. What could it be?"

"Quick, Arthur! Get up!" Stewart gleefully shouted, scrambling to his feet. "It's a grizzly!"

"I see two tasty little boys." Austin lifted his arms over his head. His fake bear roar echoed in every corner of the house. His happiness outshone the lamplight and the firelight combined as he launched at his nephews.

"Run, Arthur. Run!" Stewart squealed and grabbed his little brother's hand. The two made a mad dash around the sofa. They stayed safely a few feet ahead of the grizzly, glancing over their shoulders to laugh and shriek and run harder.

"And what did I just tell them?" Berry rolled her eyes and dropped the tea ball into the pot. "Honestly."

He is going to make a good father. Understanding surged through her on a deeper level, seeing once and for all her husband's dreams. Austin slowly closed the distance between him and the boys, who shrieked in delight as he grabbed them and drew them into his brawny arms. The threesome went down together, rolling and wrestling on the floor. The boys yelped, dissolving into giggles as the grizzly tickled them. Fits of delighted resounded through the room.

It was so easy to see the future. With Austin giving little tummies a final tickle, his laughter a deep-noted harmony to the sweet, high music from their children's giggles. In the future, it would be his sons and not his nephews that he lay down on the floor beside, claiming to be a bear too tired to eat the prey he'd captured. She could picture how this child she carried one day would leap up the way Stewart did.

"I'm not tuckered out," he said and crawled on Austin's chest, ready to wrestle some more. "Look, Pa! I caught a grizzly."

"Me, too," Arthur chimed in, apparently not one to be left out of the fun as he leaped into the fray.

Footsteps knelled close by, drawing Willa out of her thoughts, but nothing could drag her attention away from the man with the little boys. A man who had waited so long to be a father. Not waited, she realized, for that was the wrong word.

He had hungered. He longed to be a pa more than

anything. Her hand slid to her stomach where her child lay. Austin's child now and the reason he cared for her.

"Are you going to do something about that?" Berry asked, amused, as her husband drew her to his side. "They are going to be too wound up to go to sleep tonight."

"Either that, or they'll be worn out and drop off like two little logs," Brant quipped. "I'm an optimist. I don't suppose any of that tea is for me."

"Perhaps I can be persuaded to give you a cup." Berry leaned into her husband's embrace, tipping her face up to smile at him. Love resonated in her gaze with unmistakable strength.

Austin's words came back to her, what he'd told her on the second evening of their marriage. *Happy marriages run in my family. It's a family trait.*

She'd never wanted anything more.

"Fun evening, huh?" Austin hung the hearth shovel on its hook. The happiness from Brant's family visit lingered in the air, and contentment filled him. Although night had closed in with its chill, it was not freezing.

"I had a great time." Willa sat on the couch with knitting needles in hand, the toes of two tiny socks taking shape in shades of green. "I've been invited to Evelyn's house tomorrow. We're knitting and sewing baby things."

"Sounds like just what you need." Emotion that had built up through the evening threatened to brim over now. He ambled toward her, his boots echoing in the open-beamed ceiling overhead. "My sisters-in-law seem to adore you. You fit right in with them."

"I don't know about that, but they've been so nice. Did you see the things they knitted for the baby?"

"Yep. I'm not surprised. You are very welcome in this family. We've all been waiting a long time for you." He loved looking at her like this, luminous and radiant, her shadows forgotten.

"I just got lucky," she said, putting down her knitting. "Very lucky."

She had no idea what it meant to him when she held out her hand. He took her slender, elegant fingers in his to help her up from the sofa. Her rose scent suffused him and he breathed it in. His soul silenced at her smile. The look of caring in her eyes did not waver.

Love thundered through him. He pulled her into his arms and she came willingly, walking beside him. Their hearts beat in synchrony as he stopped to turn out the last lamp and open their bedroom door. His gaze trailed to their bed, and at least he could hope that the night would soon come when she would turn to him and accept him into her arms. A night where he could show her how much he loved her and make them truly man and wife.

Desire for her stormed through him, but he knew this wasn't the night. He turned up the lamplight and released her hand. "I'll fetch wash water while you change."

"Thank you, Austin. I'm more tired than I realized."

"You'll feel better after a good night's sleep." He couldn't help tracing the pad of his thumb along the line of her jaw. Tenderness wasn't what he felt, not any longer. It had transformed into an infinitely more tender emotion and a dozen times stronger as he traced the outline of her full and lush bottom lip. He felt her tremble not from fear this time, but from the intimacy growing between them, an intimacy that glinted true blue in her eyes full of caring.

She cared for him. Overwhelmed, he lowered his mouth to hers in a brief kiss. She was soft satin and sweet woman and he wanted more. His blood sang with need but he broke the kiss, wanting what was best for her. Exhaustion bruised the skin beneath her eyes. She'd had a long day but a good one. That's what he wanted to give her. Good days for the rest of her life.

"I'll be right back." He hated letting go of her. He grabbed the empty pitcher and strode from the room, begrudging every step that took her farther and farther from his sight. As he filled the pitcher from the stove's reservoir in the dark kitchen, his ears picked up her movements. The rustle of clothes, the pad of her feet, the squeak of the wardrobe's door.

The future hovered all around him, so close he felt as if he could almost touch it. He'd built this house for the family he would have one day. He could almost hear their children's laughter in the air as he headed back to Willa's side.

She stood in her snowy white nightgown brushing her long, sleek hair that fell like ebony silk down her back. He set the pitcher next to its matching basin and left her to her ministrations. By the time he'd stepped out of his clothes and finished at the basin, she was in bed, breathing softly.

But not asleep yet, he realized as he slipped between the sheets. She rolled to face him, a sleepy smile lovely on her dear face.

"I hope you have a clean work shirt for tomorrow," she told him, her voice tantalizing in the dark. "Berry said you had to make do one more day."

"Luckily, I have lots of shirts. I should be okay."

"Good, because I forgot to check when I was hanging up my clothes." She yawned.

"Come here." He held out his arms and nothing could be more inviting or wonderful. Settling against him was the most marvelous thing she could imagine and the comfort she needed.

"Good night." His words filled her, becoming a wish.

"Good night." There had to be a way to bring her heart to life. She wanted to love him and be all that he needed. She laid her cheek against his chest and fell asleep listening to the steady beat of his heart, glad to be close to him.

Chapter Eighteen

Something invaded her sleep. Something ugly and dark dragged her out of the cozy warmth of dreams and into consciousness. A sharp, deep ache brought her awake in the darkness. Not even a sickle moon's light crept beneath the ruffled curtains to cast a silvery glow in the room. Something was wrong. She felt wet. When she sat up, her nightgown clung to her thighs. The pain came again in a hard cramping twist that radiated through her abdomen and streaked down her legs.

Her cry brought Austin awake. "Willa, are you all right?"

"No." She squeezed her eyes shut but she couldn't stop what was happening. She felt sick. She felt terrible. Tears squeezed between her eyelids.

"What is it? Is it a bad dream?" His arms came around her. He sounded too groggy to realize what was happening.

How could she say the words? The twisting cramp eased, but the ghosts of pain remained. The wetness remained. She knew what she would find even before she peeled back the covers. Blood shone black in the night's deep shadows. She hung her head. "I'm losing the baby."

"Oh, Willa." His eyes popped open, fully awake now. His body warm and relaxed with sleep tensed against her. "You need a doctor."

"The baby." That's all she could think of. Those little garments her new sisters had made. The little socks she'd started, still on her knitting needles. The child Austin would not be tickling on some future evening or chasing around the sofa pretending to be a hungry grizzly.

The baby.

Hot tears burned her face and plopped onto the covers. Her abdomen cramped again, making her shaky and weak. Pain streaked through her so hard she couldn't breathe.

"C'mon." Austin loomed over her. She caught a glimpse of a shirt—he'd already stepped into his clothes—as his arms lifted her from the bed. "We're riding for the doctor."

"It's too late." Misery battered her, more intense than any pain. What was Austin thinking? What was he feeling? How disappointed was he in her? She buried her face in his shoulder, holding on as he rushed through the house. Every step he took rocketed agony through her. Her hopes fell like stars from a bleak sky as he carried her into the night, running to the barn as fast as he could.

* * *

Waiting was agony. It was killing him. Austin surged up from the sofa in the doctor's parlor, hands fisted and jaw clenched so tight his molars ached. He'd never been so scared in his life. If anything happened to her... He shook his head. No, he couldn't even think it. She had to be okay. She had to.

"She's resting quietly now, poor dear." Bea, the doctor's wife, padded into the room with a cup of steaming tea. "Silas says you ought to be able to see her in a bit. Here, now, this will soothe you. It looks like it's raining again out there."

"Another storm is blowing in." Lightning snaked in the distance as Austin stared at his reflection in the darkly gleaming window. He accepted the cup from the middle-aged woman. "Thanks, Bea."

"She's young. There'll be other children." Kindly, she patted his arm, a motherly gesture. "Drink the tea. Breathe deep. She'll need you calm."

"Thanks."

Bea slipped the cup and saucer onto a fancy little table and sauntered away. The stairs creaked as she climbed them, going up to check on the doctor and on Willa.

This was all his fault. He rubbed a hand over his face. He should have made sure she ate more. He should have put his foot down and forbid her to do so much work. No, he should have hired a cleaning woman to come in every day from town. That's what he should have done. He should have taken better care of his bride. His beautiful Willa.

He swallowed hard, staring out into the endless void of night. Hours had ticked by. Soon the darkness would begin to wane and it would be a new day. Soon he would have to climb those stairs and face her. He thought of those tiny socks she'd started knitting and his heart crumpled.

"Austin?" Silas Wetherbee ambled into sight with his graying hair mussed, his clothes wrinkled and sympathy in his eyes. "I suppose Bea told you your wife is fine."

He nodded, too choked up to say what was on his mind.

"I know that look. I've seen it on many a husband." The doc nodded slowly, his eyes wise. "There was nothing you could have done. Sometimes these things happen. There's no point blaming yourself for this."

He knew the doc meant well. Even if Silas was right, it didn't take away the tangle of guilt, regret and grief that had taken him over. Austin rubbed the back of his neck, where tension and worry had knotted his muscles into an unyielding knot.

"It feels like it's my fault." The confession tumbled out of him. "It's my job to take care of her."

"You have. No one could have done better. Now why don't you head home? She's sleeping now. You can come back in the morning. It's only a few hours away."

"No, I need to see with my own eyes that she's all right." He squared his shoulders, filled with a need so great he couldn't begin to measure it. It held him up as he followed the doctor across the parlor. Every step he took on the stairs brought her closer to him. Nothing had terrified him more when he'd scooped her off their bed, imagining all that could have happened to her and the baby.

The baby.

Grief struck like a punch so hard his knees gave out. He grabbed the banister, holding on when the rest of him threatened to go down. That loss was hard to bear. He couldn't imagine how Willa must have felt.

"We don't want to wake her. She's had a tough row." Silas cracked open the door and stepped aside.

Austin peered into the room, where a lamp's low wick tossed a sepia glow over the wisp of a woman asleep beneath a quilt. She hardly made a bump beneath the covers. She looked as if the most substantial part of her had left, lying there pale and quiet. It didn't even appear as if she were breathing.

Strong love for her coursed through him, greater than any ocean wave and more immovable than any mountain. The stars in the sky would burn out long before his love for her ever would.

"Austin?" She stirred, as if she could feel him even in sleep. Her eyes fluttered open. The pillow rustled as she turned her head. When her gaze caught his, her sorrow hit him. Another blow he had to take as he shouldered into the room.

"I'm right here, darlin'." He was at her side without remembering how he'd gotten there, sitting on the edge of the mattress to take her hand in his. It was cool and lifeless, as if she had no strength left in her.

"I'm so sorry." Her voice broke on a sob.

"You have nothing to apologize for. Not one thing.

I'm grateful you're all right." He wrapped both hands around hers. The low lamplight behind him cast him in silhouette and shadow, but she could read the sorrow heavily marking his face as if he stood in broad daylight.

"I let you d-down." She choked on the words. She couldn't endure seeing the grief stark in his eyes. "You wanted the child. I know you did."

"I can't lie. I'd already started looking forward to being a pa." He brought her hand to his lips and kissed the backs of her knuckles. She felt the heated brush of his lips, the fan of his breath and the agony he sought to hide from her.

Disappointed him? No, she'd done something much worse than that. She could feel his heart. The connection between them remained strong, a tie binding their souls. The total anguish of his grief rushed through her with enough darkness to wipe out the light in the room.

The loss had devastated him. She couldn't feel her own grief over the tidal force of his. Nothing she could do could ever make up for this failure. She felt hollowed out, empty, as if there could never be light in the world again. Tears welled behind her eyes but she did not dare let them fall. If she did, she might never stop. She might come apart into a thousand pieces. She might never be able to put those pieces back together.

She'd lost her baby. Sorrow left her too weak to say anything more at all. Seeing the desolation in Austin's eyes, she feared she had lost him, too. Wasn't the baby the reason he'd chosen her advertisement out of a newspaper filled with so many others?

It was the reason he'd proposed, brought her here and married her. Every kindness he'd shown her and every loving look he'd given her was because she carried the baby. He wanted to be a father, and she'd failed at the one thing she could give him. To Austin, the only one in her life who'd shown her true kindness.

"All that matters right now is you." His voice knelled with gentleness. "You need to rest."

She nodded, her throat too tight to speak. Defeat filled her, adding to her own grief, threatening to overwhelm her self-control. Tears slipped into her eyes, blurring her vision. Austin's face swam in front of her, but she couldn't let them fall.

"Do you want me to stay?" His question rang tenderly, but she was sure it was pity she heard layered in his tone. Sympathy, yes. Concern, yes. But pity out rang them all. The distance between them felt as wide as it had been when she'd first stepped off the train.

She shook her head, not daring to do more. If she spoke, she feared her self-control would break like a dam and all her sorrow and defeat would rush forth and he would see it all. She couldn't be that vulnerable to him, not now, not when there was no baby to bind them together.

"Are you sure?" His hands tightened around hers. "I worry about leaving you alone."

Proof of what a good man he was, she thought, swallowing hard. He'd lost everything, too, and he was still trying to do what he thought was right. She blinked, determined to clear her vision. It didn't work. Tears stood in her eyes, refusing to retreat. All she could do was look through them at the man who sat protectively at her side, braced as if he'd taken a blow he refused to let break him.

A wave of emotion she could not hold back washed over her with flash-flood force. Overwhelmed, she lifted her chin, determined to be strong. She could not let it drown her. She pulled her hand from his. The one thing she could not do was give in to her weakness and rely on him.

"You g-go." She croaked out the words, each one cutting like a blade. "I don't need you."

"Are you sure?"

She nodded. The pillow rustled as she turned her head away. She squeezed her eyes shut, holding her emotions as still as she could so it wouldn't hurt when he walked away. When he never wanted to see her again.

But he didn't move. He sat beside her as the silence lengthened and the sounds of the night deepened. Somewhere a coyote called to its mate, a lonely sound that echoed faintly in the room and lingered between them.

"All right. If you're sure." His hand came to rest on her shoulder. He squeezed lightly, leaning in as if he had more to say but nothing came. Only more silence as he drew his hand away, breaking the connection between them, breaking it forever. He didn't need to tell her that it was over between them.

The bed ropes creaked as he stood. She squeezed her eyes shut tight, to keep in her gathering tears. Need for him rolled through her, but she had to fight it. She couldn't reach out for him. Not now. Not after this.

His footsteps struck like hammers in the quiet, taking him away from her one step at a time. Pain cracked through her chest, radiating from the center of her chest. She held her breath, afraid she would make a sound that would have him turning back to her. If she didn't let him go now, if he didn't walk out that door, then she would never survive letting him.

Just keep on walking, she pleaded silently, willing his feet to carry him out of the room. She tightened every muscle, holding back both her need for him and renewed grief at his leaving.

"She should be able to go home midmorning," the doctor said. "She'll need rest. Maybe one of your sisters could do the housework for the next couple of days."

"I'll find someone." Austin's words came clipped, like he was angry. Or maybe he was holding back a world of grief, the same way she was.

Everything had been going so well, things were finally wonderful between them, and then this. Good things in her life did not last. She should have known. She should have prepared herself better for a blow like this. How could she have been so naive? She knew better. She'd learned to be practical long ago.

It was Austin. He'd made her believe. His kindness and steadfast strength had lured her into thinking she was safe, she could relax and the hard times in her life were over. This—losing her baby and her husband in one night was the hardest thing ever. She swallowed hard, forcing her grief down.

The door closed quietly and she knew Austin had not taken one look back at her. She listened to the rustle of his clothing, the murmured conversation continuing with the doctor, one she couldn't quite make out. No sense of awareness flitted over her, as it often did when he gazed upon her.

Only when she could no longer hear the drum of his boots on the steps walking away from her did she let herself breathe.

I don't need you, she'd said. Austin tried not to read anything into her words, but they haunted him all the way home. They gnawed on the exposed wounds of his broken heart. They clung to his grief, growing larger as the house came into view. By the time he'd unhitched and put Calvin up in his stall, her quietly spoken words had taken on an edge sharp enough to cut with every step. He shouldered open the front door, standing in the absolute silence of his home, listening to the absolute loneliness settle around him.

It felt as if she were already gone. He couldn't explain why exactly as he shrugged out of his wraps and hung them by the door. It was just a feeling he had. He paced through the chilly house, his movements echoing around him. The place felt as empty as he did. He'd never forget the sight of her in the doctor's bed, hardly able to look at him. She'd turned away as if they were strangers, as if there had been no laughter or closeness between them. As if there had been no kisses or the desire for more.

He saw the baby's things sitting on the end table by the sofa, where Willa had left them. Wee things, so soft the calluses on his finger pads caught on the fine yarn. Grief pummeled him like the meanest blizzard, cold and heartless. His eyes burned as he thought of all his dreams he'd had for their baby. Willa must be feeling like this, too.

I don't need you. Her words slipped into his thoughts, hardly more than a whisper. He sank onto the sofa, shivering in the cold. He knew what she'd meant—that there was nothing he could do for her but let her sleep. That was all. She'd said the words gently. He shouldn't read anything more into them than she meant.

But he feared it was a turning point. That the closeness they had begun to share wasn't strong enough to endure this loss. He buried his face in his hands and breathed deep, fighting a wave of pain and mourning that could drown him. He couldn't shake the terrible fear he was going to lose her, too.

Or, worse, he already had.

Chapter Nineteen

"I know this is hard, Willa, but as I told your husband, there will be other babies." The kindly doctor held her hand as he saw her down the stairs. "I have high hopes that by this time next year, you'll have the start to your family you both want so much."

How did she tell the man she couldn't see the future? She couldn't get beyond this moment, the one she dreaded so much. Austin was waiting for her at the foot of the stairs and she would have to face him.

Family? Those dreams were shattered, at least for her. She, who'd been so afraid to believe in dreams, wanted them back more than anything.

But it was impossible. The baby was gone and so was her reason for staying.

"You rest up for the next couple of days." Wetherbee's fatherly tone echoed in the stairwell. "Take it easy. I don't want you doing anything more strenuous than needlework, you hear, young lady?"

"Yes." She couldn't think about the project she'd started knitting. Those little socks…

Grief arrowed through her worse than any pain, filling the empty caverns of her heart. Her foot slipped on a step, but the doctor held her upright.

"Easy, now," he crooned. "You've been through an ordeal. Don't rush."

She gripped the banister with white knuckles, knowing the doctor couldn't understand. She wasn't rushing to be with her husband. She dreaded the moment when their eyes met and she could see how greatly she'd failed him.

"Willa." Austin's baritone filled the narrow stairwell, but she refused to look up. She glued her gaze firmly to the steps in front of her. One foot, then the other. His clothing came into view. She stared at his belt buckle and braced when he took her hand from the doctor.

"Take good care of her, now," the older man said. "I'll be by tomorrow afternoon to check on her."

"Thanks for all you've done, Silas."

She let go of the banister. Her shoes padded on the floor, and the front door loomed ahead. She turned to the doctor but couldn't find the words to thank him. He seemed to understand and patted her gently. Her feet dragged when Austin gave her a gentle tug.

"C'mon, let's get you home." Warmth layered his words, but she could hear the hollow notes and the grief he tried to hide. How did she tell him she didn't want to go with him? That since it was over, it would be much better for her to stay here? But his strong arm came around her to support her, perhaps thinking she needed it. He eased her along, so big and strong she couldn't stop him. This was only making the inevitable harder. Couldn't he see that?

"Evelyn is home right now getting everything ready for you." He stopped at the door and held her coat for her. "Keeping the fires lit, the house warm and fixing a hot meal."

"That's nice of her." The words tumbled across her tongue and over numb lips. Every part of her felt numb. As if she would never fully feel again. She stared at the garment he held for her, gave a sigh of resignation and slipped her arms into the sleeve. When he moved in to settle the garment on her shoulders, his heat fanned over her. Her body shivered involuntarily.

You do not want the comfort of his arms, she told herself. *You can do this just fine on your own.* She ignored the sheltering plane of his chest and tried to forget how it felt to lay her cheek there, above where his heart beat. She focused on buttoning the coat, but her fingers didn't want to cooperate. She fumbled, aware of his nearness pulling at her as if nothing catastrophic had happened. As if it wasn't over between them. Finally she fastened the last button and tugged the sash around her waist.

"All set?" he asked.

When she nodded, he opened the door. Warmish air breezed over her but she didn't breathe it in. She didn't know if she were breathing at all as she stumbled onto the porch. The sun shone too brightly, tearing her eyes as she took the steps without waiting for Austin. She heard the door click shut, his boots drummed on the porch boards and squished in the greening grass next to her.

"Let me help you up." He seized her elbow, a man determined to do his duty. She didn't know how to stop him and she didn't have the strength to argue, so she let him. She collapsed onto the seat, stared at the dashboard as he tucked the driving robes around her. She heard Calvin blow out his breath in a horsy whoosh and stomp his foot, impatient to be off.

"It's okay, buddy. We'll be on the road, just wait." Austin climbed aboard, took up the reins and released the brake. The vehicle rocked forward, rolling down the driveway and onto a residential street.

When the town gave way to the forested countryside, she didn't notice. She was vaguely aware of the sunlight dimming as it hid behind a cloud, the green smell of growing grass and the shadow of the trees falling across the road. A smart woman would be making plans to do the right thing. It's what she had to do. Austin had married her for the child that was now gone.

He sat beside her, stoic and motionless, like a mountain veiled in a winter storm. The distance between them felt immeasurable. She didn't dare look up and see what emotions were carved into his face. She'd failed him in all ways and he knew it.

After a while, the wagon stopped. She stared at the new tufts of grass poking up in the yard as she slipped off the seat. Not waiting for him to help her, she gathered her skirt hems, swished up the steps and into the house, where warmth and light greeted her. The front room had been tidied of all evidence of baby things and the door to the baby's room was shut tight.

"Willa." Evelyn swept into sight, wearing a pretty apron over her beautiful spring dress. "Oh, my dear, come. I've got your bed all ready."

"Th-thank you." The words felt wrenched out of her. Genuine caring for this woman, her sister, hurt like a fresh wound as she slipped out of her coat. She tried not to notice the man who caught the garment for her. She tried to ignore her body's yearning for him. She hated to think how much he was hurting. He'd lost dreams, too.

She let Evelyn lead her away. Every step she took felt like an end that had no beginning.

And never would.

Austin hung her coat and listened to the sounds of Evelyn settling Willa into bed. He stood in the entry way, too disheartened to move. She barely responded to him at the doctor's. She hadn't made eye contact with him once. She hadn't said a single word on the drive home. He knew she was grieving. He was, too. But he wanted her to turn to him, not away.

"She'll need rest." Evelyn closed the bedroom door behind her. "I'll bring her meal to her on a tray. Do you want me to set a plate for you at the table?"

"I don't know." He couldn't think right now. His brain was in a fog of uncertainty. The chasm between him and Willa had widened until it felt as if there was no end to it. Could it ever be bridged again? He rubbed a hand over his face, hurting in too many ways to count. "I should stay here in case she needs me."

"Likely she will rest and nap. It's what she needs to heal." Evelyn came to him, and her touch to his arm was pure loving kindness. "I know you want to be here for her, but she wants to be alone right now."

"Is that best for her? She's suffered a loss. She needs family." *And me*, he thought, wishing with all his might. *Please let her need me.*

"Why don't you go to the livery? No, don't argue with me. Just think it over while you're eating. I'll get the meal on the table after I see to Willa." Compassion shone in her gentle gaze. Compassion...and pity.

She wasn't telling him everything. He knew it in his gut. "She doesn't want to see me, does she?"

"She didn't say it like that."

"No, of course not. Willa is too kind and gentle for that, but it's what she meant." He clamped his molars together, tension roaring through him. He didn't know how to stop Willa from pushing away from him. He wanted to charge into their room, gather her up in his arms and hold her until her pain eased. But would she let him? He hated not knowing how to fix this or how to take away her agony.

"She was up a good part of the night. She needs to catch up on her sleep." Evelyn looked so certain. "She's exhausted. Things will be better in the morning."

I can't wait for morning. He bit back the words because he knew Evelyn wouldn't understand. She couldn't sense the way he could that something was terribly wrong. This was more than grief. Willa had a right to her grief. In fact, he shared it. But his heart felt cut off from hers. It felt as though if he didn't reach out to her right now and repair the damage then he never could. It would be too late and they would live out their days in polite distance, never able to experience closeness again. What if their chance to find love was gone?

No, he had to fix this now if he could. There had to be a way. He fisted his hands, ready to move mountains if he had to. He'd lost enough. He couldn't lose Willa, too.

"Austin." Evelyn caught him, her loving plea stopping him. "I know you love her, but trust me on this. Let her be."

Air whooshed out of him as he nodded. He hung his head in defeat. He understood then what Evelyn was saying. The fight was already over. She stared at the bedroom door, shut against him. Was she lying there able to hear his words? Was she listening in, knowing how he felt about her? Anguish jolted through him like lightning and he turned on his heel. He needed fresh air. He needed space. He needed some way to stop feeling so much.

"Please pack my meal to go." He grabbed his hat off its peg and opened the door. "I'll be at the livery if you need me."

"All right." Evelyn nodded as if she thought he was doing the right thing, but her eyes filled with apology. It couldn't be easy for her standing in the middle.

"Thank you for everything." He swallowed hard, wrestling to keep his heartbreak from sounding in his voice. "Take good care of Willa for me."

"You know I will."

He stepped into the sunshine, so bright it hurt his

eyes. He blinked hard, walking fast and sure away from the house. New grass sprung beneath his boots as he made a beeline for the wagon. Calvin nickered, instantly concerned, chocolate-brown eyes full of silent questions.

He didn't know what to tell the horse. He patted the gelding's nose and leaned his forehead against the animal's sun-warmed neck. Nothing could comfort you like an old friend.

"Austin?" Evelyn padded down the steps, her skirts swaying around her. "Here's your lunch."

"Thanks." He lifted his head and patted Calvin's nose a final time. The gelding nickered deep in his throat, an encouraging sound. Austin took the lunch tin from his sister, not that he was hungry, and climbed into the wagon. He could see the bedroom window as he snapped Calvin's reins. Those cheerful yellow curtains were closed tight so he knew Willa wasn't watching or wondering about him as he drove away.

An afternoon of work didn't make a dent in the hole that had become his heart. Folks dropped by to check on him—his brothers, the reverend and even Mrs. Pole—and while he appreciated their kindness it was another reminder of what he'd lost. He'd loved the baby. He loved Willa. Loneliness settled around him like a cocoon, greater than it ever had before. Charlie had stopped by to fetch him, on Evelyn's orders. She was still at the cabin, making supper for everyone. He'd declined and worked until dark.

He recognized Berry's buggy parked in front of the barn when he pulled Calvin to a stop. Berry must have stopped in to relieve Evelyn. He knelt to pick a few wildflowers from the grass in the yard. The night sky stretched above and he could see every star overhead. Those distant lights twinkled, unchanging, as he tripped up the steps and opened the door.

"Hey." Berry blinked, sitting up on the couch. "Goodness, I drifted off. I can heat up some leftovers, if you're hungry."

"No, thanks. It was good of you to stay." He hung up his hat and coat, grateful for the shadows hiding him.

"My pleasure. Delia will be over first thing in the morning." Berry stood and scooped up her sewing basket. "Willa is looking much better."

"I'm glad." He squared his shoulders. "Did she ask for me?"

"No." Apology rang in her tone. "Maybe things will be better after a good night's sleep."

"Maybe."

He waited until Berry was gone before putting the flowers in a small tin cup and adding water. He banked the fires, locked up the house and headed for bed. He put the cup on Willa's bedside table.

A faint stream of stardust slipped between the curtains to fall over her with a silvery, majestic light. His beautiful bride. Endless tenderness welled up, overflowing as he watched her. She slept on her side, her dark hair a cascade over her slender shoulders and her white pillow slip. She'd chosen to lay at the very edge of the mattress, leaving most of the bed untouched. It seemed she wanted the most possible distance between them once he'd climbed into bed with her.

At a loss, he took care not to make a noise as he disrobed and readied for bed. He slid beneath the covers, keeping to his side, knowing this would be a night where she *wouldn't* come to him. She would not ease into his arms and rest her cheek upon his chest. Heartbroken, he closed his eyes.

Sleep did not come.

Chapter Twenty

When she opened her eyes, she saw the cheerful yellow flowers peeking over the rim of the small tin cup. A fistful of buttercups opened their blossoms to the rays of light falling all around the closed curtains. Sunbeams, as if determined to find their way, crept around the edges of the ruffles, squeezed beneath the curtain hem and streamed through the gap between the curtain and the wall, filling the room with light. Unstoppable light.

She levered up on her elbow, blinking against the brightness. How had Austin known? Those were her favorite flowers. She blinked, waiting while the dregs of sleep faded and her mind cleared. Watching those yellow blossoms shine along with the light almost made her wish she could forget her plan. The plan she'd made yesterday on her ride home from the doctor's. Her plan was the only remaining kindness she could show Austin.

Austin. Tenderness warmed the cold places within her as she slowly sat up in bed. The covers rustled, too loud in the silent room. No noise penetrated the wall. Was no one home? It was early. Perhaps Austin had already left for work and Delia, who was promised to come, had not yet arrived.

No matter. That would save her the difficulty of convincing Delia to go home. What she needed to do this morning was best done alone.

It took all her inner strength to push off the bed and take the first step toward the closet. Little pieces seemed to break off her heart as she opened the door and pulled out her old dresses. Their wash-worn fabric felt familiar against her fingertips as she placed the clothes on the foot of the bed and began folding. She chose her most serviceable one to wear before going up on tiptoe to yank down her battered satchel from the top shelf.

She left her new dresses hanging. Perhaps they would fit Austin's next wife or Evelyn, after her baby was born. If sorrow burrowed deeper in at the notion of leaving the women who'd been so welcoming and caring to her, she had to ignore it. She had to set aside her feelings. She had to do the right thing. Austin deserved that. She owed him that.

The woman who gazed back at her in the mirror looked different from the one who'd arrived here. As she washed, brushed and braided, she thought of the gifts Austin had given her, especially the intangible ones. She would take with her the knowledge that good men were more common than she'd thought. That, at times, real life could be better than any fairy tale.

The way Austin had treasured her helped heal the hurt Jed had caused. Because of Austin, she'd belonged to a real family. Because of him, she could see all that marriage could be. As she grabbed her satchel off the bed, she was only sorry that she hadn't been able to give him all he deserved. But maybe in leaving, she could make way for that to happen.

Her fingers felt numb when she reached for the doorknob. Warm air met her when she stepped into the front room. The fire had died down—the hearth had gone dark—but the sunshine tumbling through the windows warmed the room nicely. The curtains had been tied back, crisp and bright throughout the room. She'd been right. They did make the house cheerful. It would be hard walking away from this lovely place—her home.

Don't think about it, she told herself. *Just do it. Just go.* She steeled her spine as she crossed the room and didn't dare take one look back. She folded up her old coat and tied on her bonnet before slipping into her patched shoes, tying them well. The clock's steady tick-tock echoed in the stillness. It was nine-thirty. If she hitched up the mare and left her at the livery, then she could catch the ten o'clock train. This time she wouldn't be traveling by passenger car, but it would be easy enough to sneak into one of the freight cars. She didn't care where she was going, only that she was gone.

The warm, early May morning greeted her like a summer's kiss. Birds chirped and flitted from porch post to fence post as she eased down the steps. Gripping her satchel tightly, she blinked in the radiance of the day. Green grass spread like a carpet at her feet, where new blades waved in a temperate breeze. Greening trees shaded the edge of the lawn, where the cow grazed. How could such a sad day be so beautiful?

Rosie lifted her head, her jowls working as she chewed. Her brown bovine eyes twinkled a friendly hello. A robin hopped from the fence rail to the ground, head cocked, hopping along as he searched for a midmorning snack. A jackrabbit froze in the tufts of wild grasses near the corner fence post, nose twitching. When she took another step, the rabbit darted away, tail bobbing.

Every step she took felt like loss. Rosie leaned over the fence, mooing merrily, and the little black mare eased cautiously into sight. Timid brown eyes searched Willa's, as the horse put one cautious step in front of the other. The wind rippled the silky ebony mane and sunshine polished her velvet coat. The animal ventured closer, her long legs poised as if ready to fly at any frightening movement.

"Thank you for being such good friends to me," she told the cow and the horse.

Rosie nosed in, bumping Willa's hand to beg for a pat. Hard to resist those sweet pleading eyes. She rubbed the cow's warm nose, ignoring the hard squeeze of sorrow in her chest. She was going to miss Rosie very much.

A horse's tentative nicker caught her attention as the black mare inched up to the fence. Star lifted her nose over the fence rail, offering it for petting. Willa couldn't believe her eyes. Air trapped in her lungs as she transferred her hand from Rosie's nose to the mare's. The horse tensed but she didn't move away when Willa's fingertips touched that silky-soft muzzle. Her heart gave a little flip as she stroked in gentle caresses.

"You're such a good girl. Such a good, sweet girl." She choked out the words. Big chocolate eyes met hers, framed by long dark lashes. Hope shone there, tentative but amazing. After all Star had been through, she found a way to open her heart again. "I'd never thought you would let me do that."

"I had faith." Austin's voice thundered behind her, deep and rich, a treasured sound. Her body responded with a honey-sweet richness that spilled into her blood, making her heart beat faster and harder.

Oh, no. What was he doing home? She squeezed her eyes shut for a moment, gathering her courage for what must be done. She squared her shoulders, hoping she had the strength to look him in the eye, see there was no caring left for her and end this the right way. But how? How was she ever going to recover from having to leave him?

"What are you doing up?" His voice sounded nearer. His boots crushed the grass, making his way from the barn. "I was just coming in to check on you. It's such a nice day, I thought the animals might like to stretch their legs in the pasture."

"Yes, so I see." She faced him with her chin set and her spine straight.

This would be the last time she would see him, so she drank him in. She memorized each detail she'd grown to adore. The way his dark hair tousled in the breeze, thick and silky beneath his Stetson's brim. The flash of blue in his expressive eyes, the fullness of his heart. The handsome planes and angles of his face that spoke of integrity and kindness. The confident, easy stride that brought him closer.

All she wanted to do was to press into his steely arms and get as close to him as she could. Until there was nothing between them.

Until they were one.

She saw the exact moment when his gaze fell to the satchel in her hand. She watched the smile die on his lips. The sparkle faded from his eyes. His step faltered. He froze, staring at her across the expanse of rippling grass, his jaw slacking in surprise. Hurt washed across his features, stark and undisguised.

No, she decided. Hurt was too mild of a word for what she read on his face. Devastation. It crinkled in the corners of his eyes and hung on his shoulders. Then he shook his head, swallowed hard and it was gone.

"Don't suppose you want to tell me what you're doing with that satchel?" He paced toward her, moving slow and stiff as if he'd broken a rib. His voice rang hollow as his boots padded through the carpet of grass. "Maybe you are fixing to add it to the church's donation barrel?"

"N-no." The word was torn from her throat. "I thought Delia was coming."

"I suppose it would be a lot easier for you if she had." His shadow tumbled over her, substantial and bold. A muscle ticked along his jaw. "I wanted to stay home with you. I have trouble saying no to Evelyn, but I have better luck with Delia. I'm here to take care of my bride."

"Oh." Her chin wobbled, and she felt as if the air had been let out of her. She leaned back against the fence post, barely noticing the cow lipping her sunbonnet brim. "That's what I have to talk to you about. I'm not your bride, not any longer."

"What do you mean?" A hint of the devastation resurfaced in heartbreaking shades of blue as his gaze latched on to hers with a force as strong as a punch. Air rushed from her as she fought back a gasp. She had expected so much pain. Why wasn't he relieved? Isn't that what would be best for him? Wasn't she simply saving him from having to ask her to leave?

"There has to be an attorney in town you can use to annul our marriage." It wasn't easy keeping her chin up and sorrow from taking over. She blinked hard, surprised to find tears pooling in her eyes.

Do not let them fall, she told herself. *You can be stronger than this.*

"You want to leave me?" He swiped a hand over his face, hiding all emotion from her. When his hand dropped away, his features were a granite mask, impossible to read.

"Isn't it for the b-best?" She choked on the word. Pain stabbed through her, as if every bone in her body had cracked. Never had she felt such pain. Walking away from Austin would be like eternal winter, like never being happy again. "The baby is g-gone."

"I'm grieving, it's true. I wanted that baby. But that's

no reason to leave." Tendons corded in his neck. He looked harsh, but she knew it wasn't from anger. She could feel his anguish like her own. The connection between them remained. She could see into him. That hadn't changed.

"But it's why we married. It's why you were so good to me. It's why you cared about me. It's why I came to Montana in the first place."

"So, that's it. You don't need me anymore, and that's why you're leaving?"

No. How did she tell him she was always going to need him? She wanted him like no other. But what about his needs? What about his dreams? She'd failed him in every way. How could he want her now? She fisted her hands, fighting hard to hold it together, to keep her heartbreak out of her voice and her stubborn tears from falling. "I can't give you what you want most. I can't be the wife you deserve."

"You are the wife I have. I don't want another. I knew it the moment I saw your words in the newspaper. *I'm a pregnant widow needing a husband,* you wrote. *Please.*" He blew out a breath and shook his head, his emotions hidden. "It was the please that got me. Not because you were pregnant. I wanted you."

"You said it yourself. Sometimes a heart is too broken." Tears stood in her shadowed eyes full of pain. "I told you from the start. I've tried, but it's nothing, just an empty, silent place within me. You are everything I've ever wished for. You are every dream I've ever had. I never thought those things could come true until I met you. And I'm not right for you. I've f-failed you."

"Willa, you saved me. Can't you see that?" If those tears brimmed her eyes and trailed down her cheeks, he was going to be in trouble. No way could he hold back the tides of his heart. No way could he keep a rein on his emotions. The thought of her leaving killed him. It slayed him to the core. "I was alone until you came. You gave me a home and a new life. You made me a husband and you are every dream I've ever had. Don't you walk away and leave me grieving you, too."

"But my heart." Her chin wobbled, her dear little chin. Her teeth dug into her lush bottom lip, reminding him of every kiss and all the others to come. "I closed it up long ago. There was simply too much loneliness and pain. Nothing has opened it again. What if nothing ever does?"

"If it's so empty, then what are those tears for?" He swiped the pad of his thumb against her ivory cheek, where one drop trailed slowly. Love for her blazed brighter than the sun above. He could not accept the fact that their union was doomed. "You can't answer that, can you?"

"I don't know." She shook her head, furrows digging into her forehead. Dismay dragged the corners of her mouth downward into misery. "I don't know what is wrong with me. I hurt so much."

"Then don't go."

"I don't want to fail you again." Her ardent gaze fastened onto his and he could read there what she didn't know about herself. Relief rushed through him as he watched her struggle to find the right words. "You matter so much to me. You deserve to be happy, Austin. I want that more than anything."

"Darlin', caring about someone more than yourself? That's what love is." He knelt to pluck a few flowers from the carpet of grass at her feet. "I hate to break it to you, but you do love me."

"No, it's too late for me." She shook her head at the blossoms he held out to her, their fragile cheerful beauty a sign that life always renewed itself, that it always found a way. She swallowed against the rising tide of emotion new and strange that struggled upward through her grief.

"It's never too late. Love can heal anything." He pressed the flowers into her hands—her favorite flower.

When his fingers brushed hers, her heart clicked. So long it had stayed silent, but now it spoke with the power to rival the sun. Recognition swept through her and she knew he was the one. He was the man she would love for the rest of her life. Tenderness lifted through her like the breeze through the trees and felt as tangible as the buttercups she held.

"I believe you're right." Now she knew what the emotion was that had been curling around her heart and filling her with a summery glow. She let the satchel fall to the ground, forgotten. "Love can heal anything."

"I love you, Willa. You are my everything. Please stay with me." His hand cradled her chin, and on his face she could read this abiding devotion to her. An affection so grand nothing could outshine it.

"I love you, Austin." She smiled with her entire soul. When he slanted his lips over hers, she put her whole heart into it. Into his flawless, amazing kiss. He made her toes tingle. He made her believe. She could see their future as he took her into his arms and she laid her cheek against his chest. Spending her days and nights loving him, laughing at his humor and welcoming their children into their lives.

Happily-ever-after was no fairy tale. It was going to be her life as this man's bride. Her hard times were over. Spring had come to her life and to her heart.

Epilogue

❧❧❧❧❧

May, one year later

"Look at him go!" Delia laughed as she bounded after Kyle, who tottered on both feet as fast as he could go. Her laughter rang like music on a flawless afternoon as Willa crossed the porch and tapped down the steps.

Rosie leaned across the fence rail and mooed, her sparkling brown eyes eagerly watching all the excitement. Another horse and buggy rattled up the driveway, Brant holding the reins. Both Stewart and Arthur assisted him in pulling their horse to a stop.

"Willa! Oh, look at that sweet little face." Berry eased down from the wagon with her husband's help. Her baby was expected in a few months' time. Merriment twinkled as she ambled slower. "How is your little angel today?"

"Excited. She knows something is going on. Look at her bright eyes." Willa held her baby daughter up so she could take a look at everything—her cousins racing across the grass, her uncle unhitching his horse and her aunt's smile. "She's been the perfect baby."

"They all are." Berry glanced over her shoulder. "Look. It's the proud papa."

Willa didn't need to turn to know Austin strode into sight. The brilliance of his smile, the magnificence of his physique and the click opening her heart affected her like nothing else. Her life as his wife was bliss. Incandescent happiness lit her up as he drew near.

"I'd best go find Evelyn and leave you alone with your husband." Berry swished off toward the house, leaving them alone.

"Hey, beautiful." His baritone rumbled low, deep and as richly warm as buttered rum.

"Sophie is particularly beautiful today." Willa gazed down at their daughter cradled in her arms, named after Austin's mother. Big blue eyes, rosy cheeks and button face were topped by soft black curls. The baby's rosebud mouth stretched into a toothless grin as she recognized her papa. "Pink is her best color."

"She looks like a little rose. Hello, sweetheart." He took one wee outstretched hand. Tiny fingers curled around his forefinger, holding on. Tenderness gleamed on his granite features, the kind of love that shone bright and forever. "But I was talking about you, my beautiful wife. Seeing you standing in the sunshine reminds me just what a lucky man I am."

"No, I'm the lucky one." Her entire being jittered with a rapid-fire tremble when their gazes fused. Her throat went dry. She couldn't catch her breath as the golden sunshine bronzed him, illuminating his thick brown fall of hair, bluebonnet-blue eyes, high cheekbones and a chiseled rugged face. The face of her beloved. Because of him, she had everything. A family, a child, a joyous life and the best husband she could imagine. "I love you so much, Austin."

"I love you more." His hand cradled her chin, a gentle touch. A reverent touch. The pad of his thumb traced the curve of her bottom lip. "Remember what I told you? Happy marriages are a family trait. When a Dermot marries, love reigns. And my love for you will last forever."

"Mine, too." She sighed, longing for a kiss. She thought over the last year where grief had given way to hope, where sadness had turned to joy. She'd spent every day adoring Austin more and having the privilege of being cherished by him in return. The future stretched ahead of them, full of hope and joy. Happiness was hers and always would be.

His lips met hers in a kiss that outshone all the others. Infinitely gentle, deeply intimate and poignant enough to stir both her desire and her heart. With their daughter between them, she gazed into his eyes and saw all the promises he meant to keep. She gave a sigh of contentment. What a good life they had, and an even better one waited in store.

"Look at the two lovebirds," Evelyn called from the porch with her baby son in her arms. "Come out back. The meal is ready. Let's get this picnic started."

"I guess we'd better join them. My stomach is rumbling," Austin quipped as he slipped his arm around

Willa's shoulder. Together they walked through the sunshine in the meadow where buttercups bloomed.

And love reigned.

* * * * *

COMING NEXT MONTH from Harlequin® Historical

AVAILABLE AUGUST 21, 2012

WHIRLWIND COWBOY
Debra Cowan

With a hardened heart, cowboy Bram Ross doesn't want to trust beautiful Deborah Blue again. But as her past unravels, Bram must protect her—by keeping her *very* close....
(Western)

HOW TO DISGRACE A LADY
Rakes Beyond Redemption
Bronwyn Scott

When shameless rake Merrick St. Magnus almost compromises Lady Alixe Burke's reputation, he's tasked with making this bluestocking marriageable. Never before entrusted with a woman's modesty, Merrick sets about teaching her *everything* he knows....
(1830s)

HIS MASK OF RETRIBUTION
Gentlemen of Disrepute
Margaret McPhee

Held at gunpoint on Hounslow Heath, Marianne is taken captive by a mysterious masked highwayman. Her father must pay the price—but Marianne finds more than vengeance in the highwayman's warm amber eyes....
(Regency)

THE HIGHLANDER'S STOLEN TOUCH
The MacLerie Clan
Terri Brisbin

With a broken heart Ciara Robertson accepts another man's hand, but formidable Highlander Tavis MacLerie is the one she's always loved. Ordered to take Ciara to her husband-to-be, Tavis is tormented—and tempted—every step of the way....
(Medieval)

REQUEST YOUR FREE BOOKS!

 HARLEQUIN® HISTORICAL:
Where love is timeless

2 FREE NOVELS PLUS 2 FREE GIFTS!

YES! Please send me 2 FREE Harlequin® Historical novels and my 2 FREE gifts (gifts are worth about $10). After receiving them, if I don't wish to receive any more books, I can return the shipping statement marked "cancel." If I don't cancel, I will receive 6 brand-new novels every month and be billed just $5.19 per book in the U.S. or $5.74 per book in Canada. That's a savings of at least 17% off the cover price! It's quite a bargain! Shipping and handling is just 50¢ per book in the U.S. and 75¢ per book in Canada.* I understand that accepting the 2 free books and gifts places me under no obligation to buy anything. I can always return a shipment and cancel at any time. Even if I never buy another book, the two free books and gifts are mine to keep forever.

246/349 HDN FEQQ

Name _____ (PLEASE PRINT) _____

Address _____ Apt. #

City _____ State/Prov. _____ Zip/Postal Code

Signature (if under 18, a parent or guardian must sign) _____

Mail to the **Reader Service:**
IN U.S.A.: P.O. Box 1867, Buffalo, NY 14240-1867
IN CANADA: P.O. Box 609, Fort Erie, Ontario L2A 5X3
Not valid for current subscribers to Harlequin Historical books.

Want to try two free books from another line?
Call 1-800-873-8635 or visit www.ReaderService.com.

* Terms and prices subject to change without notice. Prices do not include applicable taxes. Sales tax applicable in N.Y. Canadian residents will be charged applicable taxes. Offer not valid in Quebec. This offer is limited to one order per household. All orders subject to credit approval. Credit or debit balances in a customer's account(s) may be offset by any other outstanding balance owed by or to the customer. Please allow 4 to 6 weeks for delivery. Offer available while quantities last.

Your Privacy—The Reader Service is committed to protecting your privacy. Our Privacy Policy is available online at www.ReaderService.com or upon request from the Reader Service.

We make a portion of our mailing list available to reputable third parties that offer products we believe may interest you. If you prefer that we not exchange your name with third parties, or if you wish to clarify or modify your communication preferences, please visit us at www.ReaderService.com/consumerchoice or write to us at Reader Service Preference Service, P.O. Box 9062, Buffalo, NY 14269. Include your complete name and address.

HH11B

celebrating **15 YEARS** *Love Inspired*™®

If you liked this story by *USA TODAY*
bestselling author

JILLIAN HART

you'll love her Love Inspired Books title

Montana Dreams

Bumping into her ex-fiancé shatters Millie Wilson all over again. Now
that she's back in Montana to care for her dying father, her real burden
is the secret she's never divulged to Hunter McKaslin. Millie can't blame
Hunter for his anger upon learning he's a father. He's never gotten
over opening his heart, only to have it broken. Yet Millie senses a new
goodness in Hunter. Finding their lost dreams now seems possible—if
forgiveness and trust can find a place in this fresh start.

THE McKASLIN CLAN

Available August 21 from Love Inspired Books!

*PLUS, celebrate the 15th Anniversary of Love Inspired
Books with 4 bonus short stories this September 2012!*

*The mischievously witty Bronwyn Scott
introduces a brand-new trilogy,*
RAKES BEYOND REDEMPTION.

*Three deliciously naughty books, with three equally
devilish rakes. They are far* too *wicked for polite society…
but these ladies just can't stay away!*

*Read on for a sneak peek of book one
HOW TO DISGRACE A LADY.*

Available in September 2012 from Harlequin® Historical.

"You're a beautiful woman, Alixe Burke."

She stiffened. "You shouldn't say things you don't mean."

"Do you doubt me? Or do you doubt yourself? Don't you think you're beautiful? Surely you're not naive enough to overlook your natural charms."

She turned to face him, forcing him to relinquish his hold. "I'm not naive. I'm a realist."

Merrick shrugged a shoulder as if to say he didn't think much of realism. "What has realism taught you, Alixe?" He folded his arms, waiting to see what she would say next.

"It has taught me that I'm an end to male means. I'm a dowry, a stepping stone for some ambitious man. It's not very flattering."

He could not refute her arguments. There *were* men who saw women that way. But he could refute the hardness in her sherry eyes, eyes that should have been warm. For all her protestations of realism, she was too untried by the world for the measure of cynicism she showed. "What of romance and love? What has realism taught you about those things?"

"If those things exist, they don't exist for me." Alixe's chin went up a fraction in defiance of his probe.

"Is that a dare, Alixe? If it is, I'll take it." Merrick took advantage of their privacy, closing the short distance between them with a touch; the back of his hand reaching out to stroke the curve of her cheek. "A world without romance is a bland world indeed, Alixe. One for which I think you are ill suited." He saw the pulse at the base of her neck leap at the words, the hardness in her eyes soften, curiosity replacing the doubt whether she willed it or not. He let his eyes catch hers then drop to linger on the fullness of her mouth before he drew her to him, whispering, "Let me show you the possibilities." A most seductive invitation to sin.

Don't miss book one of this seductive new trilogy
HOW TO DISGRACE A LADY

Available in September 2012 from Harlequin® Historical.

And watch out for:

HOW TO RUIN A REPUTATION
Available October 2012

HOW TO SIN SUCCESSFULLY
Available November 2012

HARLEQUIN®

SYTYCW

SO YOU THINK YOU CAN WRITE

Harlequin and Mills & Boon are joining forces in a global search for new authors.

In September 2012 we're launching our biggest contest yet—with the prize of being published by the world's leader in romance fiction!

Look for more information on our website,
www.soyouthinkyoucanwrite.com

So you think you can write? Show us!